TUNNEL
VISION

TUNNEL VISION

A STONE'S THROW MYSTERY

ELOISE CORVO

This one is for my parents, Jim and Flavia. If you didn't buy the cottage, or if we didn't go on all those camping trips, these books wouldn't be the same. Heck, neither would I.

*I'm not going to lie, I was *this close* to including some of our more eventful camping memories in this book, like when we arrived at the campsite on the wrong day or when Dad tried to duct tape a tent to a tree.*

I love you both.

Praise for Tunnel Vision

"A twisty, page-turning delight that kept me guessing until the very last page. Maudy and Marty are my new favorite crime-fighting duo!"—**Cate Conte**, author of the Cat Cafe Mysteries

"Corvo has done it again. *Tunnel Vision* is a twisty mystery chock full of surprises, small town intrigue, and friendships tinged with secrets—all in the coziest of fall settings. Maudy Lorso and her adorable dog Martin Short make a clever and determined investigative team."—**Bailey Cates**, *New York Times* bestselling author of the Magical Bakery Mysteries

"Author Eloise Corvo captures all the best aspects of a cozy mystery in this sequel to her debut novel, *Off the Beaten Path*. Corvo's descriptions are so finely crafted they transport you immediately into crisp October nights spent stoking a fire and hanging out with friends. If you love hiking in the woods, visiting small towns, and solving mysteries, don't miss Tunnel Vision."—**Anna St. John**, author of the Josie Posey Mysteries

"Cozy meets thriller in this delightful mystery that puts the fright into Halloween. *Tunnel Vision* blends the right touch of spooky small-town vibes with murder during the scariest holiday of the year. A fun book to get lost in, with secret tunnels and a haunted hayride through the woods, it's a perfect read for lovers of the fall season."—**Ivanka Fear,** author of the Blue Water Mystery and Jake and Mallory Thriller series

"In this second installment of Eloise Corvo's Stone's Throw Mystery series, Ranger Maudy Lorso has her hands full with Homecoming week and a campaign for town council that someone is trying to sabotage. She's a spunky heroine, loyal friend, and devoted protector of her adopted Michigan town and its surrounding state park."—**Sharon Marchisello**, author of the DeeLo Myer Cat Rescue Mysteries

Chapter One

Heaping piles of brilliant red and orange maple leaves littering the forest floor don't put up a fight. They crunch and crumble under the thumping footsteps of children on a mission. The ones left clinging to branches paint a blazing backdrop, as if the canopy were on fire. I hide behind a rotting stump, sneaking a peek at adorable costumes, watching the kids' faces glow with discovery as they uncover their next clue.

An ancient, gray wizard looms at the edge of the woods, partly shrouded by dense trees, patiently waiting for the children. I nod to him, signaling that the next group is on their way. How lucky am I that this is my job? It's too much fun to be work.

"Halt, ye fellow travelers!" The wizard (Zach) picks a large stick up off the ground, waving it like a magic staff. His scraggly beard and pointed hat give off a thrift-store Gandalf vibe, especially with his blond hair and stubble poking through.

Giggling second graders jump wildly, costume accessories flying everywhere, in eager anticipation. I shuffle through the leaves, joining them.

"Give us our clue, give us our clue!" A small Transformer jabs Zach with a plastic glove.

"Ah, but first! You must answer my riddle. If you guess correctly, you will receive the clue that you seek. Kyle, stop poking me." He straightens his beard and takes a step back, avoiding further poking.

"Hey, I know you!" A *Minecraft* character of some sort points a blocky finger at me. "You're the lady from the posters! My mom says you're trouble!"

"Oh yeah!" A *Star Wars* character chimes in. "Wait…you have front teeth?"

Heat rises up my neck, and a weak grin spreads across my face. *Roasted by grade schoolers. Awesome. Maybe this is work, after all.*

"I don't know about trouble," I reply quietly. "And yes, of course I have my teeth. Someone just blacked them out on the p—"

"Now, now, boys." Zach interrupts, clearing his throat. "Focus up. One, two, three, eyes on me."

I step back, avoiding more attention.

"What starts in the water," Zach asks slowly, "moves on land, and is all around us?" Using the staff, he gestures to the small pond behind him.

Impressed with himself, Zach keeps waving the magical staff and makes *ooooo* noises, playfully goading the kids. As the Stone's Throw State Park naturalist and environmental education instructor, he works with local elementary teachers all the time. In his last set of class visits, he talked about amphibians, preemptively giving them the answer to this riddle.

This scavenger hunt kicks off a week-long Homecoming rivalry between our Stone's Throw school and the neighboring town of Hemlock Pond. Each year, the towns switch who hosts. It's our turn this year, and the kick-off event is an elementary school scavenger hunt through town. Like all events of the week, the scavenger hunt is between the Stone's Throw Skippers (a horrible name but loved by all) and the Hemlock Pond Hawks.

"Frogs! Frogs!" Lydia raises her hand. My best friend's daughter dresses like a knight in shining armor, covered head to toe in cardboard boxes and milk cartons, haphazardly spray-painted silver.

"That's correct, Lydia! Can anybody else tell me what other animals could answer my riddle?" Unable to pass up an educational opportunity, Zach spurs a lively chat about salamanders and toads before handing each of them a small toy frog, their trophy for the clue.

"That will never get old. I could do without the extra commentary, though," I laugh, standing up from behind the stump as the kids trot back into town, joining Zach on wooden rocking chairs on our ranger station's porch.

"If there's one thing kids know how to do, it's how to poke at insecurities," he chuckles back. "Last week, a kindergartener announced that I had a pimple on my forehead to the entire class."

The old one-room cabin was retrofitted into our park office before I started as Head Ranger a few years ago. As the only full-time employees, Zach and I share it and use some of the space as a small visitor center and storage.

As the next group approaches, a groan leaves the safety of my mind and escapes my mouth. "Ugh, not him." I pull myself out of the comfy rocking chair and brush the mud from my pants. Smoothing down my frizzy ponytail, I spackle on a smile and approach the man escorting this group. Zach resumes his post as riddle master.

"Next time, *I* get to be the wizard," I joke, walking over to meet the Grinch of a man marching towards me.

"Works for me. I'm not lasting much longer in this itchy thing." Zach messes with the beard and jogs back to the water's edge.

"Colin, great to see you today." I guide the man a few steps away from the kids, not wanting the perpetual rain cloud over his head to dampen their fun.

"Well, if it isn't Ms. Maudy Lorso. It's lovely to see you." He grins wider than I have ever seen the man grin, as the kids rush past us to Zach.

"What brings you to the scavenger hunt? Is one of these little ones yours?" *Let's get the small talk over with.*

"Oh, no. Just doing a good deed for the community. This group's chaperone canceled, and I was pleased as punch to step in. The principal is a friend of mine, plus it gives me a great opportunity to garner last-minute campaign support. You never know what kooky things can happen in the last week of an election. Shaking a few hands goes a long way in this town." He smirks, almost devilishly.

What is up with him today? He's usually such a pushover, so spineless and sniveling. Maybe he's been possessed by a demon. It'd be a step up for him, personality-wise.

"Well, Colin, I think making real changes and listening to people's needs is more important than shaking a few hands. Your policy stances help tourists, not the people who live here. Local tax breaks on vacation homes? What a joke!"

I stick out my hand. "Might as well shake mine, too, if you're giving them out freely. May the better candidate win."

His grin curdles. "Might as well." He obliges, frowning at my dirt smudges. I shake the man's clammy hand and cross my arms over my chest.

Zach concludes his herpetology lesson and joins us. "Hi, Colin." He scratches at his beard.

"Zach," he curtly acknowledges with an upturned nose. "Maudy, you're exactly right. The better candidate *will* win." He claps his hands twice, and the kids line up behind him like ducklings. They promptly traverse the gravel parking lot and over the Birch River Bridge into town.

"Yikes, how'd that go?" Losing the war with the beard, he rips it off and rubs his face as we return to our rocking chairs, waiting for the next group to arrive.

"He's just so smarmy." I shake my head. "Should I be worried? He seems more…confident. Something is different. I don't like it."

"Nah, don't sweat it. The Village Council seat is yours, hands down. Don't give him another thought." He waves dismissively. "What do we have, a little over a week to go? Kevin already endorsed you; the town begged you to run. Everyone thinks you're perfect for the job. Especially after how you handled Memorial Day weekend."

"I hope so," I mutter, a little unsure. "I'd feel better if my signs weren't constantly mustached and unibrowed."

"Colin will burrow back into his weasel hole after the election. I've known that guy forever. He's spineless. Don't worry about him."

Zach and I take turns playing the riddle giver as groups of kids filter in and out of the park all afternoon. After about three o'clock, with every group checked off our list, we close up shop early.

"They're the cutest, aren't they? I love Halloween." Zach smiles.

"Me too. Especially up here."

Past Halloweens flip through my mind like a comic book. Home-made costumes held together with safety pins when I was young, four years in a row as *Buffy the Vampire Slayer* in college, and quiet, chilly nights passing out candy on The Den's porch, sometimes bundled in snow gear. Those are my favorites.

"Are you going out tonight?" I ask him as I crunch on an apple from one of our many fruit trees. I lock the ranger station door behind us and turn to walk into town.

"I think I'm going to stay home and pass out candy. What about you? Are you taking that pint-sized knight in shining armor and her little sister trick-or-treating?" he asks.

"Yep, I'm walking with Nellie and her girls. Lydia was cracking me up today. I love that spitfire." One of my best friends, Nellie, and her two daughters, Lydia and Gemma, have become more like family over the last few years. I met Nellie in the park during my first week as Park Ranger. We've been practically sisters ever since.

"Oh, I know! That costume is so perfect for her. She wouldn't be caught dead as a princess. If there's a dragon to be slayed, that girl is going after it."

We part ways over the bridge, the barrier between downtown and the park entrance. I meander along Main Street through town, enjoying the weather. After hanging out with the kids all day, I'm curious which school won the scavenger hunt.

"Not again," I mutter, pulling down one of my vandalized campaign signs, in its full devil-horn and goatee glory. At least this one is still here. Most are gone. Someone keeps stealing them. *Colin or resident witch Charlotte Roth?*

Orange and black streamers lazily drape between lamp posts, serving a dual purpose: Halloween decorations and school spirit. Fuzzy tarantulas the size of car tires cling to lamp posts, each wearing an orange Stone's Throw football jersey. Storefronts feature spooky displays in their windows, and pumpkins flank the doors. Dancing leaves add the unmistakable *woosh!* and *crunch!* of autumn.

Anna, my friend and daughter of the local surf shop owners, agreed to handle all my campaign messaging. She designed catchy flyers and big posters in shades of dark green and orange to "match my vibe," whatever that means. She did a much better job than I could've done on my own.

I placed brand new signs in front of a handful of supportive businesses, like Peyton's bakery and Anna's family surf shop, just yesterday. Most are gone, along with the paper flyers we stapled to the bulletin board outside the Sheriff's Office. *Whatever. Hopefully, Zach is right, and these don't even matter. This is a problem for tomorrow; time to enjoy tonight with friends.*

Walking a block further, I make it to Pop's Bar, my favorite (and the only) bar in town. Written in paint marker in big bubble letters, the school rivalry scoreboard is on full display across the bar's front windows. Stone's Throw's tally is in our orange and black, and Hemlock Pond is in their signature royal purple and white.

Young kids mill about, trading trinkets and candy gathered during the hunt, while parents chat about the hectic week ahead.

"*Three* days in different costumes? And I have to bake a treat for Wednesday's class party. Who has the time!"

"Jamie is just going as different ghosts. Sunglasses ghost, baseball hat ghost, he's obsessed with ghosts this year. It makes it easy for me, at least."

"I found the cutest recipe for eyeball cupcakes last night."

The parents continue to quibble.

"Hi, Eli." As he walks out of the bar, I bid the strawberry-blond chef hello, scrambling to tie my snarled curls into a messy bun. As one of the Pop's proprietors and *supposedly* one of my friends, he adds the first tally to Hemlock's scoreboard. Behind him, a mix of groans and cheers percolates as the mark is added.

"Looks like Hemlock Pond takes the first point of the week with the scavenger hunt," he says more to himself than to me, but I take it as an opening.

"We had one of the clues in the park today. Lydia almost skewered poor Zach with a cardboard sword," I laugh. "How'd you finagle the job of scorekeeper?"

"Eh, it comes with owning the window." He's trying to ignore me, but is fighting against the Midwestern instinct to be polite. "My graduating class is doing a lot of the event planning this year with the Alumni Association, so I'm helping out a friend." He jams his hands in his pockets as his shoulders tense. The cloud of awkwardness is so thick it could choke someone. *Me, actually. It could choke me.*

"Oh, cool. Do you know if they figured out whether or not they want to do the hayride? I still haven't gotten confirmation, and we're getting down to the wire."

"Oh, I don't know. Sorry." He puts the bright purple paint pen in his apron pocket and sheepishly retreats before I can bring out the jaws of life to keep the conversation going.

It's been what? Five months? I know I turned him down when he put his heart on the line, and that must've been hard for him. It was hard for me, too. When will things go back to the way they were? How long will the weirdness linger? I miss him.

Cutting around the block to the small neighborhood adjoining downtown, I return home to my little, red A-frame in plenty of time to straighten up and get dressed before everyone arrives.

Unlocking the heavy wooden door, a *scruff* and friendly *yip!* bombard me, quickly followed by the forceful smack of a black, fuzzy tail and a toothy dog grin.

"Well, hey there, Martin Short! How are you, buddy?" With tons of scratches behind his crimped ear fur, I fill him in on my day and apologize for not bringing him to work. He's still a little miffed, but it's nothing a treat can't fix.

"How was your day, buddy? Did you work on your cancer cure, or focus on rising inflation?" He grumbles back to me, an expert conversationalist (unlike a certain chef I know), and trots around the house as I tidy up for company.

I love this house, which I dotingly named my Den. It's my safe space. My snug, dark red haven. It's not much, but it's mine. The living room greets me on the other side of the front door, covered head to toe in mismatched picture frames, stacks of records, throw pillows, and blankets. The forest green walls carry through to my eat-in kitchen and out to the maple and oak trees in my backyard. A small bathroom hides under the stairway that leads to a sleeping loft.

After feeding Marty dinner, I open the sliding glass door to let him out into the backyard. Kitty-corner from me is Eli's house. Our backyards connect through a gate we installed to make getting between homes easier. It's a gate I haven't used all summer. Tall grass weaves through the wooden slats; neither of us has bothered to weed-whack it all season.

Dwelling on that bummer of a thought, staring into space, my eyes pick up on movement in his back window. I just saw him at the bar minutes ago. He's not home right now.

This isn't your business, Maudy. He's set boundaries and made them clear. If he wants to keep things weird, that's his prerogative. You've tried to fix it for months.

On the other hand, someone could be stealing all his stuff right now. If the situation were reversed, I'd want him to call me, right?

Ignoring the nagging voice in my head and judgmental scrutiny from the dog, I shoot him a quick text letting him know someone's in his house. He responds right away. I read it out loud to Marty, rubbing it in his nose (snout).

"Thanks for looking out," I read. "It's all good. High school buddies are staying with me this week for Homecoming."

"See that, Marty? He's *glad* I'm keeping an eye out. All hope is not lost yet, my friend. We'll get back to where we were eventually. Just you watch. I might have gray hair by then, but it'll be worth it."

Chapter Two

With the house decorated, festive drinks made (of both the adult and kid-friendly variety), and costumes adorned, I welcome the girls to The Den's back porch. The sun is about to set, and trick-or-treating will pick up in an hour or so.

"Die, ugly beast!" Lydia clanks around in her valiant armor, saving everyone from the evil dragon (her little sister) that stalks these treacherous lands (my backyard).

Preschooler Gemma is none the wiser and looks adorable in a plump, overstuffed green and gold dragon onesie, happily minding her own business. She is completely unbothered, scrunching leaves in her round hands and rolling around on the grass. The girls' moms, Nellie and her wife Emma, round out their family costumes: Nellie as a pink, glitzy princess and Emma as a court jester.

Marty and I are going as Sherlock Holmes and Professor Mori-*Marty*. My big, dark curls spill out from under the plaid hat, refusing to cooperate even for the sake of the costume. With an oversized magnifying glass in hand, I blow up my dark brown eyes and olive complexion, making silly faces at Gemma. She instantly commandeers my pipe, which blows bubbles, and keeps it for herself.

Marty is, and always has been, obsessed with these little girls. I rescued him right after moving here, around the same time I grew close to Nellie. I think Marty sees them as siblings. The girls reciprocate that love, too.

Completing tonight's squad is Peyton, in full green body paint as Medusa, with springy ringlets coiled around googly-eyed pipe cleaners.

Sipping neon green Franken-tinis, we sit on my back patio and watch the two littles play with Marty before heading out. Emma slices a pepper-crusted salami onto a sprawling charcuterie spread, her nails almost matching the handle of my navy-blue paring knife.

"Euchre, anyone?" I grab a deck of cards and start dealing. We play every week. It's what we do while catching up. At this point, it almost feels odd not to.

"Deal 'em." Peyton's competitive side reveals itself as the cards hit the worn, wooden table.

"Peyton, did you see who took my signs from your storefront today? I walked through town on my way home from work, and they were gone. Again. I swear, I don't know why I even bother." We sift through our cards.

"I saw that!" Peyton sets her drink down and starts the first hand with an off-suit ace. "It was there when I started baking. But, you know, that was like five o'clock this morning. We should ask Anna when we get downtown. She's passing out candy in front of the shop tonight."

"Honestly, I wouldn't worry about it," Nellie replies. "People have made up their minds already. You're going to win." She tosses a long, blonde Rapunzel braid over her shoulder, laying down the right bower. "Beat that." She smirks.

"I don't know," I lament. "I saw Colin today, and he seemed to have something up his sleeve. His attitude was weird. He would suck in that job! He's so weaselly. He's never made a tough decision in his life. His whole platform is about attracting tourism."

"Man," Emma sighs. "How about a decent daycare or roads without potholes?" She shakes her head.

"Right?" Nellie agrees. "I get it; we need their money, but what about working to improve life for the people who *live* here?"

"Exactly." I throw away an off-suit nine with the hint of a frown. I'm not winning this hand. "I don't want to shoot myself in the foot and give up. I want that Meals on Wheels program. I want to expand daycare options."

"You're going to win. How could you not after what you did this spring? You're a legend," Emma laughs in between tastes of the radioactive cocktail.

"I don't know about *that*," I chuckle. "But I hope you're right. I just want to help, you know? I've been at odds with the council for so long over the park, it'd be nice to change it from the inside."

"Kevin practically begged you to run in his place. He's endorsed you publicly. He's *Kevin*. What he says goes," Peyton states, taking the cards and adding one to her and Nellie's score. "Your deal, Nellie." She hands over the deck.

"I don't want to disappoint Kevin. It'd be like letting down your dad," I smile.

"Speaking of Nett men." Peyton leans in, leading the next hand with an ace. "How are things going with Eli? Has he thawed out yet? When I met you all last Friday at the bar, it was like a magnet repelled him from our booth. It feels a little *middle school*, don't you think?"

"Aw, man! That was the only heart I had," Nellie groans, tossing in a king. "Why do we keep playing this dumb game?" she laughs.

"Eli is still the same," I reply. "He's as big a weirdo as he's been all summer. I saw him earlier, and he couldn't run away fast enough. He has friends in town that I didn't even know about. Normally, we'd all be hanging out with them, you know? I hate it. I miss him."

Peyton looks at Nellie over her cards, seated across from her. She pops an eyebrow. I feel my cheeks flush before tamping it down and playing a card.

Last spring, after a particularly harrowing week, Eli told me he loved me. The guy took both of my hands and ruined our friendship with one sentence. I just couldn't do it. I couldn't jeopardize what we had at the time.

"Men," Emma says, laughing, giving a big wink to her wife. "Is Jeremy joining us tonight? Is he the Irene Adler to your Sherlock?"

I lightly shove her, almost spilling her drink, before playing another card. "Oh, my god, could you imagine him in a dress? No, he's working late. He said if he can get out early, he'll try to join us for trick-or-treating, but I'm not holding my breath. He's a workaholic."

"Huh, just like somebody else we know," Peyton adds, Medusa snakes pointing right at me.

"I may not have a job this time next year, so might as well throw everything I've got into it," I retort. "Or should I just start sleeping on your couch now?"

"I hope Jeremy comes," Nellie replies. "You get so embarrassed at his PDA, and I love teasing you for it."

"I'm not *embarrassed.*" My cheeks warm even more, my personalized version of Pinocchio's nose. The entire table smirks. "Okay, maybe I'm a little embarrassed. I'm still getting used to it. That's all. He's a good guy. He's smart, and so driven, it really challenges me to step up my own game, you know?"

They mumble vague support.

I get up to grab my phone to see if he's texted an update, taking the opportunity to peer over the fence into Eli's yard. He's got the same setup as we do: friends on the back porch, and a kiddo playing in the yard. They're all in matching Power Rangers costumes. I wave, and Eli tips his matching tumbler to me in acknowledgment before returning to his conversation.

"Jeremy is going to meet up." I sit back down as I scroll through my texts. "It won't be for a while, so we shouldn't wait for him. He'll find us when we're out." I smile. "Hang on, sorry. I have a couple of emails to answer."

"It can wait until tomorrow! It's your turn. Play a card," Peyton insists, grabbing my phone out of my hand and tossing it onto the table.

"It's about the hayride this weekend." I grab it off the table and twist out of her reach so she can't take it away again.

"For the Homecoming stuff?" Emma asks, clapping with excitement. "I love a good hayride. How scary are we talking? More of a family-friendly *Haunted Mansion* feel, or full-on *Saw*?"

"It probably won't be good for those two." I point to the girls in the yard. Lydia is pretending to stab Gemma with the cardboard sword. "I'd know more if *somebody* would let me read my email…" I jokingly glare at Peyton and pull up the message.

"Dear Ms. Lorso," I read out loud. "The Stone's Throw Alumni Association is thrilled to confirm the hayride event, as previously discussed, for this Saturday evening in Stone's Throw State Park. We will handle all decorations; we simply need access to the park and logistical assistance from you and your staff. There will be no actors, all mechanics and props. Below you will find relevant details and event itineraries.

"I know our alumni are excited—there used to be an annual hayride back when we were children. It'll be a wonderful throwback to our time growing up here. We're linking this to our class reunion at the marina clubhouse, and shuttling guests between spaces. We are excited to work with you, and our deepest apologies for such a short timeline. There has been a lot on my plate these last few weeks. Warm regards, Danielle Mauer, Stone's Throw School Alumni Association President."

"Fun!" Nellie leans over and hugs me, careful not to slosh her drink on my secondhand tweed jacket. "Maybe this will help drum up some attention for the park. Get people out there that aren't the usuals."

"For sure, it will be fun." I sink into my chair as an enormous anxiety settles onto my shoulders. There is a lot to work out in just a few days.

Even after a pretty great camping season, all things considered, the state slashed the park budget. Starting in January, I must be entirely self-funded to keep the park open.

"Euchre!" Peyton sings, sweeping the cards and adding enough points to win the game.

"Every single game," Emma laughs.

Glimpsing over the fence, tossing the rest of my hand to Peyton, I watch Eli (presumably, based on his build) and another Power Ranger play beer pong. They're all in masks, ready to trick-or-treat. I wish he'd drop everything and walk over. Just to say hi and ask how we're doing.

As the *Monster Mash* bounces in the background, we put the finishing touches on our costumes, down the last of our drinks, and venture into the fall twilight. Lydia and Gemma grab their pillowcases and make a mad dash to my next-door neighbor's house, impatient to start hoarding candy.

We amble down the sidewalk as I take in the night sky, settling in from above. Brilliant pinks and purples cling to the horizon. There is no place I'd rather be.

With the sun fully set, I clutch my cider-filled thermos, trailing Lydia and Gemma from house to house with my friends.

Professor Mori-Marty is a hit, almost too much. I stop every ten or so steps for kids to pet him and tell him what a good boy he is. It's on perfect pace with the girls' trick-or-treating, so I indulge the mutt. He's such a diva; you'd think I never pay him any attention.

"That's one good-looking dog you have there, Maudy." A deep, gruff voice, attached to an older, portly body, emerges, accompanied by a gaggle of children and a couple of younger adults orbiting him like satellites.

"Leonard, nice to see you." I extend my hand, which he formally shakes as the current President of our Village Council. *Jeez, why did I wear such a dorky Halloween costume? Unprofessional, much?*

He's running for state Senate this year; his face is plastered all over the town (like mine should be if somebody weren't trying to thwart my campaign). I signal the rest of my group to keep walking; I'll catch up in a minute.

"You as well, you as well," he replies. "Perfect weather we've got tonight, eh? I remember a few years ago, it was blizzarding, but thankfully Mother Nature is looking down on us favorably this year."

"Yes, it's beautiful. I'm out with my friends and their little ones. I know they're thrilled not to have ski jackets covering their costumes. Are these your grandkids?" I take in the half dozen children kneeling on the ground, rubbing Marty's curly, white belly fur. They're mini clones of the man; the genetics run strong in this family.

"They are indeed. My pride and joy, along with keeping this town, and hopefully the entire great state of Michigan, afloat." He smiles, but not without an undertone of suspicion. "You sure you're up for the job of Councilwoman? It's a big responsibility, you know. A lot of priorities to balance and consider. It's not as easy as your Park Ranger job."

Easy? He thinks my job is easy? Oh, this stronzo, if only he knew...

One of his grandkids tugs on his neatly creased khaki pants leg, urging them to keep moving.

"I believe that I'm the right person for the job. I know how to make tough decisions, have a vision for what we should prioritize as a community, and have a good handle on what our locals need to thrive." I lift my chin, squaring my stance. "I look forward to working with you on the council if you're not in Lansing next year." I tip my Sherlock hat as he pulls away like a sled behind a pack of dogs, onto the next house with a lit porch light.

"Don't let all this praise go to your head, Marty. The last thing you need is a bigger ego." The dog regards me with the innocence of a fallen angel, perplexed at my accusation. "Uh-huh. Don't give me those puppy dog eyes." I bend to pat his head when someone grabs my shoulder from behind.

Chapter Three

"H ey, watch i—" I spin around, gripping the wrist and forcing it off me.

"Whoa, whoa. It's just me." A tall, tanned, trim man dressed in an old-timey suit, bowler hat, and cane holds up his hands saying, *I come in peace*. He pulls me in for a quick kiss and gives me a once-over.

"Well, well, well, if it isn't Dr. Watson, in the flesh," I say as I twist myself out of his arms to a chorus of *oohs* and smoochy noises from my friends, watching us from a couple of houses down. "We're about to head downtown. You're just in time. And impeccably dressed, may I add."

"It's not the nicest suit I've ever worn, but it isn't the worst either." Using his cane as an anchor, he spins around, showing off the tailored get-up. Even after months of dating, I still haven't seen a single hair out of place.

"Sorry about the wrist grab. You alright?" I ask as we walk towards the rest of our group. I shamefully peek at the red mark I left on his skin.

"Oh, yeah. It's fine. I should know better than to sneak up on you like that. Sorry for scaring you. At least you know those self-defense classes this summer paid off."

"Hey there," Nellie greets, calling us as we meet back up. "Dapper as always, Jeremy."

"Hi, Nellie. You all look quite festive. A medieval theme?" He takes in the rest of her family.

"Yep," she replies, smiling back at them.

"What's up?" Peyton nods to Jeremy, a fake smile on her face, before she turns to the girls. *What is her deal?*

When we pass Nellie and Emma's house, Emma grabs a garden wagon to empty the kids' candy bags. They're amassing quite the haul, and it's getting heavy for their little arms to carry. It's also much easier to sneak pieces from the wagon than directly out of their pillowcases, so it's a win-win.

About halfway through the block, my cider woefully empty and a snap growing in the air, I find myself in front of Eli's house. I'm not the only one who realizes that, either, as Jeremy *coincidentally* drapes an arm over my shoulders as we wait on the sidewalk for the girls to get their candy. We idle near his trout-shaped mailbox as they scamper up his concrete driveway and grab a piece of candy from a bowl sitting on a table on his front porch.

"How was your day?" Jeremy asks as we wait, fingers laced in mine.

"It was okay," I reply. "Someone stole my signs again. The rest have unibrows and blacked-out teeth. A kid called me out on it in the park, which was a little embarrassing. Other than that, it was good."

"Again? You just put those up."

"I know, but whatever. I'm glad you were able to come tonight. That's definitely the highlight." I smile up at him. He watches Eli's porch as the little girls retrieve their candy.

My insides lurch as he kisses me on my forehead, reeling at the public display. "Forget the signs, we'll figure it out later."

Eli's house is much quieter than it was a couple of hours prior. Most lights are off, and only one lone Pink Power Ranger lounges in an Adirondack chair on the front porch, monitoring the candy bowl. The rest must be out with the kid I saw earlier.

The girls gallop back to us, candy bags swinging wildly. We continue, waving to friends and neighbors, stopping for candy and Marty's adoring fans along the way, until we hit the edge of town.

The business district of Stone's Throw, the grand epicenter of industry that it is, is four blocks long. The northernmost block is townie territory. The Sheriff's Office stands in one corner, not far from the library, whose second floor doubles as our community center. We hold everything there, from town meetings to breakfast fundraisers. Beyond that, the Birch River Bridge arches gracefully over the rushing river, straight to my home-away-from-home, Stone's Throw State Park.

The other few blocks are a little more fun. Java Jones, the coffee house; Pop's Bar, run by Eli and his dad Kevin; a pizza place that hasn't changed its menu since 1998; a cozy little bookstore; and Peyton's bakery. To the south, the road dead-ends into a sandy parking lot along Lake Michigan's shoreline, serving beachgoers and lighthouse visitors.

East of downtown is the residential area, where year-round Stone's Throwers live. Porches are strung with lights, pumpkins rest on stoops, and the smell of fireplaces drifts between mailboxes.

The couple of blocks tucked between Main Street and Lake Michigan are rental cabins and cottages for people who vacation here, most of whom live downstate or in Chicago. They sit dark this time of year. A small, historical marina glows on the water's edge after going through a big makeover this past summer. This year's class reunion is taking place in the clubhouse: part nostalgia, part bragging about the renovation.

Emerging on Main Street near the bridge, we walk towards the heart of the action while the girls continue to clean house, seizing every opportunity to collect sweets. Emma's wagon rides low.

"What in the world are you guys going to do with all of that candy?" Jeremy asks Nellie as we walk. The temperature drops, compounded by the breeze coming in off the water.

"Well, Emma and I will steal some of it," Nellie laughs. "And don't think we haven't seen you all sneaking a piece or two." She points to each of us, smiling. "Emma takes some to the hardware store to put out by the register. Maudy usually takes some for the park volunteers, too. I don't know, it always gets eaten."

"For better or for worse," Emma chimes in, court jester bells jingling.

As the girls pander for a Reese's Cup in front of a car wrapped in toilet paper (mummy motif?), Marty's tail starts to helicopter, whipping in delight.

"Wow, if this isn't a sight for sore eyes," Peyton's voice calls out behind me. I turn to see her greet the Power Rangers.

Eli pulls off his mask, but the others keep theirs on. The child-sized Power Ranger joins Lydia and Gemma in front of the mummy car, compounding the squeal decibels.

Jeremy just so happens to once again pull me in close, winding an arm around my waist. I flick it off, stepping to the side to create a little space between us.

"Hey, Peyton, you remember the guys?" Eli claps the larger Power Ranger on the back, making room for him and his friends in our circle.

"Is that who I think it is, underneath those masks?" She examines them, trying to suss out who's who.

"Hi, Peyton, it's nice to see you again." The Red Power Ranger joins Eli in removing his mask, revealing a black-haired man with a well-sculpted beard. He goes in for a quick hug.

"Guys, this is Wesley. We went to high school together." Peyton clarifies, introducing us. "So that must be either Danni or Paige." She points to the Yellow Power Ranger, who also pulls off her mask and takes a sip from a yellow matching tumbler.

"It's Danni! Paige is back at Eli's, passing out candy. She had work to do." The Yellow Ranger smiles, also hugging Peyton. "Good to see you, Peyton." Her auburn hair is in two French braids, a little frizzed from the mask.

"You, too! So, are you all in town for the reunion this Saturday?" Peyton asks.

"Yep. They're staying with me for the week. It's been fun catching up," Eli interjects, shifting himself ever-so-slightly away from Danni. He runs his hands through his hair, like he always does when he's nervous.

What is this about? There's something between them.

"I don't live too far," Danni adds. "I'm over in Hemlock Pond now, but I couldn't pass up the chance to have a week-long party with these guys. It's not every day Paige is in town and actually has time to hang out. Anyway, we should catch up sometime while I'm here. Coffee one morning?"

"For sure, that sounds great," Peyton agrees. "You can find me at the bakery, or Eli has my number. And hey, I heard about your brother's passing. So sorry to hear, Danni. We were all thinking about you."

Danni's smile spoils as she gives Peyton another quick hug. "Thanks."

"Well, enjoy your night." Peyton wraps up her conversation as Lydia and Gemma move on to the next stop. Our two groups part ways, heading in opposite directions down the block.

"C'mon, Charlie, let's keep moving. And take that sucker out of your mouth, you know what that much candy will do to you." Danni ushers the mini-Power Ranger onward.

"I'm going to call it, guys," Peyton says as we pass her bakery, two blocks later. "I've got cupcake orders coming out of my ears and need to get an early jump on them tomorrow." She hugs the girls and crosses the street toward her storefront.

The scent of kettle corn clings to the crisp, night air as we weave between parked trunk-or-treat cars dressed up almost more than their owners. Kids zigzag in a blur of wings, capes, and plastic superhero suits as Halloween hits bop in the background. The whole town has come out to join the fun.

As the night air continues to nip, the girls begin to lose steam, and we gently start herding them home. They're so preoccupied with new toys and scarfing down candy that they don't notice the coercion.

We pass my house on the way, and Jeremy and I break off from the rest of our friends. "Thanks for a great time tonight." I hug each of them while Marty zigzags around Gemma's legs, sneaking a lick of sticky goo from her hands as she waves them in his face. "Marty, no. Don't eat that."

"We still need to make plans for the hayride this weekend. Can't pass up a good scare!" Emma adds.

"For sure. Once I know more, I'll loop you all in. Night, everyone."

Jeremy and I walk through the door with a pocketful of candy contraband. Marty runs to the kitchen, hoovering the kibble left in his bowl. It's as if he didn't lick half of Willy Wonka's factory off the sidewalk tonight.

"Did all that love from your adoring fans wear you out, Professor? You didn't get any chocolate, did you? I'd better keep an eye on you tonight."

"He did get a lot of attention, didn't he?" Jeremy asks, opening my cupboard and pulling out a bottle of wine. "More than usual."

"It's the outfit. Who can resist a dog with a pocket watch?" I sink into my lumpy couch and turn on an old, black-and-white Vincent Price movie. Jeremy walks over, two glasses of Merlot in hand, and sinks next to me.

"Thanks for coming. I know it was a hassle to come all this way so late." I nestle myself into him and open a paper pouch of M&Ms. "Also, who knew Merlot went so well with M&Ms? Dream combo.

I'm remembering this for next year." I pop a few in my mouth and take a sip of wine.

"You should try it with a KitKat," he replies, clinking his glass to mine before taking a sip. "How about dinner at my place tomorrow? I've been driving out here a lot lately."

"I should be able to swing it. Let's see how work goes." I tuck my feet underneath me, sinking further into the couch, and get lost in the laundry list of things required to run into Traverse City tomorrow. *Someone will need to come let out Marty, I'll probably need to pack an overnight bag...*

"What was Emma saying about the hayride? Did you finally get the green light?"

"Oh, yeah. I forgot to tell you. I got confirmation that the Alumni Association wants to use the park for it after all. They want to shuttle people from the class reunion party over at the new marina. It's last-minute, but I think it'll come together. Should be fun."

"That will be great," he pulls me in close. "You'll have to hold me tight if we go through it. I'm a big baby when it comes to scary stuff."

"Oh, I know. You almost cried watching *Friday the 13th* last week."

"Hey!" He playfully tackles me, tickling my ribs and coming in for a deep, long kiss.

"Well, now we'll have two things to celebrate," he adds. "I'm closing a major deal tomorrow."

"That's amazing!" I finish my glass and place it on the coffee table. "Do you want to sleep over? We could have a celebratory breakfast before you head back to the city. Congrats, babe."

"I wish I could, but I should head home." He pulls out his phone, looking at the time. "I want to get some more work done tonight. Plus, I can't find my lucky pen, and I need it beforehand; we're closing first thing. But I promise to take you out once the deal is done. For a nice dinner?" He drains the rest of his glass. He stands up to leave, the once perfectly pressed suit, not so anymore.

"Okay." I'm slightly miffed. He never stays. To be fair, I also hardly ever stay overnight in Traverse City, but that's because I have Marty, and dogs aren't allowed in his condo.

Distance is what killed me and my ex-boyfriend, Nate. Should I be worried it's killing this relationship, too? Maybe I should go to his place more. It's just tough with Marty and work. Or am I making excuses?

"Mind if I change before I head out?" He points to the loft, pulling me out of my spiraling thoughts. "These pants are a little tight for the drive."

"I noticed," I tease, wagging my eyebrows. "Go for it. And check for your pen. Maybe you left it here. Take a sweatshirt, too." He climbs the narrow staircase, ducking his head as he reaches the top.

A few minutes later, he reemerges after a dresser drawer shuts and a couple of bumps and shuffles echo down from upstairs. The man is at least a foot taller than the low, lofted ceiling.

"Something is going on out back," he offers with concern, pulling one of my old Michigan State University sweatshirts over his head. It's baggy on me, and snug on him (hello, biceps).

"Huh?" I get off the couch and walk into the kitchen, peering out of the back door into the yard. A half-awake Marty joins me, scruffing.

My small, fenced-in yard is undisturbed. Well, no more disturbed than usual. Marty has a dozen holes he's currently working on, with small piles of dirt crowning each. Bits of silver cardboard from Lydia's costume litter it, too. In the back, my single-car garage sits quietly, lights off and door closed, as it should be.

Behind it, though, blue and red flashing lights create a halo effect around the roofline, shrouding everything in an unnatural glow. I can't tell if it's a police car or an ambulance, but something is wrong.

Something is wrong at Eli's house.

Chapter Four

"Marty, remind me to buy blackout curtains," I grumble to the dog, exhausted. After a long night of flashing lights penetrating the safety of my loft, I yank myself out of bed far too early and make a pot of coffee.

Two police cars and an ambulance were at Eli's last night. I tried to get a hold of him after I saw the lights, but he never answered.

"What do we do, Marty? Should we go over there and see if Eli is okay? Offer our support?" The pup gives me side-eye, calling out my ulterior motive. "I just want to see if he's alright, I swear! He thanked me last time for keeping a lookout over his place, remember?"

He shuffles over to his food bowl and starts chomping on breakfast.

"Maybe I'll stop by Peyton's bakery first. He'd appreciate that."

I quickly get dressed in grubby work clothes and head out the door, a grouchy dog in tow. Hit with a frigid wind, I run back inside and grab a hat and scarf before venturing out again into the early morning. These shoulder seasons can be so annoying to dress for. This afternoon it'll be in the mid-sixties, but it's hovering around freezing right now.

We hustle the few blocks to the bakery, which is warm and steamy, smelling of fresh cinnamon rolls. Peyton slices loaves of bread behind the counter.

"Morning, Peyton," I shout over the rumble of the oven and bluegrass music blaring over the speaker. She turns around, surprised to see anyone this early.

"Good morning, sunshine." She goes over to another counter in the back and pours two cups of coffee from an industrial-sized maker, handing me one. *I need one that big for my house.*

"You're amazing, thank you," I gush, taking the cup. "I barely slept last night. Something was going on at Eli's. There were police cars and an ambulance there all night." I grip the cup in both hands, warming my fingers and savoring the bitter smell.

"Yeah, he called me this morning." She lowers her voice as her eyes dart to her delivery driver walking through the back entrance. "A girl we went to high school with died. One of his close friends." Her eyes bug out, and she leans in over the metal counter.

"What happened?" I whisper back. "Is Eli okay?"

I should've been on the receiving end of that phone call.

"He's not doing great." She shrugs with sympathy. "It was Paige. You didn't meet her; she stayed behind to pass out candy. I guess she had a heart attack. Eli didn't have details when I talked to him. They're doing some tests to learn more."

"Oh, my god. That's awful. I can't imagine. How are you? Were you two close?"

"I'm okay. No, we weren't that close, but it's still weird. We're too young to worry about friends dying."

"Yeah. For sure." I'm at a loss for words. "Think he'd appreciate a box of pastries? I was thinking about taking some over there before heading to work."

"You sure *you* want to go over there? You haven't been his favorite since well, you know." She slices the last loaf and brushes crumbs from her hands. Taking a long draw from her cup, she arches an eyebrow.

"I know, I know, but he's still one of my best friends, theoretically anyway, and it feels wrong to ignore something this big. He'd do the same for me. He looked a little cozy with Danni last night. Maybe it's not as big a thing now."

"I don't know, dude." She folds her arms in front of her denim apron. "He was pretty upset when I talked to him this morning. What's Jeremy going to think?"

Jeremy. I didn't really think about Jeremy.

"Jeremy will be fine. Just let me do something nice, okay? If it makes a difference, I'll say the food is from both of us."

"Fine, here." She folds a white cardboard box and starts loading doughnuts. "But for the record, I think you should give him space." She turns to the glass pastry case.

"Noted," I reply.

"Take these. Nobody can be too upset by a doughnut delivery." She smiles and hands me the box. "Keep me posted, yeah? I'm here all day, and already behind. If he needs anything, I can swing by this afternoon."

"Good luck. I'll try to remember to call you later, but if I get caught up, see you for spaghetti dinner tomorrow?"

"Eh, probably not this week. I'm slammed through Halloween. But hey, Maudy," she calls as I walk out the door, "just because you aren't his favorite right now, doesn't mean he still can't be yours." She tilts her head with a sad sort of smile as I walk through the door into the crisp morning.

What is that supposed to mean? Is that a slight on Jeremy? A little rude.

As the glass door shuts behind me, she calls out one more time. "I snuck in a little something special for you in there." She waves me off into the day.

Marty and I hustle through the whistle of the wind and the small leaf tornadoes swirling in the street. We make it to Eli's after devouring the lone cinnamon roll in the box of doughnuts on the way. After all the Halloween candy, I'm a little sick of sweets. Not too sick to *not* have the cinnamon roll, but sick enough to not go back to Peyton's later for another.

Eli's street has returned to normalcy. No ambulances or police cars in sight. Now that the sun peeks over the horizon, kitchen lights and TVs shine brightly through living room windows as I walk down the block. I have about an hour until I need to get to work. That should be plenty of time to check in and offer our condolences.

I tap quietly on his front door, not wanting to wake anybody. It cracks open with a reluctant *squeak!* as he jiggles the lock. A sliver of Eli's face appears in the small opening. He is red and puffy; the circles under his eyes are darker than usual, almost masking his freckles. Almost.

"Hey," he mutters through the two inches of space. "Now isn't a good time." He turns to shut the door.

"I brought doughnuts," I whisper, raising the box so he can see it. "From Peyton and me. She told me what happened. I'm so sorry, Eli."

He sighs and opens the door.

"Hi, Danni, it's nice to see you again." Marty and I walk through his living room and set the box on his counter.

The Yellow Power Ranger from the night before holds her legs tight, coiled in a ball on the couch. Her face is blotchy; makeup smudged like bruises. Her two braids fall lopsided.

"Hi," she murmurs, wrapped in a fleece blanket.

"Thanks, Maudy," Eli replies. "Sorry I didn't answer your text; I just saw it a minute ago. It's been a weird night." He sits down on the couch next to Danni. I hear the clanging of his upstairs bathroom pipes through the ceiling. Somebody else is getting ready.

"How did this happen? We—I saw the flashing lights and was worried." I deflate into an armchair while Marty makes himself at home at the pair's feet. He puts his head on Eli's lap. He hates that his buddy is upset.

Danni sniffles, quickly grabbing a tissue from a side table to blow her nose and dab the corners of her eyes. Eli considers her before responding.

"They think she had a heart attack or a stroke, maybe." His nose reddens. "They're doing some tests."

"I'm so sorry." I lean back, tearing up, seeing them this upset. To save face, I grab the doughnuts from the counter, set them down on the coffee table in front of us, and fuss over a handful of napkins. "Was she sick?"

"Not that we knew of. The EMTs think it could be stress-related. When we got back from taking Charlie trick-or-treating, she was on the porch where we left her, but she wasn't answering us when we were talking. I thought she fell asleep. She looked normal. It was getting late, and she's been working a ton."

"Oh, Eli. That's horrible." I cup my hand on my mouth, waiting for him to continue. Danni quietly cries into the folds of the blanket.

"Yeah, it is horrible. When she didn't wake up, I called the police." He swipes his fingers through his hair, unable to calm down.

"Charlie is going to be scarred for life," Danni sobs after a stint of silence. "I've ruined him. First his dad, and now all this. He's too young."

"You didn't ruin anything, Danni. Don't say that. Charlie will be okay." Eli gets up off the couch and pours three cups of coffee, giving one to each of us. As he hands me the cup, he offers a weary, beat smile as a peace offering, implying he's too tired to make this awkward right now.

Returning to his spot on the couch, Eli hands Danni a doughnut. "Here. You need to eat something." She appeases him and takes a small nibble before setting it down on the coffee table.

A door closes softly upstairs before Wesley appears in sweatpants and a Pop's Bar t-shirt, at least a decade old. He strokes his beard and takes a seat on the armchair opposite mine.

"Charlie is still asleep." He puts his index finger to his lips, signaling us to stay quiet. "Did you bring these doughnuts?" he asks. "Thank you." He grabs a Devil's Food from the box.

"I heard about your friend," I say quietly. "I'm so sorry for your loss."

"Thanks. It's unbelievable." He rubs his palms on his sweatpants. Then, turning to Danni and Eli, "I tried calling her mom, but nobody picked up. I'll try again later. She's probably still asleep."

Pitter patters thump down the stairs as a small, jet-black cat makes himself known with a squeaky *meow*. Marty's ears perk up, and he jaunts over to his four-legged friend.

Last spring, this tiny, black kitten found his way to my ranger station in the middle of a horrendous thunderstorm. He took shelter with us, and Marty instantly fell in love with him. Once our veterinarian gave him a clean bill of health, Eli adopted the little guy so he and Marty could remain friends.

"Hi, Gumbo." I pet the cat as he slinks along my pant leg, saying hello back. He's now quite a bit bigger than he was when I found him. With a chef for an owner, he eats well. Better than I do.

A stillness fills the room, but it's not uncomfortable. These people just lost a dear friend. As they swim in their thoughts, I bring everyone a coffee refill and let them stay submerged. After maybe five or so minutes, Danni breaks the silence.

"You don't happen to be Maudy *Lorso*, do you? I guess there probably aren't very many Maudys in town."

"Yes, I'm Maudy Lorso. Why?"

"Because you and I have been emailing. I'm Danielle Mauer, the Alumni Association's President. Sorry, I know that's random, but I'm worrying about all the work that needs to get done. Paige was set to receive a big achievement award at the class reunion; it all seems gross now…" she trails off.

"Oh, well. If you need any help, let me know." I offer her a smile that seems cheap, unsure of what else to say.

As Danni drifts, she grabs Eli's hand and squeezes, asking for an anchor down to Earth. He fidgets a little but doesn't pull away. *They're close, eh?*

We all sit quietly for a few more minutes, as I stew in the thought of them canoodling in front of school lockers. *Their friend just died, dummy! Could you be any more insensitive? It's good that he's getting over you. Be happy for him. This could help you two get back on good terms.*

A stern, rapid knock comes from the front door, pulling everyone's attention. I gesture for Eli to stay seated and go to answer it myself.

"Kelly, hi." I tug it open, wrestling with a sticky frame and off-center deadbolt. Her hair falls out of a looser-than-usual ponytail, and her tan Sheriff's Department uniform is wrinkled. Shiny purple nail polish and a thick, silver chain necklace are the only visible personal touches.

"Maudy, nice to see you." She nods politely, saying loud and clear that she's here in an official capacity, not a friend capacity. Kelly and I have become close over the last couple of years. Not to mention, she saved my life after I was thrown from a sand dune into a grave by a deranged killer this past spring.

"Elliot Nett, Danielle Mauer, and Wesley Mortenson, I need you to come down to the station. We need to ask you all a few more questions."

The police were here all night. What questions could she have left? Unless she found something...

"I can't leave Charlie." Danni jumps up like a firecracker.

"Bring him. We need to ask him questions as well." Kelly stands stiff, uncomfortable with herself. She's sad; a slight grimace splays across her face. She opens the door, gesturing for them to step outside. They're leaving now.

I nab Gumbo so he doesn't dart out the door while it hangs open.

"C'mon, guys. I don't want to make this harder than it already is."

Kelly avoids eye contact, staring at her shoes.

"Charlie is sleeping, let me wake him up." Danni rushes upstairs before Kelly can respond.

"Kelly." Eli stands up, clearly exasperated. "We told you everything we know last night. You were here. We sat in this room for hours, going over everything. What else could you possibly need from us?" He tries to reason with her.

"Since Paige's death was unexpected and she was under sixty years old," Kelly replies, "it's protocol to conduct some post-mortem bloodwork to learn more about the cause of death. Not to mention her current position."

We all follow along, although "her current position" piques my interest. Gumbo's squirms hold most of my attention, though, so I don't question it. Kelly will fill me in later.

Danni and groggy Charlie, still in pajamas, reemerge at the top of the staircase.

"Yes, you said that was the plan," Eli confirms. "We've been waiting here all morning for more information. We haven't heard anything yet."

"Her bloodwork came back abnormal, Eli. Paige was poisoned."

Chapter Five

A chorus of sobs, gasps, and resolute protests ring from the friends. I feel like I'm watching a movie, an observer of the chaos, unable to stop it. A swarm of state troopers enters the home, sweeping for evidence.

"We have a warrant." Kelly hands Eli a piece of paper. She stands stiff, ushering the team in.

"You can't be serious, Kelly," Eli scoffs. "Hey, watch it!" He shouts as books smash to the floor, swept off a nearby shelf.

"Maybe…maybe she did this on purpose?" Wesley asks hesitantly, eyes darting from officer to officer.

"Run the tests again. There's no way." Danni pants between renewed tears.

"You guys, you guys!" Kelly shouts over the turmoil, motioning for the friends to stop. "The dose of pills in her system is nowhere near normal ranges. It's not like she accidentally took an extra couple of pills. We're talking *dozens*. It wasn't an accident. Now, Wesley, I had a similar thought. Perhaps, she did this on purpose."

"That's impossible! She'd never do that," Danni shrieks, pacing in circles, watching Eli's house get ripped apart.

"I know nobody wants to think that," Kelly replies calmly, but firmly. "We have to consider every option. After analyzing the situation, I also don't think this was the case. I don't think someone who knows the end of their life is coming spends their last moments working."

The cohort starts to simmer down and chew on this development, watching the officers tear through Eli's house like a badge-clad tornado.

"Where does that leave us?" Eli asks, confused.

"Like I said, I need you all to come down to the station." She points out the door again.

Defeated, confused, and in total shock, Eli and friends put on their jackets under the apologetic eye of Officer Kelly. She hates this as much as they do. I give Eli a sympathetic smile and hold Gumbo tight.

"Maudy, would you also mind coming down to the station later? We're collecting statements from everyone who might've seen something. Since you live so close, we'd love to hear what you saw last night."

"Of course. I'll stop by on my way to work."

"Great, thanks. The troopers should be done in a minute. They'll lock up. You should go."

"Also, Maudy," Eli adds quietly, "could you feed Gumbo before you go? He hasn't had breakfast yet, and I'm not sure when I'll be back..."

"No problem, Eli." I reassure him that everything will be fine as Kelly ushers the foursome out of the door, leaving Marty, me, and Gumbo in the doorway, watching them climb into the back of two police cars parked on the street. Bangs and crashes rain down from upstairs, where the police tornado rips apart Eli's second floor. I spy little faces darting from behind neighbors' curtains, while a couple of folks *just so happen* to get their mail at this precise moment.

"What do we do now, Gumbo?" I sigh. The burnt marshmallow of a cat studies me, one of his eyes scarred over, and trills. "Breakfast? Sure."

Kibble clangs into Gumbo's bowl, echoing the rattling from above, quickly followed by lazy crunches from the hungry cat. I scoop half-eaten doughnuts back into the box and load the dirty coffee mugs into the dishwasher, nestling them next to four *Power Rangers*-themed tumblers. A sickly-sweet smell wafts out of the machine. Whatever they were drinking last night was quite the cocktail. It reminds me of our Franken-tinis.

After a few minutes of futilely cleaning up, the tornado already hitting Eli's kitchen, I put the leash back on the dog and get ready to go.

"Let him eat in peace, Romeo." I yank Marty away from his soulmate, giving Gumbo a goodbye pat on the head, and leave through Eli's back door. Crossing the gate into my backyard, overgrown grass nipping at my ankles, I unleash the hound to run around before work.

After a good playtime and worm torture session, he joins me inside. "Martin, you're staying put this morning. I have to see Kelly, and we both know dogs aren't allowed in the Sheriff's Station. I might be in there a while and don't want to leave you tied outside too long."

He pouts, spiteful drool dripping onto my couch.

Immediately after giving him the bad news, I throw a peanut butter-flavored treat onto the rug as a hefty bribe. "Okay, don't eat the furniture, love you, bye!" While he's distracted, I pop out the front door and head to meet Kelly.

Walking into the small Sheriff's Office, my memory deluges with when I last stepped inside the sparsely decorated space. Police wrongly arrested my now-boyfriend for first-degree murder, and I was scrambling to balance a park-saving campground opening with figuring out who dumped a body onto one of my trails.

Feeling overwhelmed and a little anxious, I text Jeremy just to say hi. I wish him well as he closes his deal this morning, saving Eli's news for later. No need to distract him with that right now.

The station is small, on par with the crime level typical of Stone's Throw. The taupe-painted cinderblock room is bare bones. Kelly and

Eli sit near the corner vending machines at a round break table, while the rest of his friends wait on the opposite corner on a handful of folding chairs.

With a slight smile, I force the vision of Jeremy in that back jail cell out of my mind. His arrest this past spring feels like it was yesterday. *We should be thinking about the future, not the past.*

Not wanting to interrupt, I approach another officer at a nearby desk. "Excuse me." I knock on it like a front door. "Kelly asked that I provide a statement regarding a recent incident. Can I talk to you, or...?"

He looks up. "Take a seat, and someone will be with you shortly." He returns to his computer and points to the chairs along the wall. I plop down next to Wesley.

"Long time no see," he says. "Did Gumbo give you any problems? That little guy is something else." He tries to crack a halfhearted smile. "I'm glad Eli took him in."

"I gave him breakfast, and he was grateful. Particularly chatty this morning. The police were still there when I left."

"Crazy, eh? I'm sure it'll be fine. None of us hurt Paige. They won't find anything." He smiles. "That monster knows how to put it away, that's for sure." He switches back to Gumbo. "I swear, since I've been here, he's gotten at least a dump truck full of treats." He tries to muster a laugh, but it's more of an exasperated exhale. *He keeps changing the subject. How is he not more upset that his stuff is getting ransacked right now?*

"How have things been here?" I ask, hoping Charlie doesn't overhear. The kid is glued to a handheld video game, so it feels safe enough if we keep our voices low.

"She spoke with Charlie first, which took maybe ten minutes. It was quick. She's been with Eli since." He glances at his watch. "It's been over half an hour already."

"Looks like we might be here for a while." I text Zach to let him know I'll be late. I also forward him the email Danni sent about the hayride so he can start on some of the to-dos if he has time.

Kelly and Eli look frustrated with one another. They keep their voices quiet, but he snorts or raises his tone every few minutes, and she does it right back. Then she'll put a hand on his shoulder like she's apologizing. It's hard to tell what exactly the vibe is. Either way, it's not good. It doesn't feel like a simple witness statement.

Could Eli be involved in this? There's no way...

After another twenty minutes, she ushers him straight out of the building, preventing him from coming over to us. I try to catch his expression, but his head hangs low with his eyes toward his feet. *This isn't good.*

Kelly points at me, waving me over to the table.

"Hey." She takes a few deep breaths and shuffles papers in front of her, flipping to a fresh page in her notebook. "So, let's start with what you did last night, and what you saw as it pertains to this fiasco." She glances up with the whites of her eyes, saddened, pen poised.

"How about we start with what the hell you're doing?" I hiss through a thin line of a mouth. "Eli didn't hurt her. We both know that. A search warrant? *Really,* Kelly?" I cross my arms. "What the heck were you two saying just now?"

"I feel like such a jerk," she admits. "You know I love Eli. We've been friends for years. I feel horrible, but you don't know what I know. And, I'm not the one in charge here. The state force is pulling jurisdiction." She cringes. "Trust me, it's a bummer. I don't have a lot of authority. Even still, Sheriff Landry is breathing down my neck to edge my way in and be the one to solve this. He's flipping his lid. This could make or break his career. He wants his name on this case."

"The state police?" I ask.

"Yep. The big guns. Of course, I don't want Eli involved. But I can't ignore facts. He escalated first. He was getting defensive." She shrugs. "Not to mention that the state is itching to close this *fast*, given the circumstances. Did you see how they tore through Eli's house? Sloppy police work, if you ask me." She shakes her head. "Enough about all this, though. Let's focus on you. Spill. What were you doing last night?"

I pause, unconvinced.

"For the record," she continues, "Eli is just a person of interest right now, and he's not the only one. Nobody's charging him with anything yet."

"Fine." I cave. "But we're not dropping this."

She prompts me to start.

"I had the girls over before we took Lydia and Gemma trick-or-treating." She nods, taking notes. "It was the four of them, me, and Peyton. We all put on costumes, had a drink on the back patio, that sort of thing. Jeremy met us on the street later."

"Great. Did anything at Eli's seem off? Did you notice anything?"

How could I tell her that what was "off" was that we were having two separate parties? We would've all hung out together if he and I weren't in this bizarre limbo. "He basically had the same situation going on over in his backyard. I saw them all out on the back patio."

"Them? Be more specific for me."

"The Power Rangers. Charlie was playing in the yard, and the others were all dressed and

sitting outside. I didn't know who they were at the time, but we met later that night. They were in full costumes, too."

"Got it. Okay, so then you went out trick-or-treating. You ran into them?"

"Yes. Also, Lydia and Gemma did trick-or-treat at Eli's house. It was before we bumped into their group downtown. The girls walked up to his front porch, but none of us went up with them. We watched from the sidewalk. They grabbed candy from the bowl. A Pink Power Ranger sat with it."

"Did you see the Pink Ranger move? Was she sitting upright?"

"I don't know, but you should ask Lydia. I bet she will remember. I didn't notice anything strange at the time, but I wasn't paying that close attention, I guess. I dressed Marty up like Professor Moriarty from *Sherlock Holmes,* and everyone kept coming up to pet him in his little suit. I was distracted a lot that night."

Kelly makes a note. "Okay, so you ran into them after you passed Eli's house. How long after?"

"Oh, jeez, um…we were downtown. Maybe it was half an hour later? It could've been less than that. Anyway, the rest of the Power Rangers were all there. Eli introduced us to Wesley and Danni. I saw Charlie there; he ran around with Lydia and Gemma. We chatted for maybe five minutes, then went our separate ways. It wasn't a long conversation, just a brief hello. Peyton and Danni agreed they should catch up sometime this week. Peyton was in the same graduating class as all those guys."

"Yeah, I was a couple of years ahead of them. I remember." She continues scribbling. "Anything else weird that night?"

She's not bothering to study me as she asks questions, continuing to take notes. Her expression is calm and clearly sympathetic to the weirdness of the situation. *At least I'm not a suspect.*

"Nothing until we saw the police lights from the back window. Jeremy was up in the loft and noticed them first."

"Jeremy was up in the loft, eh?" She pops an eyebrow.

"Get your head out of the gutter, Kell," I reply. "He was changing into sweats before driving home."

"Sure, whatever you say. No judgment from me." She laughs a real laugh, a brief moment of levity in the dark situation. "One last question: Did you see Leonard that night?"

"Leonard Henley?" I ask, surprised. "Like Village Council President, Leonard?"

"That's the one." She affirms, eyes on her notebook.

"I did run into him, just before we got to Eli's house, now that I think of it. He made a snide comment about me not being ready to be on the Council." I roll my eyes. "He was with a couple of other adults, much younger than him, and a half-dozen kids. He said they were his grandchildren."

"Interesting." Her scribbling continues. "What's your impression of him?"

"Um, I don't know. He's usually grumpy. He's not my favorite, to be honest. He and Charlotte argue with me about park stuff all the time. What does he have to do with this?" I ask. She's got a thick case file next to her.

"Just exploring all the options right now. Keep an eye on him, though, eh? Especially with you running for a seat on the council. If you find yourself in a room with the man, keep your eyes and ears open for me." She taps the side of her head with her pen.

"You've piqued my interest."

"Don't go crazy. Just keep your wits about you, I don't want to have to fish you out of another hole in the woods."

After another moment, she looks up from her notes. "Alright, I think that's all I need right now. Thanks for stopping by. I'll follow up with any more questions later if needed."

"Sounds good, you know where to find me. Good luck with all of this. I'm going to keep bugging you until you give me details." I slap the top of the table in the universal Midwestern *best be on my way!* sign and wave goodbye to Wesley and Danni as I leave the building.

Chapter Six

Java Jones just isn't the same without Tracy. Ever since she left for law school, my morning trips have dropped in frequency. Her replacement is entirely adequate, but the morning chats and surprise concoctions are a thing of the past, at least until she comes home for summer break. *If* she comes home for summer break. She's bound to get an awesome internship in a law office somewhere. I'm thrilled for her; she deserves all the success that's coming her way.

With a pumpkin latte in hand, I walk into the ranger station where Zach sits behind his desk, the small fireplace crackling in the background.

"Morning, sorry I'm late. Kelly told me to blame her." I smile and set my things down at my desk, the only other one in the small log cabin.

"Tell. Me. Everything." He swivels in his chair, eyes wide, unable to resist. "What happened? Is everyone okay?"

"What have you heard?" I ask, hanging my coat on a hook near the door and settling in.

"Pretty much everything you could dream up. Laura told me a fight broke out, and Charlotte started a rumor that somebody was embezzling." He rolls his eyes and throws his hands up.

"Worse," I state flatly, opening my laptop and booting it up for the day. "Eli's friend died. She was spending the week with him for Homecoming stuff. Kelly thinks somebody killed her."

"Oh, my god. You're kidding." He leans forward, mouth hanging open. "Who was it?"

"Paige, something? I didn't catch her last name. I never met her. The only time I saw her, she was in costume, a backyard away."

"Paige Ramos?" He spins around in his chair again. "I can't believe Paige Ramos died."

"Wait, that's Paige Ramos? Like, *Ramos* Ramos? The state senator?"

"Uh, yeah. That's the only Paige that went to Stone's Throw that I know of. She's around Eli's age, so that would check out."

That's what Kelly meant by "her current position." That's why the state police are involved... Was this an assassination?

Turning back to Zach, "She's sent me nice letters supporting the park. Especially after what happened this spring. This place meant a lot to her."

I rummage around one of my drawers and pull out a typed letter, handing it to him. "It was so touching that I kept it."

He skims it, handing it back to me. "Wow. This is wild. It's too bad." He spins back around in his chair, facing his computer. "I'll work on squashing these other rumors and see if I can dig up anything helpful. She was up for reelection this year, right? I feel like I've seen her signs along the highway. Who is running against her? I wonder what will happen with that."

"Leonard is running against her," I state slowly. *That's why Kelly asked about him.* "Kelly is investigating, so send any info her way. Everyone was outside last night; it seemed like somebody would've seen something. What a shame."

"Yeah, for sure," he replies.

We return to our work for the rest of the morning. I get everything squared away for Danni, assuming the hayride is still on, while Zach maps out next week's lesson plans. Still no word from Jeremy; his meeting must be going long.

Clicking across my calendar, rearranging my schedule to jam everything into the days ahead, I work my magic to squeeze all the hayride-related logistics and obligations in.

"Coordination meeting at the marina, football game halftime announcement," I list, reviewing Danni's email, making sure everything is covered.

I stuff certificates for guided hikes and foraging excursions into a few manila envelopes and scribble *Silent Auction* on them. Making copies of the park's insurance policies and rules, I write *Park Forms for Hayride* on the other.

Danni's email reads like a master plan for all festivities on Saturday. A silent auction, dinner, and dancing at the renovated marina hosted by the graduating classes of 2000-2010, while a hayride snakes through the park. Downtown will be in full, spooky swing with old Halloween movies on a blow-up screen, and a more adult (beer tent included) party in the street.

"I'm going to stay late tonight to finish some administration stuff after my check-up," I tell Zach at lunchtime. "You might be gone for the day by the time I get back. I'll see you tomorrow."

Wrapping up his lesson plans, Zach puts on his jacket and heads into town for lunch, as I get ready for my daily walk in the park, which I lovingly call my "check-up."

I get maybe a hundred feet up the main trailhead before the *thump, thump, thump* of running feet gains on me from behind. Spinning around, I tighten the grip on the pepper spray canister in my pocket and square my hips.

"Hey," Eli pants.

"Oh, it's you," I relax my grip.

"Glad I caught you. I saw Zach on the bridge, and he said you were heading into the woods for a while." He hunches over, hands on his knees, breathing heavily. "I need your help."

I hand him my water bottle from my pack, eyeing him quizzically. A Smokey the Bear sticker stuck to the bottle watches both of us. "How'd it go with Kelly?"

"That's what I need to talk to you about. Not good." He takes a sip and hands me back my bottle.

"I can take Gumbo for a while, so you don't need to worry about him escaping with all the…comings and goings?" I offer, choosing my words carefully.

"I didn't think about that, but that would be really helpful, thanks. Charlie doesn't seem to grasp the *Keep the Door Shut* rule,and Gumbo's been taking advantage of it. That's not what I was going to ask, though."

There's desperation in his sage green eyes, on the verge of tears. He still fidgets like he did this morning. I pause, waiting for him to continue.

"I need your help to figure out who killed Paige."

"No, no, no," I insist. "I'm done playing detective. It got me into serious trouble last time." I point to my leg, which Lucas Sullivan pulverized. A weird bump on my shin bone is there as permanent proof. "I'm still not back to normal after that fiasco. I almost pepper-sprayed you right now." I pull the canister from my pocket and show it to him. "I was seconds away from breaking Jeremy's wrist last night when he came up to me on the street."

Shrugging, I put the pepper spray back in my pocket. Desperation runs wild across his face.

"Maudy, please. I'm begging you." He grabs one of my hands. "Kelly made her suspicions clear. I'm a suspect. You saw us at the station, right? She's just waiting until she's done more digging before she charges me with something. I swear I had nothing to do with this! None of us did. Paige was our friend. We wouldn't kill her." He drops my hand and paces, zigzagging across the trail, kicking pebbles in the dirt.

"No offense, but it's not like we've been the closest friends lately. I've been trying, Eli," I murmur, stepping back towards the tree line, feeling a little too vulnerable.

"I know, I'm sorry," he huffs.

"I have a lot going on right now," I waffle. *I'm trying to win an election. And I have to organize a last-minute hayride. On top of an already demanding day job, and a new relationship...*

"I don't know who else to ask." He drops his voice to an almost-whisper. "I'm going to keep trying to clear my name, but I don't think Kelly will believe anything I say."

I kick a rock myself. "Kelly's a good cop. She'll figure out who hurt Paige. And for what it's worth, the state police are in charge. Not her."

Is he hiding something? Kelly made it seem like she had a handful of avenues to pursue. Why is he this freaked out already?

He locks eyes with me in a way he hasn't in months. "Look. The four of us have a lot of history. We've been friends for two decades. Friendships this long don't come without baggage. She could come up with reasons for any of us to have hurt her. That doesn't mean we did."

What are those reasons? I don't know anything about Danni or Wesley. Why should I put myself at risk for two people I don't even know?

"No promises, Eli." I cave.

A wide grin replaces his desperation. "Thank you, thank you."

"And just a heads up, Kelly didn't just ask me about you guys. She's investigating other people, too."

He rushes me for a hug, then halfway through, releases and steps back, an uneasy smile on his face. "Sorry, that was weird."

I brush him off. "I said no promises. I'll grab Gumbo in a bit, okay? I need to do some more work today, but then I want to know more about this friendship 'baggage.'" Shuffling back, I brush away the flyaway hair from my face.

"Amazing, yes, thank you! Use your spare key, yeah? You still have it?

Let yourself in." I fiddle with my keyring in my jacket pocket, feeling for his rusted old key. "I'm going to head over to Pop's to prep for the dinner rush, so if you need me, I'll be there. I'll let you know if Kelly tells us anything else."

He waves goodbye, already jogging back to the parking lot, as I march into the woods, eager to let my mind wander under the safety of the watchful eyes of the Paper Birch trees before all hell breaks loose.

He said he needs me.

* * *

"Dammit, Eli," I mutter, wiggling the rusted key in the lock of his front door, frustrated that he never fixed this janky old thing. "How do you do this every day?" After a few shoulder checks and a death grip, I shove the door open and stumble inside. Marty leaps in behind me.

"Hello? Anybody home?" I shout, shoving the door closed. No response.

Eli's house is dark but welcoming. It's decorated in slate blues and warm browns and cluttered with word puzzle books, knick-knacks he's amassed over the years, and Gumbo's crinkly cat toys. It looks like an earthquake hit; the police raid left it in bad shape.

I walk through the living room and into the kitchen, stepping carefully around couch cushions and picture frames scattered on the floor. A small furball emerges from seemingly nowhere and chirps hello.

"Hey there, buddy. You're going to stay with us for a few days. That sound good?" He pounces over to weave through Marty's fuzzy legs and trills at us both, which I take as a resounding, *yes!* Rummaging through cabinets, I find a grocery bag and pack his food, treats, a handful of toys, and a dime bag of catnip.

Gumbo quickly loses interest and trots upstairs, sassily swishing his tail as he prances. Marty bounds after him with a full helicopter tail.

Eli did say to investigate...he wouldn't have a problem with me starting here, would he? If they are innocent, they don't have anything to hide.

"Wesley? Danni? Anybody home?" I shout again up the stairs. Still no response. *And if they aren't innocent, at least they're here.*

Convincing myself all too easily, I follow the animals up the worn, wooden stairs. Although Eli's been one of my best friends since I moved here and I've spent countless hours in this house, I've only been on the second floor a handful of times. He had a plumbing problem in his first-floor bathroom last year, and for a couple of weeks, he had guests use the one upstairs. Other than that, I've never really explored.

Walking up the pine staircase, creaking and cracking, I reach the top, facing a single hallway. Two doors are on the left, and two are on the right. The first door on the right is the bathroom, and the first door on the left is Eli's bedroom. I have no idea what's behind the others. *How do I not know the layout of his house? Was I as close to him as I thought?*

I start in Eli's bedroom. The white-painted door moans as I open it. Gumbo struts in like he owns the place, while Marty and I follow. "If I killed my high school friend, who just so happens to be a bigwig politician, what would I be hiding?"

Opening his drawers and sifting through his closet feels wrong, but curiosity gets the better of me. Almost everything is already tossed on the floor or piled on the bed anyway. *He asked me to do this, so I'm not technically doing anything wrong, right?* I poke around his t-shirts and a heap of dirty aprons on the floor.

The room floats in an airy gray paint, which surprises me given the rest of the house's darker palette. His bedspread is a black-and-white, homemade quilt, worn from time and use. It's stitched in squares like a crossword puzzle. Marty makes himself instantly at home, hopping up and pacing in circles before curling up on the bed.

"We're not supposed to leave evidence behind, butthead," I grumble at the dog. "He might notice your fur on his bedspread."

Marty replies with a look so unbothered that he starts to fall asleep.

I can't help but compare it to Jeremy's bedroom. Jeremy's swanky flat overlooks Grand Traverse Bay, right in the heart of downtown Traverse City. His bedroom has a wall entirely of windows, with a stunning view of the water. His bed is low to the ground with a solid black bedspread. It feels like a five-star hotel room, which is a fun luxury to experience. Eli's room feels more lived-in. More personal, maybe.

Rummaging through the rest of the space, I come up empty. There's nothing unusual stashed away or hidden. At least not anything the police left behind. I smile as I shut the door on our way out, thinking of him decompressing after a long day's work in this cozy nest he built for himself.

Gumbo trots ahead, tail high like a tour guide's flag, leading me to the next room. "What is this Gumbo? A guest room? A gym?" I enter a space with a clear identity crisis. Plastic storage tubs stack high in the corner. Underneath the window, looking out onto the front lawn, is an old futon, currently unfolded into a bed. Nothing is on the walls, but a dusty treadmill takes up half the floor space.

Marty ambles in after us, disgruntled that his nap was disturbed. He pokes his long nose around, circling the room with his feline friend.

A large duffel bag and a backpack are on the ground next to the futon. They've been dumped out, piles of clothes and miscellaneous travel needs strewn about. Considering the size and style of the clothes, I'm guessing these bags are Wesley's. Red Power Ranger costume pieces litter the floor under the futon, from mask to shoe covers.

Rummaging through his things, I find an old photo of the group in the same Power Ranger costumes, doing goofy action-movie poses. Their masks are off, and everyone is making silly faces. They look maybe sixteen or seventeen. Young Wesley is in red, and Paige's darker complexion pops against her yellow top.

Eli's freckles were even more prominent back then, and his reddish blond hair went down to his shoulders. "Look at his hair," I giggle to the dog, smiling. He's too busy sniffing the thick layer of dust in the air, agitated by the police. "I need to save this." I pull out my phone and snap a photo of the old Polaroid for safekeeping (and future teasing).

His high school look wasn't any better than mine. I was rarely seen without an oversized flannel around my waist, a textbook in my arms, and dark curly hair pulled into Mickey-Mouse-ear buns on the top of my head.

Continuing to look around the room, I clock a deflated air mattress folded neatly in the corner and a black carry-on suitcase tied with a bright orange polka-dot ribbon. *Paige or Danni's?*

I check the tag. It's Paige's. *So, Paige and Wesley were sharing this room. Danni is probably bunking with Charlie in the other.*

"Empty," I grumble as I unzip the suitcase. The police took all of Paige's stuff. Gumbo takes a seat on the open futon, staring at me with his good eye, the other a milky swirl. "At least we know she and Wesley were sharing this room. Maybe he knows something helpful. Alright, Gumbo, you lead the way," I order as we move on.

Moving on to the next door, I walk into an office of sorts. Over-looking Eli's backyard sits a beautiful oak desk. He has a laptop, a file cabinet, and a fleece bed for Gumbo, positioned in a prime sunshine spot. The window has a clear view of my backyard, too. I can see Marty's holes polka dotting the lawn. In the corner of the small room, an armchair and a coffee table are pushed off to the side, making space for two twin air mattresses.

"This must be where Danni and Charlie are sleeping, eh, Gumbo?"

He chirps and moseys over to the desk, stretching in the warm cat bed, purring like an engine.

Charlie's backpack sits on the armchair. They each have a purple suitcase tucked into the closet, with matching luggage tags.

I peek in Charlie's backpack, trying to keep things organized. It looks like the state troopers didn't mess with Charlie's things. Inside, he has a couple of books, school folders, and a journal.

Popping open the journal, scrawled drawings of dark shadows chasing a little kid stare back at me. There's page after page of similar pictures, over and over again. It's pretty disturbing, especially considering how young Charlie is. I'd guess he's between Lydia and Gemma, making him five or six. A typed note nestles between the pages. It has an apple border.

"Jeez," I say, unfolding the paper, taking a closer look. It's from Charlie's teacher.

Dear Ms. Mauer,

Charlie is acting out in class, which frankly isn't surprising given his current situation. He's starting to display signs of paranoia, talking often of nightmares, and is insistent that monsters are coming after him. Grief manifests in many different ways, especially in young children. I'd like to meet with you to create a game plan to set him up for success. Please stop in at your earliest convenience.

Thank you.

"Whoa, poor kid. He's having nightmares," I tell the animals. "That's probably why he's doing these creepy drawings. They're his nightmares."

Continuing to look through his backpack, I find a stash of snacks in the front pocket. Everything from apple juice to chocolate squares, to some sugar squeeze goo. The kid is set. No judgment here, I'm a woman who keeps emergency s'mores supplies in my office desk.

Danni has another bag, an over-the-shoulder messenger-style one. The worn green and gray satchel is wide open, zipper broken from years of use, or maybe a brazen officer. Inside are tons of disorganized papers, a clipboard, charging cords, loose bits and bobs like lipstick, gum wrappers, and change. It's a mess. *Did the police leave it this way, or was it already like this?*

I dig through the papers, reading as I go. Most are for the events this week, including the class reunion this Saturday. There are spreadsheets with to-do lists and notes for her to follow up on. There is also a crumpled stack that, upon quick inspection, appears to be adoption papers for Charlie. Half of the information is still left blank; she's in the middle of filling it out.

Charlie isn't her kid? She did say something this morning about his dad, didn't she? "First his dad, now this" or something? Peyton offered condolences, too. Note to self to look into what happened.

Not finding anything else out of the ordinary except for the kids' drawings straight out of a horror movie, I put everything back and move on. The last room is the only one I have been in before: the bathroom.

This is a no-frills space with small, white hexagonal tiles on the floor and the bottom half of the walls. Opening the medicine cabinet reveals Eli's toiletries, which are about as bare bones as a person can get (would it kill the man to use sunscreen?). He's got a toothbrush, a couple of prescriptions, a bar of soap, and a box of bandages.

"Well, Gum, nobody can call him high maintenance," I chuckle to the cat, who follows me into the stark room.

Gumbo slinks around the room as I riffle through the cabinet. He's as curious as I am and puts his entire head and two front paws in the small wastebasket underneath the sink. He bats at something; a rattling, tinkling sound rings out as something knocks against the metal can.

"What's that, Gumbo?" I crouch down and get a better look under the sink. Reaching into the basket, I pull out a small, clear glass vial. It's empty. "Huh. Somebody takes medicine?" I ask the cat who rubs up against my knees.

Next to the basket is a red sharps container. I can't see inside, but shake it enough to hear used needles jingle. "Maybe Paige did have an underlying condition." The cat's expression couldn't be any more skeptical. "You never know!"

Chapter Seven

With the obvious places sufficiently snooped and my curiosity awakened with the medicine vial, I head back downstairs, zip the cat up in my jacket, grab his stuff, and head out Eli's door. Cradling the cat and holding Marty's leash tightly, the three of us slip through the yard over to my house.

"What am I, chopped liver?" I asked the dog after releasing both of them in my kitchen. He couldn't care less about me now that Gumbo is here. "Wait, scratch that. You'd be all over chopped liver. What am I, a head of lettuce?" I ask, still getting nothing from him.

With a playful romp around the living room, the two catch up on the latest pet gossip as I get the cat situated for his stay at Lorso Villa. Marty and I have Gumbo-sat before; we all know the drill.

After the initial excitement wears off, the two fall asleep on the couch as I shut the door behind me, needing to return to the park.

"Kelly, it's me," I say as she picks up the phone. "Got a sec?"

"Hey." I hear her crumple up paper and lean back in her desk chair, squeaking loudly. "What's up? Remember something else from last night you want to tell me?"

"No, nothing else. But I wanted to, uh, offer my help. You said the state police are in charge here? And the Sheriff is pressuring you to figure this out? Let me help."

"Now, why would you ever offer that? Wait, don't tell me. Let me take a crack at it." I hear her rub her hands together. "Mr. Eli Nett asked you to do a bit of poking around, yes? To prove his innocence?" I hear the amusement in her expression; she lets out a dry laugh.

"Your detective skills precede you. He's worried."

"Yep, thought so. I mean, he and his friends are on the suspect list, for sure. They're not the only ones, but they're pretty high up there. The state police is still waiting on other testimonials and interviews to clarify some things."

"It couldn't be Eli," I declare, trying to hide my desperation. "Let me help. I'll buy your spaghetti every week for the next six months. Or better yet, Eli will give us both free plates for life."

If I can just do this one thing, Eli and I can get back to our usual. To best friends.

To Muddy and Coach.

As I weave through town, making my way towards the park, I look down Main Street and see Pop's weathered sign.

"I don't think so," Kelly replies. "Not that I wouldn't love an extra set of eyes and ears out there, but Sheriff Landry wouldn't go for it this time. There's no connection to the park, no clear reason to have you consult. I'd get reamed out for sending that request up the chain. Especially with the added attention on this one."

"What if I don't technically consult…" I tentatively ask, tapping the seconds as they pass with my free hand on my jeans as I cross the Birch River Bridge. Old habits die hard.

"I'm listening," she replies.

"I could just *keep an eye out* for you."

The silence from the other side of the line lingers. *Tap, tap, tap.*

"I'll tell you what," she whispers. "I'm desperate. If I don't figure this one out, or stay in the mix at least, the Sheriff will kill me. You do what you want, I'm not going to stop you. Check your email. I may or may not be sending something over."

"Thanks, Kell." The smile comes through in my voice.

"So, as I was saying, Maudy," she says much louder, "I don't think we can bring you on this case, but please keep an eye out for any suspicious behavior and report it to the police. Feel free to use my direct line if you'd like." Somebody's listening.

"Roger that, officer," I respond, understanding.

"Also, if it's not too much trouble," she continues at a normal volume again, "there is something I wouldn't mind your help with. It's not work-related, but..."

"Sure, what's up? Anything."

"The Sheriff's Department is supposed to ride in the parade on Thursday night, but we have to bail with all this going on. Is your park crew riding already? Would you guys take over our float? I guess the marching band timed out this whole big thing based on the number of floats, and we're throwing everything off by ditching."

"Maybe *you* owe *me* six months of spaghetti dinners, Kell," I joke. "But, sure. No biggie."

"How about we call it even, eh?" she whispers.

Add "build float" to my to-do list.

With the sun descending in the autumn sky, I make the quick trip back to the park office to check in before the end of the workday. Knocking the mud off my boots, I step inside. Zach has already left and put out the fire that was snapping away earlier. A note on his desk reads, *Ducking out a little early to run a work-related errand. Be back to lock up.*

"A work-related errand? Okay, weirdo." The note is strange. Usually, he'd just run out to take care of whatever it was.

I start studying snippets of the case file Kelly emailed over, reaching photos of Paige. She seems...peaceful, at least not in agony or with any visible injuries.

The picture instantly transports me back to the woods, trying to catch my stubborn dog hot on the trail of Michael Price's decomposing body, just a handful of months ago. The ticking cuckoo clock rang like a gong as I came upon his corpse. He had head trauma and was dead for a while. Peaceful was not a word I would use to describe him. Even though I didn't know Paige personally, I'm relieved she didn't seem to suffer a similar fate.

It's been less than a day, and after reading this, Kelly and her team have whittled down the suspect pool to Wesley, Eli, Danni, and Leonard. Officers canvassed Eli's block, gathering witness statements from neighbors, but nobody reported anything of interest. Paige just leaned back in the Adirondack chair, and nobody noticed since she was in a full mask. Many reported Leonard there during the appropriate timeframe, but so was everybody else. The whole town wandered by that night. By that logic, I'd be a suspect, too.

There are a few notes about a possible political motive, which is why Leonard is on the list, but the details are thin. A draft of a speech was found in her lap; she was editing it when she died.

I start reading the background information they dug up on Eli and his friends. Lots of pieces are still missing; they must still be in the evidence-gathering phase. Charlie is listed first. He's five years old, lives in Hemlock Pond, and his father recently died of a drug overdose. His mother died in a motorcycle accident when he was a baby, so his father's sister, Danielle, was temporarily given custody. She's trying to make it permanent and is in the process of adopting him outright.

Tingles shoot down my back, and I shudder, reminded of Jeremy's drunk driving accident that killed Lucas Sullivan's mother two decades ago. My stomach flips, thinking of these young children left without mothers.

"Wow, so Danni just took on caring for Charlie this summer," I murmur to myself, skimming the document.

Zach pops through the door, smiling, and sits at his desk. "Sorry about that. Had a bit of business to take care of." He wakes up his computer and settles in quickly.

"No worries… Your vagueness is killing me, though." I hold up the sticky note. "A 'work-related errand?' What kind of nonsense is that? Where'd you go?"

"Oh, you know. General things…" He grins, a hint of mischief coming through. "I promise, it's all good stuff. A little patience wouldn't kill you."

Another note to self: Dig into this "work-related business."

He searches through his backpack, unloading binders and files. "I brought you this." He hands me a to-go container of Pop's tomato soup. It's my absolute favorite.

"Nice, thanks. Late lunch at Pop's today? You were downtown for a while." I open the steaming container, pulling a spoon from my desk drawer.

"Mhm," he confirms, still a little cagey.

"I have a bit of work-related business for you, too," I admit between spoonfuls of soup that's mostly croutons, just the way I like it. Zach watches patiently, waiting for me to swallow.

"I sort of…maybe…might have been coerced into doing a float for the Homecoming parade on Thursday."

"Ugh, you didn't." He grimaces. "How did that happen? We already declined when they were looking for volunteers a month ago. I thought you had stuff to do already with the council campaign?" He immediately pulls out a new sticky note and begins writing.

"Kelly said that the Sheriff's Department has to drop because of Paige's case, and something about the marching band's timing getting messed up, I don't know. It seemed like a nice thing to do since they have so much on their plate right now. One less thing for them to worry about. But we're not starting from scratch! They're giving us their float. I can get out of the campaign stuff for the night to help."

"I have time tomorrow to assess the situation. Maybe it won't be too bad."

"Thank you, thank you. I'm happy to lead it up or follow your command. Whatever you want. I was also going to see if Jim wanted to ride with us and maybe Emma and her garden volunteers, too."

Emma, a master gardener, tends our pollinator garden near the outdoor classroom in the park. She runs our garden club.

"That sounds like a good plan. I'll focus on the float; you handle the people. No offense, but your aesthetic is a little *yard sale* to lead up the design," he laughs. The glint in his eye says he's excited for the challenge. Not that he'd ever admit it, but this is his version of the Super Bowl.

"Sounds good. And no offense taken. I call it 'maximalist chic.'" I wink, diving into the bowl of soup.

We both work late into the evening, trying to catch up on the thousand things we need to do. I chip away at a grant proposal I've been working on for over a month, but my mind keeps wandering to Danni and Charlie.

"Zach, did you hear anything about a drug overdose recently? I saw that someone died in Hemlock Pond not too long ago. I don't know how I missed it when it happened."

He doesn't need to know why I'm asking.

"Oh, yeah. You didn't hear about that?" He twirls around in his chair, chewing on the end of a pencil.

"If I did, I don't remember. What happened again?" I swivel to face him as well. The eyes of the taxidermized animals perched on the shelf judge me.

"From what I heard, it wasn't super unexpected. The guy, I don't remember his name off the top of my head, had a bad problem for a while and accidentally overdosed. I think his family tried to get him help a few times, but it didn't take." He shrugs, a slight frown on his face. "It's a sad story. Why do you ask?"

"Oh, no reason. I just overheard people talking about it and wanted to be looped in. A lot of the Hemlock Pond folks are around this week, and I don't want to say something stupid."

"Good call. Lord knows you can put your foot in your mouth." He smiles and turns back to face his computer.

Now well past the end of the work day, we say our goodbyes over the bridge, and I head east toward home. He continues down Main, maybe to meet a friend for a drink or dinner. He doesn't say.

* * *

Thump, thump, thump! I knock on Jeremy's black condo door with the toe of my boot, arms full.

"You're late." He pulls it open, a dishtowel on his shoulder, ushering me in.

"I know, I know. Sorry," I puff, dropping the takeout bag on his marble countertop, shedding my jacket.

"Glad you made it. Better late than never." He outstretches his long, tight arms and envelops me. I look back at my backpack leaning up against the door. *What else is in that case file?*

"Drink?" He hands me a lowball glass, saving another for himself.

Jeremy's condo is *stunning*. It's brand new. Everything has its place, just like him.

"Fancy," I add, accepting the cocktail, smelling a hint of toasted rosemary.

I mill around his space while he tends to something in the kitchen, poking my head into his home office. "Is that a new bookshelf?" He's got rows of beautiful leather-bound books, all shades of natural browns and tans, and others in painted rich blues and greens.

"Oh, that old thing?" He drops what he's doing and shuts the office door, guiding me back to the living room. "No, no. Just rearranged a bit. Sorry, the office is a mess right now. Let's sit. I haven't talked to you at all today."

Setting my drink down on the glass coffee table, we sit on his couch, taking in the view. "How was your day? You finalized that deal, yes?" I ask.

"Yes, it went through! Everything's signed." We clink glasses to celebrate.

"That's great, congratulations! Did you get to use that thing you were telling me about?"

"That new contract clause? I did! My clients were thrilled."

"That's awesome, hon. I'm proud of you." I lean over to kiss him. *This man's brain is incredible. He's so smart.*

"How was your day? What have you been up to?" he asks, splitting his attention between me and his phone.

Investigating Eli's house, giving a witness statement for a murder, organizing a parade float, what else?

"Oh, you know. Park stuff, campaign stuff, Marty stuff." I smile over the rim of my glass. "Do you mind if I do a bit of work before dinner?" I bat my eyelashes and cheese big.

"Maudy, seriously? I barely get to see you. You're an hour late as it is. Let's just relax." He picks up my glass and puts it back in my hand, tossing his phone onto the table.

"Something big has come up. It's a…a grant proposal I need to finish. It's due soon." Lying through my teeth, I grab my backpack and start scrolling through the pages Kelly sent me. He'd flip if he knew I was doing this for Eli.

"Fine." He's mad. "I'll get dinner heating up in the oven. Thanks for picking it up on your way over," he grumbles, swiping a few stray Marty hairs off his couch. They must have stowed away on my sweater.

Miles Davis's trumpet ambiently fills the air, coming from all directions through hidden surround sound speakers. Jeremy puts the lasagna and an unbaked loaf of bread from a nearby restaurant into the oven.

"So, what's this grant for?" he asks, mixing another drink for himself. "It must be a big one if it's worth interrupting dinner." A cut in his tone slices through the question's innocence.

"Yeah, it's a big one," I placate. My mind focuses on these notes. Scrolling past what I've already read, I land on pages about Leonard.

"You know, those big grants aren't even worth going after. They're so competitive these days," he drones. "I wouldn't waste your time."

"Oh, my god," I gasp, fixated on the case file.

"What now?" he asks, eyebrows knit together.

"He put out a public statement against her last week," I whisper. Heart racing, I read faster than I comprehend, skimming Kelly's documents. *He accused her of lying...of launching a smear campaign. Of slander.*

"What?" he asks, walking back over and leaning to look at my screen.

"Jeremy, I need to go." Scrambling, I snap the laptop shut, gather my things, and put on my jacket. "It's for the proposal. I need to do some research. Rain check, I promise."

"Uh-huh. Sure." He throws a dishtowel on the counter, exasperated. *I'll deal with him later.*

Chapter Eight

Before jumping to big conclusions, I take a few deep breaths and continue reading in my old, rusted-out Jeep Cherokee, free of Jeremy's judgment. This car is on her last legs. With Stone's Throw being so walkable and my access to the Park's work vehicles, I've extended her life well past expectancy.

"Podcasts, podcasts," I utter, cranking over the engine, and scrolling through to find one on smear campaigns. I turn up the sound and drive back home to the dry voice of a legal professor's introductory course.

I learn that smear campaigns are legal but often result in retaliation, so if you dish it out, you should expect it back. *Maybe I should start stealing Colin's signs since mine keep disappearing. He could use a little retaliation...*

Home in record time, I crack my front door, playing defense against dog and cat escape attempts. "Hi, buddies, how are you guys? What did you do this evening?"

From what I gather, Marty worked on a global peace treaty, and Gumbo pondered the clean energy transition. Both were very productive.

I pull out my computer, fingers typing away as I dig into Leonard and Paige's campaign trails. Headlines, ads, and news clips fill my screen. Paige is polished and confident, clearly experienced in the political world, speaking with conviction. Leonard's rebuttals aren't of the same caliber. He's heated, accusing her of weaponizing and twisting his words to pull ahead.

I find the ads in question. The claims Paige makes home in on his voting record—budget cuts, tax breaks, and other issues on the Town Council. This isn't scandalous; she's just airing the truth. The numbers don't lie, and looking at polls, her attacks are making an impact. His standings have been slipping for the last two weeks, since Paige started unearthing this stuff.

"Marty, Gumbo, what do you gentlemen know about political slander?" They meet me with blank stares and drift back to sleep. "You two are no help. But hear me out. What if Paige refused to back down? What if Leonard wanted to eliminate the competition, so to speak? He was up by quite a bit in the polls, and he's dropped ten points since she started running these ads. His win is guaranteed if he doesn't have an opponent. That could be a motive, yes?"

More blank stares. Gumbo saunters over and bats at pages in my notebook, while Marty sits like a good boy listening to me. He's had years of practice.

The only other piece of helpful information Kelly sent is from the medical examiner, who did the toxicology tests. The report explains that the toxins in Paige's system are barbiturates. Her blood sugar and other levels were all out of whack, too, which is unusual for barbiturate poisoning, but no other foreign chemicals were found in her system. There was evidence of a mild seizure that may not have been visibly noticeable. They mention the barbiturates could have done this, but it's not common.

"Anybody know what barbiturates are?" I ask the fluffs, who reply with nothing helpful (shocker). A quick search tells me they're prescription sleeping pills. Like Kelly said, Paige had enough in her system to kill an elephant. She didn't accidentally take an extra pill or two.

"I wonder…" Walking upstairs to my loft, I rummage through a small, woven basket beside my bed. In it is the current book I'm reading, the new Gillian Flynn, a book light, an eye mask, a small notebook, and a bottle of sleeping pills.

After almost getting killed this past spring, coupled with the surmounting job stress, insomnia has taken root. I started on the medication a couple of months ago. It helps.

"Yep, they're barbiturates, guys. I know you two were on pins and needles." They lounge on the couch downstairs but have the decency to perk their heads up as I lean over the loft railing. Wary, I pop open the bottle and pour the tiny, white pills into my palm, doing a rough count to make sure I'm not missing any. Nope, it looks like they're all here.

"I wonder who else has sleeping problems? Leonard? We all know it's not Eli, am I right?" I laugh. He's slept on my couch often enough for me to know he can saw logs. That man could sleep anywhere. He's fallen asleep sitting upright, and even at parties. Gumbo meows in agreement.

In the margins of the toxicology report, there's a note from Kelly. *Paige has Rx for barbiturates. Checked with her doctor. Drug was hers, but bottle is missing.*

"Ah. Well, there we go. The pills were hers. So, somebody had access to Paige's things."

The two black, scruffy animals grow tired of feigning interest.

"Okay, let's think more about that later. Who had access, besides the other people in the house?" I jot that question down. So far, the Leonard theory is still interesting. Eli would've absolutely let him inside if he had asked to sit down or for a glass of water. He's a town leader. It could still be Eli or one of his friends, but Leonard's political motive is compelling.

I grab Marty's harness and apologize to Gumbo for leaving him home alone so late. Promising to come back soon and give him tons of cuddles tonight, I take Martin Short on a late-night hunt for some answers.

"Peyton can help us," I tell the dog as we head downtown. "She's from here; she knows the history. I need to learn more about Eli's friends and Leonard's family. Then we'll get everything squared away, and Eli and I will go back to normal."

Flashes of Danni snuggling up to Eli burn in my mind's eye.

We cross Main Street, but instead of walking into Peyton's bakery, we loop around the block to the back alley. It's dark, but a silhouette of the marina's freshly renovated clubhouse takes center stage in the moonlight, on the shores of a black, glassy Lake Michigan.

The bakery sits in the middle of the block, and as we come around the side a few businesses over, about to turn into the alley, voices reach us first. Hushed voices.

"Marty! Shh!" I gently tug the dog close, so he doesn't dart into view. "Sit," I mouth silently and raise my fist. He does immediately, locking eyes with me. We pause, straining to listen to the conversation.

"You're doing fine, Colin. Just a few more days until we shore everything up." A piercing, high-pitched voice affirms with satisfaction. "There aren't many problems that money can't solve."

A simple grunt replies. Then a long pause.

The high voice continues, "We're handling the opposition. We have a friend on the inside, so to speak. It's important to keep *our* hands clean." The tone and formality could only be one person: Charlotte Roth. "Anything else for tonight?"

"No, that should do it. Thanks. I appreciate your support."

"On the contrary, Colin. We appreciate *your* support. Have a good night. I'm sure I'll have the pleasure of bumping into you soon." The higher voice ends the discussion.

Their footsteps grow louder, coming right for us. *Merda!* Pulling back my hood, I square my shoulders and hold my head high.

"Hello, there," I announce myself with hands on my hips, as the two almost bump into me and the dog as they turn the corner.

"Oh! Maudy," Colin snivels. "Hello. We're in a hurry, so—"

"Hang on a minute." I raise a hand. Charlotte's initial surprise wears off, and she angles her body in front of the craven man, shielding Colin. "I overheard your conversation," I press. "Are you two taking down all my signs? That's illegal." I cross my arms.

Charlotte puts an arm on Colin and steps forward, like a mama bear protecting her cub. The vitriol in her expression looks ready to leap off her and attack me.

"Now, Maudy, that's quite the accusation. We don't want to be hasty. We were just out for a late-night stroll. It's perfectly legal for me as a citizen to offer my support." She grins, but all I see is that mama bear, baring her teeth.

"Hasty? No, of course not. Just like I'm sure you don't want to be charged with theft. Or is it vandalism? I'm sure Kelly can help us figure it out."

"You can't prove a thing," she hisses. The demon-woman walks past, shoving her shoulder into mine. Colin follows suit, trailing behind, overtly avoiding my eyes.

Fury radiates off of me. These two are bigger than thorns in my side. They're entire rose bushes. Polished and poised at first glance, but wicked underneath the surface.

Marty and I proceed into the alley and ring Peyton's intercom, rattled. "Yeah?" her voice asks over the speaker.

"It's Maudy. Sorry I didn't call, I know it's late. Mind if I come up for a sec?" The lock on the door buzzes, and we walk up the narrow staircase into her above-bakery apartment.

I both love and hate her place. It's decorated so cute in a way I could never put together myself, with delicious smells wafting from below, creating a fantastic atmosphere. The massive oven downstairs makes it so hot. Even in the dead of winter, it's over seventy degrees. It saves her on electric bills, I guess.

"Hey." I step through the door and unhook Marty's leash, immediately taking off my jacket. The dog gallops over to the galley-style kitchen and sits down, searching for a scrap of whatever she's last cooked.

She's in pajamas, hovering over a bowl of ice cream on the coffee table.

"Ah, jeez, sorry. I didn't mean to interrupt." I sink into the couch, tucking my feet underneath me.

"Don't sweat it. You caught me right before bed with a little snack," she laughs and sits beside me. She points a remote at the TV, turning down the volume of whatever *Real Housewives* is on. "You okay?" she asks, picking up on the heat waving off me. "Want some ice cream? You need some ice cream. Cookie Dough or Mackinac Island Fudge?"

"No, that's okay. Thanks, though." Marty slowly migrates to Peyton's feet, realizing the action (ice cream) is here, not in the kitchen. He wags his tail, making his eyes as big and round as possible. "I just overheard Charlotte conspiring with Colin. She's trying to take me down."

"Yikes, seriously? Can Charlotte ever just mind her own business?" she scoffs.

"I know. Whatever. That's not what I came here to talk to you about. I wanted to ask you about Leonard. What do you know about him and his family?"

"I don't know, he's old and cranky. Is that helpful?" She eyes me suspiciously. "Why?"

"So...it turns out that Paige's death was no accident."

"Oh, my god. What?" She leans in, almost dipping her *Girls Just Want to Have Fun-damental Rights* t-shirt into her bowl. "I've been working all day and haven't heard! You were supposed to call me!" She throws a pillow at me.

"I know, I know, sorry! I'm not sure how public that is, but when I went to deliver those doughnuts this morning—great job by the way, they were phenomenal—Kelly and a whole mess of state troopers stopped by. Eli asked that I poke around, so here I am, poking around. He's hoping I'll find something that'll exonerate him since the police have all three of them high on her list of suspects."

"Wow, okay." She pauses, staring into space. "That's a lot to take in. Kelly thinks our Eli, as in Elliott Nett, chef at Pop's Bar, here in Stone's Throw, could've *killed* someone? *That* Elliott Nett?"

"Apparently." I throw my hands up. "But I'm interested in Leonard. He has a political motive; he's running against Paige for the state Senate seat. So, what do you know about him?"

"Huh." She thinks for a second. "Well, he's lived here forever, and the Henley family goes back generations. Like, before Stone's Throw was Stone's Throw, his family was living here and farming, I think. He's got a couple of kids older than us; I don't know them well. I don't think they live here anymore, but they're not far. Maybe Traverse City or Cadillac or something," she says, between bites.

I nod along. "What about him as a person? Nice guy? Not-so-nice guy? Murderous guy?"

"Ha, I don't know about *murderous*, but I wouldn't call him a 'nice guy.' Pretty stern, and a little cutthroat. Doesn't take no for an answer," she says. "We were all afraid of him when we were little. He would scold us for making too much noise." She rolls her eyes. "He's a run-of-the-mill town curmudgeon."

"Well, this town curmudgeon went on public record attacking Paige. He claimed she was lying about him in her campaign ads. Like a smear campaign. And she didn't back down."

"Jeez, what'd she say about him?"

"I didn't think it was that bad, or lies, from what I can tell. It was just about his voting record on the Village Council and things he stood for in the past. She was basically pointing out how he's sort of shady."

"Well, yeah, he is a little shady," she agrees. "His family's got a lot of money. And I think some of that has come from Town Council decisions. He's from a long line of Stone's Throw big shots."

"So...what if he killed her to eliminate the competition? His polling numbers tanked. He was probably going to lose."

"I don't know. It seems drastic." She bites her cheek, clearly thinking this train of thought is destined for Crackpot Station.

"Totally, but I'm still suspicious of him. The political angle here seems compelling."

"That's a big leap to murdering someone. But hey, if the other option is Eli, I'm on board. I don't think he, or any of his friends, could do something like this."

"Leonard is just an idea. And I hope you're right about Eli. I'm realizing I don't know him as well as I thought. I don't know his friends at all."

"Well, what do you want to know? I've known him since we were infants. Kevin changed my diapers."

"What was he like in high school? What about these friends of his? Were you a part of their group?" I finally stop pretending I'm not having ice cream and walk over to her kitchen to scoop a bowl.

"The four of them were tight. I was only really friends with Eli. I wasn't like, in their posse. There's hot fudge in the fridge, just microwave it for thirty seconds."

I hit the buttons and put the ice cream back in the freezer. "Were they popular?" I ask, talking over the mechanical whirr.

"No, but they were nice, so they got invited to parties, you know?" She takes another spoonful before continuing. "There weren't a lot of us, so it wasn't super cliquey. I think we had like thirty people in our graduating class? Anyway, they were a little messy. Eli and Danni were on-again, off-again all through school. Before you moved to town, I would've bet money that they would've gotten married eventually. And divorced," she chuckles.

"I think they might be more *on-again* right now. I was picking up on something when I was over there this morning."

"Yeah, well, it wouldn't surprise me." She shrugs. "Can't blame the guy for looking for a little comfort. Something familiar. Especially with you two all weird." She swipes a finger into her empty bowl.

"Fair enough. Anyway, continue. You were saying they were messy." I rejoin her in the living room, leaning back into her squishy couch.

"Right. Yeah, exactly. There were rumors that Wesley and Paige were also a thing, but I don't know if that ever really happened, or if it was just talk. Paige was the smart one in our class; she got straight A's. She didn't really date. She and Wesley were more into academics, but maybe their late-night study sessions were a little biology-focused." She grins. "Eli didn't care much about school, and Danni partied a lot. They were more like two pairs that hung out, rather than an equal foursome."

"Anything notable with any of their families? Anything that comes to mind that's unusual for people around here?"

"Mm…no, not really. You already know Kevin; he owned Pop's back then, too. Danni's family was pretty poor. They had a small farm outside of town. I don't know about the others."

"Any reason they might want to kill Paige? Deep-seated grudges or anything? Tell me if I'm way off-base here, but Eli said their friendship has 'baggage,' and he's worried Kelly will use it as a motive."

"Um…no major grudges that I can remember. Like I said, they were just sort of messy. They'd go on stints of someone not talking to the others, someone would break up with another, or whatever, but it wasn't anything weird or unusual for teenagers."

"Okay, okay. Good to know." I mull this over. "What about now? I heard you say Danni's brother died?"

"Yeah, isn't that horrible? I was sad to hear that. He ODed. I didn't know him well, but he's had a drug problem ever since I can remember." She absentmindedly scratches Marty's back.

"Totally awful." I shake my head. "Do you know what he did for work before he died?"

"You know, that's a great question. I'm not sure. I don't think it was legal, whatever it was. He gambled a lot. There's a high-stakes poker game in Hemlock Pond that I think he played in. I don't know for sure, though."

"How the hell do *you* know about an underground poker game?" I ask.

"Hey! I know things! I've lived here forever; you'll pick up on it eventually. Give it another decade, and you'll be up to speed on all the goings on." We laugh, and Marty sneaks a lick of ice cream while he thinks we're distracted. We both pretend not to notice.

"Well, friend, you've been a wealth of information. Thanks, and sorry for interrupting bedtime." I sigh, unsure where to go from here.

It starts to drizzle as we walk down the alley.

"Marty, c'mon. It's starting to rain." The dog's nose picks up on something as we pass a dumpster. I even smell the putrid trash coming out of it. "It's just garbage, come on, dude. I want to get home. It's late, and wet."

I begin walking again, tugging him along with me. My patience grows thin; I feel like I'm facing a dead end here. Not to mention the campaign gang-up I just uncovered. *I need to figure out what to do about that, too.*

Marty hunkers down on his short little legs and gives a stern growl and sharp *"yip!"* right at me. Pulling up the hood of my jacket, I look around to make sure we're alone.

"Okay, fine. What is it?" I give him slack on the leash, and he beelines to the dumpster, jumping up on his hind legs. "You're about five feet shy, dude." He yips again.

"It's just garbage! I promise!" If looks could kill, his stare-down would incinerate me on the spot. Something's in there. "If this is another squirrel carcass, you're going to pay big time. Be quick."

Against my better judgment, and thankful to be under the cover of a dark sky, I pick up the dog and place him gently on top of the trash heap. He traipses around, sniffing like a madman.

While I wait for him to do whatever he needs to do, I replay the last hour. The devious whatever-the-hell-that-was with Charlotte, and the history lesson from Peyton. Both leave me confused.

"Marty, hurry up! I hear thunder, we should go. You hate thunder, remember? What could be *so* exciting that you want to stand out in a thunderstorm?" I try to coax the dog out to no avail. Leaning against the dumpster, arms crossed, and jacket hood up, I simmer.

"So, it was Colin and Charlotte. But Charlotte used 'we' a couple of times…I wonder if she's working with someone else? Charlotte is already on the Town Council and conspiring to help Colin win the open seat." I talk to the dumpster as Marty continues to root around. "Should I report them? Would that get me anywhere? Kelly is already swamped. She couldn't do anything about this with Paige's case still open. What'd they say about having someone on the inside? Did they mean on *my* inside? Like a friend or something?"

No response from the dog.

After another few minutes, the rain picks up, and my patience grows thinner. "Time to go, Marty. This is gross, even for you." I balance on a lip of the green metal and peer into the garbage heap. His head pops up between two bags, with a couple of long, floppy things dangling out of his mouth. "What is that, bud?"

He crawls up, tail wagging and stinking up a storm as I hoist him onto solid ground. He drops long pieces of cloth at my feet, with half an avocado and a bunch of unknown brown goo smashed into them. *Tube socks?*

I pick them up, holding the reeking things as far away from my face as possible. Recognizing the subtle diamond pattern covered in revolting trash, I immediately drop them on the ground and call Kelly.

"Kelly, it's Maudy. I'm in the alley behind Peyton's bakery. Marty found parts of a Power Ranger costume in the dumpster."

Chapter Nine

After giving statements and assisting the state troopers in screening the rest of the dumpster, Marty and I return home, completely drenched. A hot shower does me good. We both fall asleep to the whistling wind through dead leaves as soon as our heads hit the pillow.

Sleep comes fast but is restless; those costume pieces haunt my dreams. How did they end up in a dumpster across town? How coincidental is it that Charlotte and Colin happened to be there right before Marty found them? By all accounts, Paige didn't leave the house that night; why would someone take pieces of her costume off her?

Reluctantly, after stewing over this for over an hour in the middle of the night, I take a sleeping pill and a healthy dose of dread as I'm reminded of Paige.

The next morning, listening to the gurgle and hiss of my coffee pot, waiting for it to finish, I stare out my back door, trying to get a plan together for the day.

This morning is blocked off with a coordination meeting for Saturday's events. Danni's running it, so it might also be a good opportunity to learn more about her.

"Marty, it's time to go! Want to see the new marina? According to Danni's latest email, it's supposed to be 'utterly spectacular.'" I slide the door closed behind the chipper dog. He mumbles to himself, sitting politely while I put on his harness. Time to start the day.

The marina sits out on a small peninsula surrounded by Lake Michigan on the edge of town. The clubhouse overlooks the docks along with a small concession stand, jet ski rentals, and a public restroom.

The original clubhouse was a small, dark red brick structure that, from the outside, didn't look like much. Surprisingly, though, it's a fascinating piece of prohibition-era history.

The home was built by Al Capone's gang back when the Great Lakes were a bootleggers' blessing. They ran liquor up and down the coast by boat, even making runs up to Canada.

Capone and his mobster cronies sent their pregnant mistresses up here to have their babies away from Chicago, to keep from upsetting their wives. At the time, there wasn't much out here. Stone's Throw was a small farming settlement with a few established families. Capone's crew built out downtown, essentially running the village for a while.

By the 1960s, the gangs were a memory; tourists discovered the phenomenal sand dunes and perfect summer weather. Around the same time, the town rebranded to "Stone's Throw."

I often walk past the back of the house, but haven't yet swung around lakeside to see the full scope of the renovation.

"Holy cow."

Walking up to the home blows me away. The old brick house now stands with a quiet pride that comes from outliving its secrets. I half expect to see the ghost of a flapper in the upstairs window.

"Welcome, *Maude*. How lovely of you to join us." The disdain drips from a familiar, shrill voice.

"Charlotte, hi," I murmur, distracted by the building. I almost forget about overhearing her conspiring against my Village Council campaign. Almost. "You know, I'm not one to pay you a compliment, especially after what just happened, but you've done a phenomenal job with this place."

The house's original integrity still shines, paying tribute to its history. There's a significant addition and a new, sprawling patio. Intimate wrought-iron cafe tables sit beneath a pergola, with creeping grapevines newly planted at the base. Meticulous garden beds line the cobblestone path down to the boat docks.

"It is marvelous, isn't it? It's been my entire life for the last few months. You should see the inside. I found a few *interesting* historical artifacts. I'm sure you've heard the rumors."

I nod absentmindedly, still taking it all in.

"They're true," she whispers, clapping her hands. "I'm so excited to show everyone."

"Wow," I reply, still distracted from the grandeur. "How did you pay for this? The upkeep alone must be a fortune, let alone the actual renovation. The house was barely standing..."

"Oh, you know. Grants, donations, the usual. It's not hard to find money for good work," she muses, reading through papers on a clipboard as I fester in jealousy. "And Maude," she bristles. "Let's keep that little conversation you overheard between us. I'd hate to have to defend myself in the court of public opinion. I assure you, you wouldn't like that either."

Is that a threat?

She dismisses me before I can respond, as other meeting attendees approach behind me. "Head inside. I'll be in momentarily." She glances at her watch and glowers down at Marty as we walk up the steps.

Wow. Just wow. Walking into the house is like taking a step back in time, but still with a modern glamour. With new amenities and sleek furnishings, the design is quintessential 1920s, from the shape of the floor tiles to the gold, tessellated wallpaper.

"Hey." I approach Peyton and Eli, who hunch over a pad of paper scrawled with Peyton's notes. They're with a clump of others waiting for the meeting to begin.

"Morning, Maudy." Eli jams his hands in his pockets and steps aside, making space for me to join them. "We're just going over the menu, but *somebody* has major control issues." He jokingly glares at Peyton. I can tell this is a welcome distraction for him.

"If you honestly think I'm serving chocolate brioche bread pudding after a *fish* course, you are certifiable." Her mouth is as thin as a pencil line as she meets his glare with equal fervor. "Hey, girl." She turns to me briefly, then shifts back to him.

"Alright, everyone, now that we're all here." Charlotte claps her hands and shuffles through the door to the front of the group. She walks up a couple of stairs to see everyone. A few mumbles wrap up conversations, including more of a snake-like hiss from Peyton to Eli.

"We're gathered here to do a run-through meeting for Saturday's class reunion. You all are involved in hosting the event, and we must be on the same page. I'll begin with an overview of today's agenda. First, we will tour the home to familiarize you with its new layout. It's bound to be the talk of the party, and as hosts, you need to know about its history and recent revitalization."

Peyton turns to me, sticking her finger in her mouth, making the universal *gag me* sign. I stifle a giggle.

"As I was saying," Charlotte peers over her glasses at Peyton. "After the tour, we will briefly review roles, responsibilities, and call times. Now, I know many of you are leaders of our great town and are very busy. I hope to adjourn in an hour to let you all move on with your day. Any questions before we begin?"

Met with none, she proceeds up the stairs. We follow one by one, like schoolchildren on the way to class. We get a brief tour of the four bedrooms, learning how the gangsters used them as birthing rooms.

Now these rooms are offices. One is for a water-sports rental company; another is Charlotte's as the Chamber of Commerce Chair. The other two sit vacant. She shows us a secret panel inside one of them where they allegedly stored booze and weapons.

Back on the main floor, two construction workers hammer away at a small stage towards one end of the ballroom. Danni will make all announcements there.

Where is Danni? She should be leading this meeting, not Charlotte. Tied up with Kelly, maybe? Or making funeral arrangements? I wonder if this party will actually happen, given the circumstances.

I risk getting scolded by the Lilly Pulitzer-clad crone to shoot off a quick text to Kelly. *Is Danni with you? Charlotte is running the class reunion walk-through at the clubhouse, and she's not here.*

I jam the phone back in my pocket before she notices.

"Now, here's where the fun begins." Charlotte ushers us towards the back door. On the floor of the back landing, she pulls on an inlaid wooden ring, revealing a rectangular door: a secret basement.

"We're going to make a public announcement at the event, so I ask that you kindly keep this all to yourselves until then. But I'm thrilled to say, the rumored tunnels are real."

The group's excitement swells, swirled whispers filling the small foyer.

"We'll be giving tours for those who want a peek at history. Crews are working to make sure it's safe right now. Please watch your step." Charlotte turns back with a puckish smile as she leads us down the wooden stairs.

"As many of you know, this house was rumored to be the hub of a tunnel network, winding underground all over the area. These tunnels were said to have been how the mob ran illegal substances and evaded a police officer or two." Charlotte's voice grows fainter the deeper she descends.

One by one, we clamber down into the rocky basement. The walls are made of large lake stones stacked and haphazardly grouted. Every few feet, I spot a baseball-sized Petoskey Stone worth well over five hundred dollars.

The maze of decrepit rooms gives me the creeps. Ceilings loom low, and the air hangs damp, claustrophobic. We're so close to the lake; I'm surprised there isn't standing water flooding the space. It smells like that happens regularly, though.

"I apologize for the condition; it will be safe and cleaned up by the party on Saturday."

From quietly behind, I hear, "Hey, babe." Turning, I tangle my legs in a coiled string of lights. The satin sound of Jeremy Gray's voice echoes again. "Whoa, be careful." He pulls me in, preventing me from falling, but sacrifices his bag and an armful of papers to do so.

"Well, this is a surprise," I say, teetering in the mess of lights. "Sorry about that."

I find my footing, and we both crouch to pick up his things from the grimy, wet floor. "Here you go," I hand him an old, green book now covered in slime, along with a handful of file folders.

"Thanks," he grunts, wiping it off on his jacket before packing it back up.

"Hope none of that was important," I whisper. Nobody seems to notice my almost-fall; everyone's roaming on their own, amazed at the real-life gangster history in front of them.

"Nah, just a little business. Hope it's okay, I saw this meeting in your calendar and wanted to join. I'm sorry I was so curt with you when you left last night. I know your work is important," he apologizes, pulling me in closer. "I have a lot going on right now, too, and I took it out on you."

"I'm sorry for blowing you off," I whisper back. "I didn't mean to." I pull his shoulder closer to mine as we hang back. "Isn't this an invite-only thing? Charlotte's going to kill you. Duck down, I don't want her to see."

"It'll be fine." He scrunches down, obliging me, nonetheless. "This place is stunning." He lets me go and takes it all in. "Getting a sneak peek is every real estate agent's dream. When my morning meeting got done a little early, I figured I had time to swing by."

"It's gorgeous, isn't it? Well, not this part, I guess. But the rest of the house. The history behind it is wild."

"Yeah, they did an amazing job on the restoration. So, what'd I miss?" He leans in, whispering in my ear. Eli steps to the other end of the room, suddenly taken by old booze bottles cemented into the foundation.

"I'll fill you in later; we're just wrapping up," I reply.

Charlotte notices the new addition to the tour group and gives him a terse sign of acknowledgment. Jeremy curtly nods back.

"Down here was rumored to be the headquarters of the infamous 'Trail Blazers.'" She uses air quotes. "A secret society, of sorts, that pulled strings throughout the region. Al Capone was the supposed founding member. Stories of the group have surfaced now and again ever since.

"I regret to inform you that there was no evidence of such a group, but we did find quite an intricate underground tunnel network. Most are collapsed or barricaded off with pieces of old barrels, but they were a fun find, nonetheless. I'll point out a couple of entrances as we move through. Where they go, we're unsure. Their other ends are lost to history and development." She beckons us forward through claustrophobic, dank rooms.

Eli's face scrunches and brow furrows. There's a fifty-fifty shot it's either from the rotting algae smell or Charlotte's condescension. We continue to explore the labyrinth, which extends well beyond the meager footprint of the above-ground home, before reemerging outside in the blustery fall weather. The lake rumbles loudly as waves crash on the sweeping, sandy beach.

"Maude, before you go, may I speak with you?" As the meeting begins to disperse, many still taking in the view, Charlotte calls me over.

"Sure," I reply before turning back to Jeremy. "Give me one sec."

"I just wanted to coordinate the hayride with you. It didn't seem proper to waste everyone else's time discussing the matter with the entire group."

We wrap up after ten minutes of agreeing on the trail route, safety measures, and parking logistics.

"What's the rest of your day look like?" I ask Jeremy. "Are you sticking around town? I'd love a date for spaghetti dinner tonight. Plus, I think there's another goofy homecoming competition thing."

He pulls out his phone, scrolling through his calendar.

"That should work. I set up a showing not too far up the coast and then have a few meetings, but I should be able to meet you at your place after work." He pockets the phone as I lean into him, grabbing my hand in his.

We pass Pop's and see the tally on the bar's windows. Hemlock Pond is up two to one. Pausing by Jeremy's sleek little Audi, parked on the street, he pops his trunk and tosses his leather messenger bag inside.

"Hey, my signs." I point into the trunk. My campaign signs and flyers are strewn all over his trunk.

"Ah, shoot! It was going to be a surprise. I had more printed for you at work. We get a big discount with all the For Sale signs we print. He holds one up to show me. Placing it back in his trunk, he wipes dirt from his hands, smiles at me, and opens the driver's door.

"Aw, thank you! Let's put them up later," I gush, as he gives me a peck on the cheek before driving away.

* * *

Stepping through the park's ranger station reminds me of the stark differences between this historic building and the one where I spent my morning. Both are around the same age, but ours has leaky windows and a fireplace chimney in need of serious repair. Marty hops onto our mildewy couch and curls into a ball, looking like a miniature black hole opening up to another universe right on the cushion.

Eli huddles over Zach's desk, the two poring over papers.

"What are you doing here?" I ask.

Like deer in headlights, they shove the papers in a drawer and try to act casual.

"Uh, nothing. Zach was just helping me with some new plans for Pop's. Don't worry about it." He throws on his jacket and rushes out the door, shooting Zach a thumbs-up. "Later, Zach."

Was that a little smirk? What is up with those two?

"What was that?" I ask Zach. "Are you two planning to rob a bank?"

"None of your business," he retorts as I get up to chase Eli. "You'll find out soon enough. It's a good distraction for him after what happened to Paige. Don't worry your curly little head about it."

"That's not at all concerning," I mutter sarcastically, shutting the door behind me. Lucky for them, this is low enough on the list of concerning things not to push much more.

"Eli! Hold up a sec." I flag him down; he's already way up ahead. Standing in the gravel parking lot, he turns and waits patiently for me to catch up.

"What's up?" Right then, his phone buzzes, and he reaches to read a text message. A little squint strikes his eye, and a subtle frown briefly shows itself.

"Is now not a good time? We could talk later if you'd rather."

"No, no. Now is fine." He's distracted, still sneaking glances at his phone. "Sorry, hang on."

"No problem." I pause, waiting for him to look up.

"Okay, shoot."

"I've done a full day of snooping and think Leonard could be our guy. He's got a political motive, and a recent conflict with Paige."

"Interesting. That makes sense." His eyes stay on his phone as I describe what I've found so far. His mind is elsewhere; he's not paying attention. *Making funeral arrangements? Letting other friends know? Maybe just grieving.*

"The only thing is," I continue, "I haven't found anything solid yet. I haven't found his access to Paige's sleeping pills, unless he got into your house somehow. I also *technically* haven't been able to rule out your friends either… Are you sure Wesley or Danni didn't have a reason to hurt her? I heard that she and Wesley used to date. Maybe a scorned lover-type thing?"

I intentionally leave out that he's still a major suspect, too. I haven't found a clear alibi for any of them. He types away on his phone.

"Are you sure now is a good time? We can talk later," I offer, wanting to be sensitive to his situation. *His friend just died. He's a suspect in her murder. I can't imagine what's going through his head right now.*

"I said now is fine," he states through a clenched jaw. He puts his phone in his back pocket, faking a smile. "Sorry." He takes a deep breath. "I'm not mad at you. What were you saying?"

"Okay," I stammer, unsure how to take that. "I found pieces of a Power Ranger costume in a dumpster in town. Behind Peyton's bakery. Any idea how that got there?"

His expression morphs to pain as his face droops ever so slightly. "First, Danni's on my case, and now you, too?" He swipes his hands down his face, drained. "No, of course I don't know anything about that. I promise, we didn't do this. I appreciate your help, Maudy. I really do. But if you won't believe me, I'd rather you not get involved. I'm sorry I asked for your help." His tone isn't angry, it's disappointed. It's tired. He's overextended. I wish there were something I could do to help.

He backs off, shamefaced, and turns towards downtown. He pulls out his phone again and calls someone. "Can we talk this out, please?" I hear him say as he walks away.

"I still think Leonard's our guy!" I shout after him. "I'm just saying I'm not positive. I'm sorry!" He's paying me no mind. He's talking with his hands, the phone call absorbing his full attention.

"Well," I mutter under my breath, "that could have gone better. I just made tonight's spaghetti a lot more awkward..."

Watching him walk down the street, I see him get smaller and smaller as he wanders down the block. He passes a window covered in giant posters that look...*no.*

Is that my face?

Chapter Ten

"*Merda.* It's worse than I thought." I'm fuming, fire practically spouting from my nostrils as I stare up close at the flyers, smattered all over downtown. It's a horrible photo of me at a Park Stewardship Committee meeting we had last year, with my mouth wide open and an accusatory finger pointing at the audience.

The background is a bright, jarring red, with the headline, "*Hot head Maudy Lorso is bad for our parks and bad for our town! Vote Colin.*" The tiny font in the bottom corner reads, "*Paid for by Tiller Brazas.*"

Who the hell is Tiller Brazas, and what did I ever do to them?

These things are everywhere. I couldn't have been gone for more than forty-five minutes. Probably even less. How did these get up so fast? My vision blurs with oncoming tears, welling from frustration and embarrassment. I scramble down the street, ripping dozens of flyers and posters down as I go.

The photo is taken wildly out of context. At that meeting, Zach presented with our local bird rehabilitation center. They took in an owl who couldn't be released into the wild and were training him to be comfortable around people. This way, he could take the bird into classrooms for educational purposes. I arranged a trial run for the meeting to showcase the new addition to our parks programming.

My arm was outstretched, not to point fingers, but so the bird would perch on me.

As I proceed downtown, I move slower and slower, encumbered by the growing stack of flyers. I feel the heat of questioning stares as people pass by. Their eyes bore into my back like lasers. Folks who usually say hello keep their distance. Panicking, I pick up the pace, desperate to get these eyes off me.

I race down one side of the street, ripping them down, thankful to see someone already cleared Pop's block, and begin making my way back around the other.

Colin smugly hands out Halloween candy, seated behind a card table in front of Charlotte's art gallery. His campaign banner flies above the entryway in blue and white font, a calming contrast to the red of my blown-up face behind him.

"I can't believe you stooped this low, Colin. It's pitiful, even for you. Actually, I take that back. I can believe it." The part of my brain that filters thoughts before they reach my mouth has closed shop for the day. He smiles coyly and hands me a mini-Snickers Bar. The awkward stares from onlookers bolster my anger, funneling it straight into the wiry man.

"Believe it or not, *I* didn't do this, Ms. Lorso. I see why you might think I did, especially given our little chat with Charlotte, but I promise I'm not the disgruntled citizen you're looking for." He continues to pass out candy, the town buzzing with late-morning shoppers and folks on lunch breaks. I scoot out of the way so as not to block the sidewalk.

Crossing my arms, I wait for him to turn his attention back to me. "I'll take this up with Kelly, Colin. Charlotte can't interfere in our race. Do you want to get disqualified?"

This gets his attention. He crosses his arms as well. "Like Charlotte said, you have no proof. Kelly can't do a thing. Don't waste your time."

He's right, and I huff off defeated, continuing to rip down the flyers as I go. I get another block before bumping into Jeremy again.

"Hey there, gorgeous." He pulls off his sunglasses as he shuts his car door, stopping to chat for another moment.

"Hi," I say flatly. I feel just as red and puffy as I look in these ads, and my arms tire from the weight of the signs.

"I'm in between appointments. What happened?" His expression softens, registering my mood. He looks around, landing on the stack of papers in my arms. "What are those?"

He pulls one from the stack and examines it. "Oh, no," he mutters quietly. "These are awful." His pity grows, not knowing how to fix the situation. "Let me take these off your hands. I have my car, so you don't have to walk around town with them for the rest of the day."

I hand them over, and he puts them in the trunk of his Audi alongside my much nicer yard signs. "Thanks, Jeremy. Today has not been my day." I sink into his cashmere sweater, holding on longer than the average hug. It's like a soft, buttery shield I can hide behind for a minute.

His attention is elsewhere; I feel it in his tense frame, likely watching Colin behind me. Eventually, he pulls me back a bit and squeezes my hands.

"I wish I could stay and help you, but I need to get to my last appointment. To be honest, it's not my best day either. This one is with Charlotte. My clients are interested in a commercial space, and as you know, everything business-related in this town goes through her." He rolls his eyes. "They want to open a toy store, which I think fits Charlotte's vision. Hopefully, it won't be too much of a pain. Anyway, still good to meet at your place in a bit? That is, if I can function after spending an hour with her?"

"I bet that'll be okay," I agree. "I doubt she'll send you another nasty letter this time."

"Ugh, don't remind me about that fiasco." He rolls his eyes, still bitter about Charlotte's petty involvement in his business dealings with the now-deceased Michael Price.

We agree to meet up before dinner, and he walks towards Colin, keeping his car parked on the street. I turn to see the two men conversing before Jeremy walks through the art gallery doors, behind Colin's table. I imagine him telling Colin off, intimidating the corrupt louse of a man. Their brief exchange looks cordial enough, but a girl can dream.

As I finish the last few windows at the north end of downtown, Wesley rides by on a bike, and I flag him down.

"Hi, Wesley." My arms are once again loaded with flyers and posters, now done with the whole town. "I noticed you have a basket; would you mind if I put these in there? I can pick them up at Eli's later and dump them in the recycling bin."

"Sure, no problem. That's a lot of paper you got there." He peers over the top of his basket, getting a better angle on the gross photo.

I barely know anything about this man. I've been so preoccupied with Eli and Danni that he's gone under the radar. He's a black box that I need to dig out of the rubble.

"Yeah. I'm running for a seat on our Town Council, and some jerk plastered these all over town. Have you been out for a while? Any chance you saw who put them up?"

"I just left Eli's, sorry. But I'll keep an eye out. Are you walking home now? I can ride alongside you and drop these off. Wow, that picture is gnarly…"

"Ugh, tell me about it. I don't want you to change your plans. It's all good."

He sighs. "I have no plans; I just needed some air. My head has been a mess, and I thought a bike ride would help, maybe. I don't know."

"Yeah, I can't imagine what you all are going through," I reply. "If you really don't mind, I'd love the help. I need to pop back into the ranger station really quick to grab my dog, and then I can head home."

Seizing the opportunity to get to know him better, I don't push back too hard, just enough to adhere to the unwritten Midwestern code of conduct.

"I don't mind at all. A little purpose will help me out, too."

He rides with me as we cross the Birch River Bridge into the park. "So, Peyton told me that you and Paige used to date. I'm so sorry for your loss. This must be so hard." I keep my gaze straight ahead. He bikes slightly in front of me, avoiding eye contact. His beard quivers as a quiet sniff hides behind it.

"She was special." He bows his head, confirming Peyton's rumor. "We broke it off before we went to college, but she always had a little piece of my heart."

I give him a moment to collect himself. "Did you two go to separate colleges?"

"Oh, yeah. Paige was destined for big things from the get-go. She went to Yale and did her master's at Michigan. After that, she started working for the state. I didn't want to hold her back."

"I wish I had gotten to meet her. We emailed a few times about the park. She sent me an incredibly thoughtful letter after a rough patch this spring; I still have it."

"Sounds like her." He hangs his head and pulls over his bike, resting his foot on our front porch of the ranger station.

"I'll be just a second. Want to come in?" He signals *no thank you,* and I walk into the office, shutting the door behind me. Zach left another cryptic note on his desk saying he's on more "work errands." Marty, an absolute angel today, remains where I left him, curled up on the couch. The fire is out, and the air holds a slight chill. Zach threw a blanket on the couch for the dog to snuggle up in.

"Hey, Martin," I gently jostle the sleeping pup, who pops one big, brown eye open in response. "It's time to go home, buddy boy."

He grumbles, not appreciating the wake-up call.

"Marty, I need you to do me a favor," I whisper into the dog's floppy ear as I put on his leash. "Give me a read on the guy outside. Is he okay, or is he a bad guy?"

I think back to Marty's interactions with Lucas Sullivan before I knew he was a completely deranged murderer. The two met several times, and Marty showed subtle signs of wariness toward the man. He never really warmed up to him and was always very interested in how he smelled.

"Give me a sign if he's got bad vibes, okay? Trust your instincts." He wags his tail, which I take as an iron-clad contract, and gives me a small lick on my nose. His white, curly chest fur is all fluffed up and extra adorable.

We lock up the office behind us and reconvene with Wesley, heading home.

"Wesley, I'd love to learn more about you guys back in the day. I don't know if Eli told you, but he asked me to help clear your names from the police's suspect list. I sort of got wrapped up in something similar earlier this year, so I guess he thinks I could help." I shuffle, shoving my hands in my pockets. "Any context or info you have would be great."

"Oh, sure. I mean, what do you want to know? The four of us were tight. We still are. Eli and Danni dated on and off forever. Paige and I did, too," he divulges. "We started dating on Halloween of 2002, our sophomore year. It sort of became our holiday." He looks out over the Birch River. "She asked that we stay a secret. Her parents were strict and didn't allow her to date. They thought it would distract her from studying."

He tells me all about high school, the different friend groups, the big gossip, all standard John Hughes stuff. He's now an architect, working for a small firm near the Mackinac Bridge, a few hours north of here.

He designs fancy vacation homes and lives by himself in Cheboygan, which isn't all that different from here. He never married.

His statement tracks with Kelly's police report: nobody went in or out of Eli's house until they left to take Charlie trick-or-treating.

"I think we were all a little nostalgic this year," he continues. "At least I was. I couldn't wait to feel the same way I did when I was seventeen, just hanging with my friends. When the whole world was in front of us, where we could just be ourselves."

"I get it," I admit. I was pretty nerdy in high school, but I had an awesome core friend group, too. We were on the student council together, but disbanded shortly after graduation, all of us destined for schools across the country. I haven't thought about them or the student council in ages. I let out a small chuckle, remembering my old campaign slogan: *Of course-o, vote Lorso!*

What was I thinking?

"Were you Power Rangers for Halloween when you were younger?" I ask, remembering the photo I found stashed in his things.

"Yep, this year was a throwback. I ordered them for us as a little homage." He pauses. "I can't believe Paige is dead… It just doesn't feel real. I thought…things might be different this time now that her divorce was final."

He doesn't say it outright, but I hear it in his voice. This was his chance with her. Their big rekindling. Their time to be together. This was Wesley's shot to be with the woman he's always loved.

Maybe she didn't return his affections? An if-I-can't-have-her-no-one-can situation? He's been pining after her forever. Maybe he flipped out after that fantasy died?

As we turn the corner onto my street, I well up again. Downtown wasn't the only place my mystery saboteur worked today. The mix of frustration and embarrassment swells in my chest and onto my face in big, red splotches.

Toilet paper covers the beautiful Sugar Maple in my front yard, huge signs with horrible pictures of me plaster my lawn like headstones. What must be a few dozen eggs run down my dark red siding. A big, *No hot heads! Vote Colin!* banner hangs over my doorway, bookended with cheerful balloons, like I'm hosting a child's birthday party.

"Holy shi—," Wesley trails off, stunned. He dismounts his bike as we reach my driveway, dumping the slanderous ads into my recycling bin. "Do you want help with this?" He gestures to the front yard.

"I, uh," I stammer, paralyzed. A small group forms on the other side of the street, waiting to see what happens next. "I guess. If you don't mind."

The paralysis melts, and I usher Marty into the backyard. Wesley and I move quickly, wordless. With signs stacked in the trash can and banners ripped down, Wesley sprays the runny egg off my house with a hose. We agree it's probably best to leave the toilet paper and lean into it by adding dusty Halloween decorations from my garage. Now it looks intentional, less like vandalism.

"Thanks for your help, Wesley," I thank him for unexpectedly saving my butt this afternoon.

"No problem. Thanks for giving me something to take my mind off everything," he replies and rides off.

I walk through my wet, drippy door into a dark living room. Sinking into the couch, I stare out into space, overwhelmed. Between this campaign surprise and Eli's attitude, not to mention his pending murder charge and ditching Jeremy last night, my brain buffers like a video.

I let it.

Turning on the TV, eager to cue up Buffy reruns to calm the whir and hide from the world, I'm yet again met with my scrunched-up face and outstretched hand on the harsh, red background. "A TV ad? Really? You have got to be kidding me."

"Maudy Lorso: bad for our parks! Bad for our town!" a gruff voiceover booms. Images of my face, distorted with filters, flash on the screen. After thirty seconds of absolute hell, the voiceover ends with "Paid for by Tiller Brazas" at five times speed. I turn off the TV, exasperated, and put on a record instead.

Fifteen minutes or three hours later, my phone alarm goes off, reminding me it's Wednesday, which means spaghetti. Jeremy will be here soon.

"Ugh, Marty, do I have to go?" I peel myself off the couch, looking around for the dog. He's still outside, soaking in the sunshine, blissfully asleep on my back patio. Tapping on the glass, he pops up and comes inside, groggy. Like owner, like dog.

I pour him kibble for dinner and change into non-egged clothes. Putting on a nice sweater dress with tights, and some effort into my hair and makeup, I crack open a hard cider before he gets here. Ready early, I call Kelly.

"Hey, Kell. Are you going to spaghetti tonight? Want to go a little early and catch up?" Hearing a gentle tapping on the front door, I check the peephole and see a Greek statue waiting patiently. I open it for him and beckon him inside. He sits down at my kitchen table. "One sec, Jeremy," I whisper.

"I wanted to talk to you, too," Kelly says quietly. "I can't chat right now. The Sheriff is going ballistic. The state police are here. I'm at the station; I'll walk over to Pop's once they leave."

"Yikes, okay. You got it. Jeremy just got here; we'll head out the door in a few minutes. See you soon."

Chapter Eleven

We walk through the doors to Pop's, taking two stools out of earshot on the far end of the bar. Kelly isn't here yet, and it's a little soon for dinner, but a few early birds twirl noodles and crunch on garlic bread already. The bar drips in school colors. The left side of the room is in Stone's Throw orange and black, and the right is in Hemlock Pond's purple and white. Each team claims one of the long community tables, topping them with matching centerpieces and covering them with football-shaped confetti.

"Hi, Kevin," I greet the older man in a Detroit Tigers baseball cap as he approaches us from behind the bar.

"If it isn't one of my favorite patrons." He smiles, but it's tainted with worry. I remember when Eli would smile at me like that, when something bothered him. They have the same head tilt. "What can I get you two? Besides a healthy dose of school spirit." He throws a handful of Stone's Throw Skipper temporary tattoos on the bar, along with a clean, damp rag.

As we order a round, I add a block letter S and T to each cheek.

"I'm going to go wash up. Be right back." Jeremy heads to the bathroom.

"How are you holding up, Kevin?" I ask the bartender. "I'm sure you knew Paige. I'm so sorry for your loss."

He looks around the room, then back at me, not answering my

question. "Here," he whispers, sliding an iPad across the bar. It's in an orange polka-dot case.

"What's this?" I pick it up.

"Keep your voice down," he whispers. "It's Paige's."

"Whoa. Why do you have this, Kev?"

"She left it here on Monday by accident. She ate lunch here. I thought Eli might look suspicious if I handed it over now…" He blushes and fiddles with his hat. "They tore through my boy's house. They think he had a hand in this."

Jeremy returns, and Kelly walks in not long after. I quickly stuff the iPad in my bag. *We'll talk more about this later, Kevin.* Seeing her, too, Kevin pours an IPA and slides the glass in front of us.

"So, what's the competition thing today? I can't keep up," Kelly asks Kevin, taking a seat on the stool next to me.

"Oh, come on! Do you mean to tell me you're not familiar with the Rigatoni Race?" Kevin laughs, folding his arms. He's got a good poker face.

"Can't say that I am, Kev. A little busy these days. Is this a new one? I don't remember it from past years," Kelly says.

"Fill in us out-of-towners," Jeremy adds.

"Oh, stop that, Jeremy," Kevin replies. "You're no out-of-towner. I remember your grandparents like it was yesterday. I was sorry to see them move to Traverse City. Your grandma would always give me free penny candy from their store when your grandpa wasn't looking." He laughs.

"I didn't know your grandparents lived here," I play punch him in the arm.

"Of course you did," he laughs. "I told you I had roots here. They moved before they had kids, though. I'm a Traverse City boy born and raised."

"But to answer your question, Kelly," Kevin continues, "It's new this year. It's a pasta-eating contest. Each school nominates three seniors, and the team that eats the most wins. Eli's getting their food ready right now. He doesn't waste the good stuff on this nonsense."

After a few minutes of small talk, the bar gets crowded. I feel stares growing on my back. The flyers were up long enough to get their intended job done. All eyes are on me, and not in a good way. Kelly notices the shift and watches me curiously, raising her brows.

"I've got a bit of business to take care of," Jeremy interjects. "I'll be right back." He leaves, heading toward a booth on the far side of the room.

Kevin clocks him leaving and walks back over to us, pausing for a moment. "I'm sure I don't need to tell either of you this, but I wouldn't be much of a father if I didn't say it, anyway." He leans in, speaking quieter. "My son didn't have anything to do with that tragedy you're investigating." He taps the bar in front of Kelly, frustrated. "You both know him just as well as I do. There's no way."

Kelly and I look at one another. I waver and nod my head ever so subtly. "I believe you, Kevin," I reply, heartbroken for the man.

"Nobody is charged with anything yet, Kev. I'm holding out hope that he's not involved. I'm doing my best," Kelly adds, patting the man's hand. "But I'm not the one in charge."

"Well, I trust you. And Maudy, I have something for you. For the parade tomorrow. Remind me later."

"Whatever it is, no thanks. I'm going to be on the Park float. Rather not mix campaign stuff with work stuff," I reply. I have a hunch I know what this is, and I'd rather not, given the circumstances.

He frowns and pours a pint. "I don't know, Maudy. Seems like the tides have turned against you today," he nods to the rest of the bar. "I'm not letting you off the hook." He winks at me and turns to Kelly, his expression softening. "I know you'll do the right thing, Kelly. And I know this puts you in a hard spot. I don't envy you. My boy is innocent.

He wouldn't hurt a fly. You two know that."

Eli must have told him that he asked me to poke around. Is there anything worse than disappointing Kevin?

He leaves us to wait on others trickling in. We continue to drink, both exasperated, while I reel from embarrassment at everyone's stares. I try to keep my eyes on Kelly as we talk, but I still catch glances and whispers. Electricity charges the air.

"Everything's pointing at Leonard," I confide. "The political motive runs pretty deep, and that slander accusation is a little ill-timed. Something seems so fishy there."

"I don't think it was him," she sighs, dejected.

"What? Why?"

"I talked to the medical examiner this afternoon." She takes a long pull from her pint glass. "Time of death doesn't line up. Based on the dosage and the nature of the drug, they're pretty sure that she ingested it a few hours before she died. Before the rest of them left to go trick-or-treating. It took a while to, uh, take effect."

"That afternoon, when I saw them in the backyard."

"Did you notice anyone come or go?" she asks.

"No, I didn't see anyone else. It *was* one of them," I whisper as the house of cards falls.

"It looks that way. We just ordered a full autopsy. So far, they only did a tox screen." She looks at Kevin, who is talking to another customer down the bar. "None of them has a legit alibi. They just have one another to corroborate where they were that afternoon. Gah, this sucks." She tightens her ponytail and puts her elbows on the bar.

"Eli's going to kill me." I drag my hands down my face and tap my head against the bar top in frustration.

"Gonna kill *you*? I'm the one who might have to arrest him. Like I said on the phone, the Sheriff is going nuts. He wants me to make an arrest now and scoop the state force, so we get the credit. The town is going to exile me." She takes another pull.

"Ugh," I pout. "This isn't looking good for that trio."

"Speaking of those three," she adds, "sorry I didn't text you back this morning. Danni wasn't with me during that meeting you had at the marina. She probably had something with Charlie. They're working through the court system to finalize his adoption."

"Good to know, thanks."

"By the way, I'll be at the class reunion this weekend. We're going to be surveilling the property in case something else happens. I'm an alum of one of the classes. I think it's from 2000 to 2010. Anyway, I'll be there with bells on." She rolls her eyes.

"I think I'll be in the park most of the night, but I might pop in and out with the shuttle." I pause, still thinking about the timeline developments and Danni's whereabouts this morning. "Yeah, maybe Danni was with Charlie," I mull over. "Or doing funeral arrangements. Last I heard, they couldn't get hold of Paige's family. Jeez, Danni has a lot going on, eh?"

"She's President of the Alumni Association. Paige was Vice President, so I'm guessing she's got extra stuff dumped on her. On top of everything with her family," Kelly adds over the rim of her pint glass.

"For sure. She's working on full custody of Charlie, right?"

"Yes. A complete adoption. Could you imagine? Going from single to single parent is a mega life change."

"I bet," I mutter, taking another pull from my pint glass.

By the end of our second round, the bar is shoulder-to-shoulder. The Rigatoni Race is about to begin, taking the heat off of me (thankfully).

Three testosterone-filled football players from each school sit in the middle of a long community table, facing each other. The audience swarms, people forced to stand on the booths along the sides of the bar, and others kneeling on their stools to get a better look.

Warring chants ring throughout the room. As they crescendo, Eli emerges, a huge stock pot and ladle in hand. He climbs up on the bar, towering over everyone, and bangs on the pot, silencing the rabble.

"Let the Rigatoni Race...BEGIN!"

The room roars in excitement. Kelly and I stay small in our corner. In the span of ten minutes, the racers scarf down plate after plate of pasta.

Soon enough, they slow down. One Stone's Thrower runs to the bathroom. Eli calls it, taking final plate counts and ruling in favor of Hemlock Pond. Stone's Throw has officially fallen behind.

The whole town is here, now settling into seats to eat their own spaghetti dinner. How appetizing, after watching a bunch of kids stuff their faces with it. But as Kevin said, that wasn't Eli's good stuff, which is hard to pass up.

Danni sits at the far end of the bar with Charlie and Wesley, leaning over and talking to Eli, whose face draws to hers as well. I feel the heat rise again in my chest. *It's a good thing! He's getting over you. You can be friends again.*

Charlie plays with a little device, probably another game, occupying himself. After a minute or so, he pockets it before diving into his plate. Red sauce immediately splatters all over his shirt.

Eli's face looks a little...disgruntled? Upset? He's not smiling and snaps the dishtowel from his apron pocket to wipe the bar, creating space between him and Danni. She glances at Charlie and leans further over to Eli, waving a piece of paper in his face. He pulls away even more. *They're not flirting, they're fighting. Is she holding one of my campaign flyers?*

Nearby, Anna's straw blonde hair comes into view, alongside Nellie, bobbing through the crowd.

"Kelly," I ask, "did you ever ask Lydia if she spoke to Paige that night? When she got a piece of candy?"

"Not yet, but we should." She shifts in her stool, making room for someone squeezing in behind her.

"On it." I climb off the barstool and slink down the room, trying not to draw attention to myself.

As I snake through the bar, the radio station cuts to a commercial. "Hot head Maudy Lorso isn't even from here! She's bad for our parks and for our town! Vote Colin for Stone's Throw Vill—" Eli turns the station, scowling at the radio, pointing a remote.

All eyes swivel to me like I'm a magnet they're unwillingly pulled to.

"Hey, guys," I grumble, giving Anna and Nellie each a side hug, shrinking into their tight circle in the bustling room.

"Hey, hey." Anna gives me a big hug, burying my face in her hair. "Colin sucks."

"Yeah, thanks." I cringe. "It's been a day."

"Have you seen the poll Channel Seven put out?" she asks, handing me her phone. "Nellie and I weren't sure if we should show you, but I feel like you'd want to know."

"It's that bad, eh?" I take it and look. Colin has the lead. I've dropped from having sixty percent of the vote just last week to forty-eight percent today. That's the thing about small towns. A handful of people make a big difference.

"Let's go for a nice fall paddle soon," Anna offers. "I got new sea kayaks in stock. We should test them out on some of these waves."

"I'm not going to say no to that, but I'm alright." I muster a smile and hand her phone back.

"You're hanging with Kelly tonight?" Nellie asks, changing the subject. "Peyton filled us in on Eli's little request for your help. You really want to do this again? Are we all forgetting what happened last time?"

"Reserve your judgment, please. I'm just trying to get Eli and me back to normal."

"Normal, *right*," Nellie replies doubtfully.

"Speaking of," I retort, not indulging her sarcasm, "I wanted to ask you something about that. Did Lydia talk to Paige that night? When she was trick-or-treating?"

"I'll be right back. Going to grab a drink," Anna excuses herself, shuffling towards Kevin.

"After I heard what happened, I asked her," Nellie replies, answering my question. "I guess she said, 'trick or treat' and didn't get an answer, so she and Gemma just took candy from the bowl and left." Nellie shrugs. "Paige was probably already dead, but I didn't tell her that. No need to traumatize the poor girl."

After a few more minutes of catching up, I turn to make my way back to Kelly and fill her in.

"What the hell is this?" I ask myself, faced with a booth across the room occupied by Charlotte, Leonard, Colin, and Jeremy. *My* Jeremy. Anna stands in front of them, shoulders tense and fists glued to her sides.

Fortified by hard cider and desperation, I pull myself tall and use the oncoming stares as fuel to walk into the lion's den. Folks step back as I approach the booth, giving me a substantial berth.

"Isn't this an interesting group?" I smile wide, tone shriller than intended, draping an arm around Anna's shoulders.

"My thoughts exactly," Anna agrees, staring each of them down one by one. "I went to get a drink, and what do I find?" she asks. "A snake in the grass."

"Honey, why don't you join us over here?" I squeeze Jeremy's arm, yanking him out of his seat. *Is Jeremy the "man on the inside" I heard them talk about? He wouldn't undermine me...would he?*

"Of course." He stands up politely. "Great speaking with all of you." He nods curtly.

"I hope I have your vote, son. Michigan government needs men like us. We see the world for what it could be, not what it is." Leonard glares over the rim of his glass right at me.

Anna follows as I drag Jeremy back to the bar. When out of earshot, I hiss, "What the hell are you doing with them?"

"Relax." He pulls me in for a hug, shielding me from the outside world for a moment. My suspicion begins to melt as I take a deep breath and pull myself out of it. He wouldn't hurt me.

"You might be able to convince her, but you're not convincing me, Jeremy Gray," Anna snaps. "Fess up."

"Look." He keeps his eyes on me, ignoring Anna's accusation. "Charlotte and I needed to wrap a couple more things up about that new toy shop I was telling you about, Maudy. Then the other two joined, and it felt rude to leave."

Anna's expression says more than enough. "Oh, so you're going with a flat-out lie? That's not what I heard." She crosses her arms over her teal, plaid flannel.

"Jeremy," Kelly chimes in before an argument breaks out. "Give Anna a second to cool off. Go get another drink."

"Sure…" He's suspicious but listens to her. He walks away.

"Okay," Anna rushes, mouth going faster than her brain. "I saw him with those jerks and went to confront him. But then I sort of psyched myself out and froze for a second. Before they saw me, I overheard some interesting chit-chat." She looks back and forth between Kelly and me. It's like she's sitting half-court at a tennis match.

"What'd you hear?" Kelly asks, setting down her glass as we scoot into the stools next to her.

"Charlotte was talking about how Danni no-showed today for a big meeting." She looks at me. "At the clubhouse this morning. Were you there?"

"Yep. I was there. I thought that was weird too, but Danni's probably doing funeral arrangements or the thousand other things she has on her plate," I explain.

"I don't know… Charlotte hinted that Danni may have had something to do with Paige's death. She was cryptic, though, and I only heard a little, so I'm not sure. Colin also mentioned a meeting with Paige on Monday, but didn't say what it was about."

"Huh," I ponder.

"Just be careful, Maudy. I don't know about him." Anna looks over at Jeremy and squeezes my arm. She walks over to get Kevin's attention, still needing that drink.

I swivel to Kelly and slap my hands on the bar top. "I'm going to deal with the fact that my boyfriend might be sneaking behind my back later. Lydia didn't talk to Paige. She tried but didn't get an answer. She was probably already dead."

"That lines up," Kelly concludes.

"I'm dying to know about the shoe things from the dumpster. Any more info on those yet?" I ask as she steals a piece of garlic bread from my abandoned plate.

"They're boot covers."

"Yeah, yeah, of course. What'd you find?"

"That's the thing. Not a whole lot." She runs her fingers through her hair, tightening her ponytail. "It's as you thought, they are covers for a Power Rangers costume. They bungee around your shoes and are worn like tall socks, meant to look like the white boots from the TV show characters. I went back and checked her clothes when she died. She wasn't wearing any when we arrived on the scene. They also didn't have any prints or DNA other than Paige's, so it's reasonable to assume these covers were hers. They were soaked through with gross dumpster juice, though, so evidence was probably lost."

"Did they match the others? Wesley told me they bought the costumes as a group set. Are you sure they match the other ones? I think I saw Danni's in her bedroom, you could compare."

Her eyebrows pop, and that oh-too-familiar scowl takes over her face. "You were in Danni's room? That's not what we agreed, Lorso." She whisper-yells at me. "Did you take anything? Did you touch anything? You could get us both in serious trouble. Why did I even open this can of worms in the first place?"

"Because you need help. And to be crystal clear, Eli asked me to cat sit Gumbo. I didn't take anything." *Do I tell her Kevin gave me Paige's iPad? Maybe later.* "I have a key; it's not like I broke in illegally." I cross my arms. "He didn't know if he'd be around regularly to feed the cat with everything going on." I shrug innocently but also smirk a little. "He asked me to do this, remember?"

"Fine," she caves. "If Eli consented, you're right. I can't do much about that." She pauses, taking another sip before continuing. "Yes, they all match. Made by the same manufacturer. Same fabric, yada, yada, yada. The yellow diamonds match the style of everyone else."

"Yellow?" I ask, trying to remember when I pulled them out of Marty's mouth. They were covered in slime, and it was dark out; I don't recall the color. "They had yellow diamonds? She was wearing the pink costume."

"I don't know what to tell you, the covers from the dumpster have yellow diamonds on them. They were definitely hers; her DNA was all over them, and she wasn't wearing any when we first responded to the scene. I have all the clothes she was wearing in evidence. No boot covers."

"Danni was in the Yellow Power Ranger costume when I saw her that night. Downtown with the rest of them. Why was Paige wearing pieces of Danni's costume?"

"Maybe Charlotte's not as crazy as she seems," Kelly replies, glancing at Danni.

Chapter Twelve

Climbing down from the loft, I amble into the kitchen, eager to get my day going. Jeremy's measured, heavy breathing drifts down from above like leaves falling from the old oaks in the backyard. That man could sleep all day. *Jealous.*

Marty scampers down the stairs, claws tapping on the floors like Fred Astaire. He stands up on his hind legs and scratches at the back door. I hear a grumble from upstairs, but silence quickly follows. He's still asleep.

"Go play outside, Marty," I whisper to him. "I'll be out in a second." He bounds out the door, tail wagging, and inspects the latest happenings in the backyard. I imagine it's a little like reading today's issue of the Birch River Current.

With coffee in hand, I join him outside, lounging on the patio. The peace and quiet juxtapose last night's chaos, spaghetti, and surprising discoveries.

Am I mad at Jeremy for whatever he was doing with those snakes? Yes. Was I going to make him drive home after drinking? Absolutely not. Do I secretly wish my coffee bean grinding or the dog's claws would wake him up? Maybe.

With a notebook in hand, I collect my thoughts this morning. Time to crack into Anna's, well, Charlotte's, theory.

"Motives, means, opportunity," I repeat the big three I learned this spring, writing them each as a heading on a blank page. Marty, done with his important business, joins me on the patio, spread-eagle, tongue hanging out of his mouth in the sun.

"Let's start with motive, shall we, Martin Short?" Paying me no mind, the dog happily sleeps on.

"Why would Danni want to hurt Paige?" I tap my pen on the blank sheet of paper, staring out into the yard. "They were friends, maybe there's some bad blood between them? They both were on the Alumni Association board together?" Without more to go on, we leave the motive there for now.

"Okay, now the means. Isn't poison a stereotypical femme method of killing?" No reply from the dog.

"And opportunity. They were all together in that house. We know she died around 6:30 p.m. and was poisoned sometime between 3:30 and 5:30 p.m. According to all four people who were in the house during that window, and are still alive to talk about it, nobody came in or out before trick-or-treating. Danni had the same opportunity as Wesley or Eli. Seems possible, Marty. We just don't know *why.*"

That got me a halfhearted grumbly "bow row row," at least.

"Maybe their drinks were tampered with beforehand? Their cups in the dishwasher smelled super sweet. It could've masked poison, maybe. Let's dig through his fridge next time we break into his house. We'll figure out what they were drinking."

At that unfortunate moment, the sliding glass door opens behind me, and I slam my notebook shut.

"Break into whose house?" a velvety voice interjects.

"I have a key; it's not what you think. I just...need to get more food for Gumbo over at Eli's."

"First, all that stuff with Kelly last night. And now," he points to the notebook, "you're snooping around this Paige Ramos thing, aren't you?"

"Hang on a minute. Are *you* the one who's upset with *me* right now?" I ask with disbelief. "Last I recall, I'm the one who caught you conspiring with Charlotte and Leonard against my campaign."

"I swear to you, I am not conspiring! I had business to finish up, Maudy." His presence grows, and I feel his exasperation. "And for the record, I'm still a little miffed you walked out on me the other night and bailed on our dinner. Was there even a grant proposal, or was it this stuff?"

The wind rattles around us, goading a fight. "Fine, I believe you," I say without much feeling behind it. "I can't just sit around and watch a friend get accused of murder, Jeremy."

"So, this *is* what you ran off to work on the other night. When you came to Traverse City for all of fifteen minutes. I don't hear denial."

"Can we talk about something else, please? Call a truce?" Memories of arguments with my ex, Nate, swirl, each one escalating more than the previous. We were both stubborn, and distrust festered with each fight. I don't want that again.

He simmers in the doorway. "Fine. For now." He walks inside to pour himself a cup of coffee, bringing the pot to refill mine as well.

"Any chance you know someone over at Channel Seven?" I try smiling at him, hoping to break the tension.

"Why do you need someone at the news station? That ad?" he asks, sitting down.

"Yeah. I want to see if they can tell me who bought the airtime. Tiller Brazas doesn't have any search results. No phone numbers, nothing."

"No, sorry. I don't know anyone over there."

"It's not you, is it?" I ask, hesitant to re-enter fight territory. "You didn't place those ads, right?"

"Wow. You're unbelievable." Anger fuels his voice; he quickly drains his cup and pops inside to get dressed, reemerging in a suit.

"I have to go to work." He walks right past me, avoiding eye contact, and follows the driveway to his car. Marty lingers at the gate, and we watch him roll himself with the lint brush he keeps in his glove box before climbing in and slamming the car door behind him.

"Ugh," I groan. *I shouldn't have gone there. I messed that up.*

Tabling what to do about Jeremy, I sit back in my patio chair and call the phone number listed for Channel Seven.

"Advertisements, please," I ask a secretary, who connects me to a gravelly-sounding gentleman.

"Yeah, Channel Seven."

"Hi, I'm wondering if you could tell me who placed a TV commercial that aired last night?"

"What's this about?"

"Someone aired an attack ad on a local political campaign. I'd just like to know who placed the ad, that's all."

"Ah, you must be that screaming chick. Not a good look, babe," he wheezes. I think it's a chuckle encased in decades of cigarette smoke.

"The photo is taken out of context. Actually, I don't need to justify myself to you. Can you just tell me who called to place it, please? I know it says, 'paid for by Tiller whatever,' but any other info would be great."

"Take it easy, no need to bite my head off. Let me see here." He pauses. "Best I can do is give you a phone number. I didn't take this call, and I don't know who was on the other line."

"That's fine, thanks."

He recites a phone number with a local 231 area code. I hang up with him and call it.

The phone rings a handful of times before an automated voice tells me this number is not set up to receive voicemail. "Please hang up and call again later."

"Alright, I'll call again later. And later. And later. Until I figure out who the hell you are."

Knock, knock, knock. Muffled calls from the front door reach me on the patio. "Out back," I yell, walking over to the gate.

Eli, Danni, and Charlie walk around the side of my house, a couple of bags in tow. *How formal, choosing not to cut through our backyard gate.*

"Hey, sorry to do this, but could Danni and Charlie shower here this morning? My hot water tank is puny, and it's already cold. Charlie has to get to school."

Doesn't she live like, twenty minutes away? Why doesn't she just go home?

I lead them into the house. "Of course. Come on in." Marty trots in behind us, grumbling for breakfast.

Danni might be involved in this somehow. Be cool. Paige was wearing a piece of her costume that night. Don't let her know you're on to her.

Eli thanks me and leaves. Charlie hops into the bathroom while Danni waits for him on my couch.

"Are you a coffee drinker?" I ask from the kitchen, unsure what else to say. *Don't be weird. Don't let her know you're suspicious; she could be dangerous.*

"Absolutely," she groans, still half asleep. I pour her a cup and join her in the living room, curling up on an armchair beside the couch. "Thanks. Not just for this, but for letting us get ready here. That's really nice of you." She attempts to tame her bedhead. Her nailbeds are all ripped up like she's been picking them.

"No problem. I'm so sorry for your loss." There's palpable friction between us, like members of two opposing teams. With crossed arms, she turned slightly away from me, a little stiff.

"It's been a tough year. Eli and I have been fighting, too, which doesn't make things easier." She closes her eyes, savoring the coffee and fighting off sleep.

"I thought I picked up on that last night. Hope you guys are okay." I jam my hands underneath my legs, feeling uncomfortable.

"Oh, yeah. We do this. Fight, make up, fight again," she explains. "Just, do me a favor?" she asks. "Would you mind keeping your distance? He gets all strange and self-conscious around you."

"Oh," I stammer. *Were they fighting about me? Is she threatened by me?* That came out of left field. "Uh. Yeah. I'm sorry about that. We've had some weirdness for a while. It's nothing, though."

"Thanks." She smiles as a pause fills the room.

"Do you mind if I ask what happened to your brother? I've heard bits and pieces." I ask, trying to change the subject. If she's going to throw curveballs, so can I.

"Uh, yeah," she replies, flustered by the question. She waits for a moment, checking to make sure Charlie can't hear us from the bathroom. The shower runs loudly. "My big brother was as sweet as can be, but had a nasty addiction problem. Like, for forever. We tried to get him help, but it never worked, or he would refuse to go. Eventually, he got into bed with some bad people to keep up with his drug habit. He overdid it…"

Her eyes glass over as they fixate on the coffee in front of her. Her phone rings from her bag. Looking to see who it is, she says, "Sorry, I have to take this," and steps into my kitchen.

"No, no, please. I just need a few more days. He's getting his own room, I promise," I hear her plead with whoever is on the other line. "Next week. Yes, come by next week." After a long pause, she ends the call with a grave, "thank you, thank you."

"Everything okay?" I ask when she returns to the couch."

"I have no idea what I'm doing. I'm floundering here." She rubs her face again and stretches out her neck and shoulders. "That was Child Protective Services. I'm fighting to get custody, barely scraping together enough money for the two of us, and… His death just changed things. There's still a lot to dig ourselves out of."

"Family trying their best is light-years better than no family at all." I smile and get up to refill my cup, sensing she could use a moment to compose herself.

"You know," she says, rubbing her eyes. "Paige was a big part of the reason the park's funding went as long as it did. She was so excited about the work that you were doing over there. She lobbied hard for you. She was bummed when they cut it."

I return to the chair, bringing a couple of Pop-Tarts as a makeshift breakfast. "I didn't know that. I'm sure she tried her best. She sent me a note now and again thanking us for our work, but she never said anything about the budget."

"Sounds like Paige." She smiles, sipping from one of my favorite mugs adorned with cartoon versions of Bill and Ted, two feisty crows that live in the park, wearing sunglasses. Zach made it for me for Christmas last year. "I think she was the only humble politician that ever lived."

"I wish I had gotten to know her better. She seemed great."

"She was. She totally was…" Her mind wanders for a moment.

"Do you know if she was doing any business while in town this week? Had any meetings or anything?"

"Probably. She knew everyone. I think she had a couple of meetings on Monday before we met at Eli's. She was the last one to get to his house." She swallows, voice cracking. "Oh, good, you're out." Charlie emerges from the bathroom in a steam cloud, dressed for school.

"Charlie, why don't you wait outside? Go play. I'll be out soon." He listens and goes through my sliding door. "I'll just be a minute." She fakes a smile and closes the bathroom door behind her.

The second I hear the water flowing, I spring into action, pouncing on her bag to snoop through her things. Gumbo and Marty patter over; their curiosity getting the better of them.

Sifting through papers stuck in notebooks and a thousand little pockets, I pull out a piece of hard plastic. "An EBT card?" I whisper, inspecting it closer. "She's on food stamps." I sigh, looking at the bathroom door. This breaks my heart.

I try to put the card back where I found it, but the God of Chaos could learn a thing or two from Danni. Her bag could've been thrown down a bowling lane and look the same. I keep searching until my fingers find a crumpled-up ball of fancy, tan-colored paper.

"Coast still clear, Gumbo?" I ask the cat, who tilts his head and rubs against me as I crouch over her bag like a gargoyle. Eyes darting towards the bathroom door, the shower water still *wooshes*. I unfurl the paper, revealing a check from Paige for thirty thousand dollars.

"Holy cow," I whisper, mouth gaping open. The note on it reads, *Pay back by Halloween.* It has a mobile deposit date from about two months ago.

The water faucet squeaks off. Hastily, I crumple the paper and toss it back in her bag.

"Marty, come here," I beckon the dog. "Hurry!" He listens, and I rip off the tracker from his collar and hide it in the bottomless pit of Danni's purse. Nonchalantly planting myself at the kitchen table, I put her bag back as the bathroom door unlocks.

After Marty darted away from me in the park this spring, I got a GPS tracker to help me hunt him down if it ever happened again.

"Thanks again. We should get going." Danni emerges *slightly* less haggard. "I need to take Charlie to school and then have a ton of work to do before the reunion on Saturday. I'll be in touch with hayride stuff." She grabs her bag and smears on a smudge of dark red lipstick before looking at her phone, noting the time. "Crap, it's Thursday! Is it really Thursday? I completely forgot."

"What?" I stand up, feeding off her sudden panic.

"The parade. Tonight's the parade." The dark circles under her eyes are beyond the help of concealer. Her color shades sallow.

"*Merda.* I also forgot." I shoot texts to friends who might be able to join us on our float, hoping I didn't drop the ball.

"Merda? What is 'Merda'?" Danni asks as Charlie comes in from the backyard.

"Italian for, uh," not wanting to swear in front of the kid, "crap." I smirk at her. "I should also get to work. But I'll see you tonight? At the parade?"

"Yep, I'll be there." She opens the front door. "Don't forget to run back to Eli's and take your medicine before school, kid! Eat some breakfast!" she shouts to Charlie, who's halfway around the block already.

With them gone, I hook up Marty and walk out the door myself. "Ready for our daily check-up, Marty? If Zach's got the float all worked out, we should have time today." The pup's ears perk up, and a pep jolts his step as we head towards the park, pushed by a cool breeze as if we have our own personal escort into the woods.

"Danni is in debt, Marty." I mull this over with the mutt on our way into the park. "This could change things."

* * *

"Oh. My. God," I shriek, unintentionally channeling Janice from *Friends*. Crossing the park entrance, absolute anarchy greets me with the kindness of an electric shock. Half of the parking lot is taken up by what I can only assume is our park's parade float. Not to mention two dozen men unloading a semi-truck full of haunted hayride props.

"Morning, Maudy." Zach's head pops up from under shiny green streamers hanging off the platform, covering the wheels and metal beams of the boat trailer holding this monstrosity up. "Is this great, or is this great?"

I'll say this: the man tried his best. Inheriting a complete Sheriff-themed float and turning it into a park theme is no easy feat. I never saw it in its full law-enforcement glory, but even now it's pretty clear that the crown jewel was a six-foot-tall police badge, encrusted with gold pom-poms.

Now that badge is a giant, gold beetle. With legs and antennae made from twisted birch branches, it sparkles with a new layer of yellow oak leaves. Unfortunately, all that really did was make the police badge look like it sprouted legs and crawled out of someone's fever dream, but the man tried his best, and that's good enough for me.

The rest of the float kind of works. The bottom is draped in layers of leaves. Little wooden chairs ring a faux campfire made of construction-paper flames and painted pool-noodle logs. Bags of marshmallows and mini chocolate bars are ready to toss to the masses. Even a fake Bill and Ted sit on one of the chair backs, our unofficial park mascots (second to Marty). The real Bill and Ted watch and squawk in support from a nearby branch, occasionally swooping down to peck at the float's glittery streamers.

Thankfully, Emma rallied her garden club kids to sit on our float today. We've got a full house: Emma and her garden club, Zach, our campground caretaker, Jim, and me.

With details hashed out, Marty and I check in with the hayride crew and make sure they know where they're going. We instruct them to store their props in a natural clearing not too far off the hayride track. It's a little closer to the action than up here and will keep our parking lot open to the public.

With everyone good to go, the scruffy pup and I set out on our park check-up, eager to clear my head and think through this Danni theory as well as how to salvage my campaign. I need to lay out next steps on all fronts.

I always say that the best days are spent with walks in the woods, and today is no exception. Marty frolics, hopping in big piles of crunchy leaves. Some of the trails are almost invisible under the blanket of fiery debris. We wade through, choosing less popular routes to stay out of the hayride crew's way, taking the opportunity to clear fallen branches and make note of maintenance needs before the first snowfall.

With the sun high in the bright blue sky, my phone alarm goes off. "Time to head back, Marty." We could've wandered all day.

"Ruff," he grumbles in protest and hunkers down on his back haunches.

"I know, bud. I'm with you. I have other work I need to do."

Reluctantly, we turn around. He's grown attached to a particular stick and carries it with him most of the hike back, occasionally getting it caught on high grasses and shrubs. We reach a fork in the trail and continue towards the ranger station.

"Eli? What are you doing out here?" He emerges from the other fork and heads in my direction, maybe twenty feet ahead. He's a hiker, but not in the middle of the day on a Thursday. He's outfitted with a daypack, carrying a water bottle, and wearing proper shoes. Not his usual Pop's clothes.

He whips his head around. "Jeez, Maudy, you almost killed me. I didn't hear you." Marty scampers over, putting down his prized stick to give the man's hand a friendly lick.

"Sorry, didn't mean to scare you," I laugh, grinning ear to ear. "What brings you out here? Need anything?"

He clasps his hands together and then wipes them on his pants, on edge. "Oh, nope. Just out for a walk."

I cross my arms and give an exaggerated, skeptical look. "Uh-huh. Sure. During one of Pop's busiest weeks. Right after your high school friend dies. You just scamper off for a couple of hours of R&R? I don't buy it. Not after I saw you whispering with Zach back in the office. What's going on?"

"Don't worry about it." He claps his hands again, signaling he's done talking about it. "So, how was this morning with Danni and Charlie? Thanks again. My house isn't built for that many people. And look, sorry about snapping at you before, I'm just...stressed out."

Danni's request that I keep my distance rings in my head.

"Forget it. We're fine. And they were fine. Everything's fine."

He's suspicious, with a solemn head tilt. "Was everything okay between you and Danni? It wasn't weird or anything, was it?"

Of course, it was weird. It was so, so, so weird.

"Like I said, it was fine. I know she means a lot to you." I force a smile, saddened by our situation, and we walk back towards the park entrance in torturous silence.

We part ways as I head to the ranger station, waving goodbye. Zach gives me the rundown of when and where to meet up later for the parade, and what Marty and I should wear. After the final touches, he grabs his things and heads out for the day.

"Alright, let's get to it." Taking advantage of a quiet office and a tuckered-out dog, I hammer out a statement in response to the attack ads and send it to all major news outlets and stakeholder groups in town.

I've seen the hateful ads my opponent has released, grossly mischarac-terizing me. I care for this town, I'm a part of this town, and I want to keep my campaign focused on what matters: the people who live here. Am I passionate? Absolutely. I'll bring that passion to our Village Council and fight for what will make Stone's Throwers' lives even better. - Maudy Lorso

With that out of the way, I chip away at other work until my focus wanders. Eventually, I look up from my screen with an achy, hunched back and a stiff neck.

"Better get going," I groan. "Wake up, Martin. We have a pit stop to make before we go home to change."

Chapter Thirteen

Walking into the marina for the second time is still just as striking as the first. This is, by far, the nicest building in town. It sticks out like a sore thumb (wearing a diamond ring) compared to the rest of Stone's Throw. I cringe walking in the door, feeling so out of place in my muddy hiking boots and work jacket.

The main floor has high-top tables scattered throughout. They've made progress on the party set-up since I last visited.

Ascending the staircase to the second level, I turn into Charlotte's office, finding it (thankfully) empty. I have to drop off paperwork for the hayride and our silent auction submission for the party on Saturday.

"I'll write her a note and leave it here," I mutter, searching for a pen and notepad. She's decorated the space in a streamlined style that office buildings are embracing lately. She has a glass-top desk, white painted walls, and two armchairs straight out of *Star Trek*. The rest of the house renovations are so tastefully in line with the home's history. She killed every ounce of personality that was once in this room.

I find a notepad and tell her I'm dropping off paperwork and our silent auction submission.

Taking the chance to poke around, I peruse her bookshelf, filled with urban planning and local history books like one titled *Trail Blazers*, the supposed puppeteers from back in the day. She has an extensive collection; as a reader myself, I'm impressed.

The only hanging artwork in the room is an old town map from the 1920s, framed in shiny black. It's a replica and shows traces of significant wear and tear from the original over the last hundred years. Most of what's now downtown is farmland, except for this building and a few blocks adjacent. Pop's bar is there, but the rest of the town is largely undeveloped.

I scan the land that's now the park to see if the old ranger station is there. A small, house-like structure marks the station, with a swirl of smoke churning out of the chimney. The level of detail on Pop's and the ranger station is incomparable to the rest of the structures. *Well, that's adorable. I should get a copy of this for our station's wall and give one to Eli, too.*

Charlotte's planner and laptop aren't here, so I can't check her email history. She *has* to be behind the attack ad. After hearing her with Colin, who else could it be? If only I had the proof.

With nothing much else to go through, I get about halfway down the stairs before pausing. *I wonder...* I pull out my phone and redial the number the TV station guy gave me. Turning towards Charlotte's office, I wait for her phone to ring. Nothing. Her office stays quiet.

Walking down the stairs, however, a faint ringing floats up from the basement.

One of the construction workers?

Sneaking around to the basement stairs, I creep through the sublevel, dialing the phone number and following the sound.

I wind through the basement maze, stone walls pressing in the further I go. Past the area marked off for tours, I find myself alone. Charlotte said the basement was bigger than the home's above-ground footprint, but she didn't say just how expansive it is. I'm probably a block over by now.

Following the ringing, I stop at forks and turns, trying to inch closer to the noise, but eventually meet a dead end. Faced with a wall of lake stones and makeshift cement, I search for loose rocks or a hidden door. The ringing persists, but this is the closest I'm going to get right now. I have more to do before the parade, and I've already spent too much time here.

How did I hear the phone from this far away? There must be a more direct path...one that carries sound.

On my way back, I slide the sole of my shoe against the corners of walls, leaving scuff marks. Next time I have a free minute, I can zoom through quicker.

* * *

Back in the safety of The Den, animals flanking me on the couch, I refocus on Paige. Time to comb through everyone's online presence before tonight's parade.

Paige's is highly curated, which is probably best for a politician. Her photos are professional, statements are grammatically correct, and all are work-related. I can't find any skeletons in the closet or any red flags that give me a reason someone would want to kill her. I can't find any nasty comments or hate accounts on social media.

I pick up her iPad and try a few dates I find in her profiles to unlock it. I try her birthday and the last digits of her phone number, but neither work. Her calendar must be in here. I bet Kelly has her phone; I could ask her to look if I can't figure it out.

Afraid of getting locked out permanently, I tuck the iPad into my backpack and out of sight. *Note to self: still need to find password.* Without any other ideas, I stalk Paige and Eli's friends to see if anything interesting pops up before leaving for the parade.

Scrolling through Wesley's feed, nothing stands out as unusual. He's not very active. The occasional birthday message, a tagged photo here and there, that sort of thing. He "likes" almost all of Paige's posts going back the last few months, which is interesting.

Danni's profile is frozen in time. She's been radio-silent for a while, since around the time her brother died: no comments, no posts, no updates, nothing. I don't blame her. Some grief doesn't have words.

Flipping through Paige's follower list, I find Colin and Leonard's names. I write, *Get into her calendar ASAP! Meeting with Colin the day she died?*

Peeling myself from the couch, brain melting into the cushion from the screen time, I put the finishing touches on my official park uniform, wide-brimmed hat and all, grab my backpack, and go to join the parade. *Let's get the public humiliation over with.*

I bring Marty, as he is a park employee in his own right, and tie a forest green bandana around his neck per Zach's request.

We meet around the corner from Main Street on the beach near the old, defunct lighthouse. Over two dozen floats fill the roadside parking lot, our giant golden beetle sitting pretty toward the beginning of the lineup. The only floats in front of ours are the official event hosts: the Stone's Throw Classes of 2000-2010, followed by their Hemlock Pond counterparts.

I catch Eli's attention from their class float. He raises his beer in a *cheers* motion. I wave back. Their float has maybe twenty people, about half of whom I know. Kelly is there, and so is Peyton, not to mention Eli and his crew.

Their float is luau-themed. They are decked out in orange Hawaiian shirts (many of which are covered in jackets) and sunglasses. It's an odd sight for October in Michigan. One guy is even wearing a coconut bra over his fleece. With music cranking, they lounge in beach chairs with beers flowing and sand covering the float's floor.

"That's a little morbid, isn't it?" I say to Zach, nodding over at their float. "One of them died, and they're acting as if nothing happened."

"I know, I was thinking the same thing. But who knows, maybe that's what Paige would've wanted. Or maybe the alcohol is to help them forget." He shrugs, loading up our float.

I unfold camp chairs around the fake fire for our garden club kiddos. Zach hitches us to a friend's pickup and jumps aboard, joining us around the campfire." We should be starting any minute.

"Maudy," a voice calls through the crowd. Kevin bobs through the idle floats. "Ope, excuse me," he apologizes to a random passerby. "Glad I caught you before we took off," he shouts. "Here." He tosses a bundled-up piece of fabric.

"What's this?" I ask, unfurling it.

"A sash, to show your candidacy in the Village Council race. I told you not to leave Pop's last night without reminding me."

"And I told you 'no, thank you' last night." I toss it back to him. "I've already got everyone's attention, not in a good way. The last thing I need is a flashy sash. Didn't you see my face on those ads?"

"I know, kid, but it's tradition. Would you rather give Colin the ammo? He could say you hate our customs or some nonsense. He's already reminding people you aren't from here. He's wearing one, if that makes you feel any better." He points down a handful of floats to a sparkly, black convertible. Colin's signs hang from each side as he basks in his glory on top.

"Hand it over." I admit defeat.

He tosses it again, and I throw it over my shoulder. The orange satin stands out against my work uniform like a neon construction vest. I shrink in my chair, trying to stay under the radar.

With everything ready, Jim, Emma, and the garden club climb aboard, and we settle around our paper campfire, waiting for the festivities to begin. Once the school marching band starts, engines crank and applause rings. We creep to a speedy three miles per hour, roll around the block, and pull onto Main Street right in front of Anna's surf shop. Tossing her a marshmallow, I wave as we pass by.

Rolling down the street, my presence is met with an interesting mix of responses. Some folks' eyebrows pop in surprise. Bolder people shout a flat *"boo!"* Eyes slide away, desperate to be associated with anyone but me. *Stupid sash.* After the first dozen interactions, I become numb to it. A few particularly obnoxious people may or may not get a marshmallow to the head.

What matters is that the kids have a great time. Our giant golden beetle is well-received, met with confusion and amusement. Marty leans over the edge, greeting his fans.

I pay close attention to the luau, trudging along behind the marching band. Danni sits on Eli's lap, slap happy, toasting everyone in sight. Wesley stares out, I'm not sure at what, and is pulled back into the party every few minutes, faking a smile absentmindedly. His mood shifts. He's darker.

Danni says something that grabs Wesley's attention, and his face scrunches. He's angry, talking to her with a stern look that wrinkles his beard. She points at him and shouts something back. I can't make it out.

"He's hurting," I say to nobody in particular, unwrapping a mini-Hershey bar for myself and handing another to the kid next to me. "Wesley really loved her."

Marty looks back at me with big eyes and licks my hand, asking for a piece of chocolate. When I refuse, he returns to the grueling demands of being a cute dog.

"Of course, he's hurt. His sweetheart just died," Jim astutely chimes in from the camp chair across from me, clocking the interaction, too. "There's no pain like it." He shakes his head.

Eli catches me staring, and our eyes meet briefly. He immediately fidgets until Danni slides off him. He grimaces, almost as an apology to me, before reengaging in the festivities. *Embarrassment, perhaps? Is he sad about Paige, or sad about him and me?*

Danni's deep in conversation with another woman, happily buzzed.

In a knee-jerk reaction to my flushing cheeks, I text Jeremy just to say hey. He's working late tonight, so, of course, no response.

Chaos slingshots around us as we continue to crawl through the heart of town. Floats rumble, dance parties break out in the street, and people swarm everywhere; the sound of it all is deafening. Wesley removes himself from his friends and steps to the corner of his float, overstimulated. He rubs his hands on his face and stares out at the surprisingly calm Lake Michigan water behind us.

His love runs deep, like an old river. They were serious. Or at least he was serious about her... What if she was still serious about him, too?

I hand Marty's leash to Jim and follow Wesley's lead. Walking to the back corner of our float, partially cloaked by the egregious beetle, I crouch down and pull Paige's iPad out of my backpack, typing in her and Wesley's Anniversary, Halloween 2002, into the password box. It unlocks.

She loved him back. It wasn't one-sided after all.

Unable to stop myself, I scan through saved documents, her email, anything I can access quickly. With the occasional candy toss, I try to keep up appearances as we go. Only two more blocks before the parade ends in the park's parking lot.

"Everything alright?" Emma asks, handing me a marshmallow.

"Yeah. Everything's fine," I answer, the iPad gripping my attention.

I open up Paige's calendar. She briefly met with Colin at the marina on Monday morning, just like Anna overheard last night. Right afterward, she had an hour-long hold for "TB." *Tiller Brazas?*

The Charlotte and Colin duo seems more and more likely to be involved in this somehow. But why would Charlotte be talking about Danni at Pop's last night?

In Paige's saved files, I find marked-up drafts of old state budgets, red line edits everywhere. The Department of Natural Resources' portion is listed, including Stone's Throw State Park as a line item. She was fighting to keep it in the budget; this draft has a big comment next to it. "Aw, Paige. You really did care about us."

The ghost of a tear forms in my eye. This draft is old. Paige's efforts didn't work, but it means the world to know she tried.

Otherwise, her email is jammed with messages from Wesley, dating back over a year. I skim a couple, feeling a little queasy at the invasion of privacy. They've been expressing feelings for one another for quite some time.

When did she get divorced? Was it before or after these two started talking? Maybe her husband found out about Wesley? Perhaps that's what caused the divorce in the first place...

A few minutes and three mini-Hershey bars later, we pull over the Birch River Bridge as I peek at her photos to see if she has any from her time at Eli's this week.

The most recent one shows all of them dressed up in their Power Ranger costumes without their masks, wearing big smiles. Charlie is doing a cartwheel with a watchful Danni right behind him. The pink costume really highlights Charlie's black. The others huddle around them. The joy on Paige's face kills me.

"Something's different." Examining more closely, I scan the photo like one of those eye-spy pictures. "Paige is wearing yellow, and Danni is in pink... But when Paige died, she was in pink, and Danni was in yellow. But Paige was wearing yellow boot covers when she died..." I pause. "They swapped costumes that night!"

Frantically looking for somebody, *anybody*, to tell this revelation to, I come up short. Taking a deep breath, I call Kelly. She's in front of me, on top of the luau float with Eli and the rest of them, chatting with a woman I don't know and tossing the last few leis to the parade watchers. Her phone goes to voicemail.

"Kelly, it's Maudy," I whisper into the phone. "Paige and Danni switched costumes that night. What if the killer messed up and killed the wrong person? We thought Danni could've been involved since Paige had the yellow boot covers on, but what if Danni was supposed to be the victim instead? Not Paige. I know this doesn't make sense right now, but hear me out. The killer went after the Pink Power Ranger, thinking it was Danni. That's why they dumped the yellow boot covers—so the police wouldn't realize they killed the wrong person by mistake."

Chapter Fourteen

A symphony of float-pulling truck engines end their song in the park's gravel lot, slowly morphing into a party as everyone unloads. A volunteer teardown crew joins the masses, with dozens of people who watched the event crossing the bridge to partake in the fun.

The eighteen-wheeler filled with haunted hayride gear is gone. All of the props and supplies have been moved into the woods. The entrance to the park is adorned with dried cornstalks and hay bales, already waiting to beckon thrill-seekers in.

Our float parks on the opposite end of the lot from Eli's, so I, with Marty in tow, do my best to push through the crowd. Half-covered in spilled beer and Fireball by the time I make it over there, I run up to Danni and pull her aside with a panicky, bug-eyed expression.

"Whoa, what's up?" she asks, turning (stumbling) to see me grab her.

"I need to talk to you," I mutter quietly. "Over here." I glance at her group of old classmates, standing nearby: Wesley, Eli, Peyton, and a handful of others I don't know. Peyton gives me an inquisitive look, asking what's up.

"I'll fill you in later," I mouth to her. She gives a thumbs-up, and I throw Marty's leash to her, telling the dog to hang here for a minute.

"Okay, okay, sheesh." Danni giggles as I lead her past the tree line, out of earshot. "Wait for me! Don't leave without me," she shouts back to them, a little slurred.

"Sorry to pull you away, but I think you might be in danger." Her smiley, giggly face contorts into a confused scrunch.

"Danger? I'm not in danger." Brushing me off, she starts walking back.

"Hang on, hang on." I tap her lightly on the arm, trying to get her attention. "Did you and Paige swap costumes on Monday?"

"Huh?" she replies, thinking for a second. Her thought flees, and she bops to the Eminem throwback playing from nearby car speakers.

"Danni, what color Power Ranger were you on Halloween?" This is so frustrating.

"Um, yellow." She beams, proud of herself for knowing the answer.

"But you started as pink, didn't you?"

"Oh, yeah. I forgot about that." The giggles resume.

Don't kill her, Maudy. Someone else already wants to do that for you.

"Danni. Did you lose your boot covers? The white sock things that went over your shoes? Were you wearing them?"

"Oh, I kept the pink covers on. Paige wanted to swap costumes. The pink one was a little bigger, and she wasn't comfy in the yellow one." She plays with her hair. "I didn't mind stuffing myself into the smaller one; I thought it showed off my curves pretty well." The relentless laughing continues, and she wiggles her butt in the air, twerking.

"Got it. Thanks." I refrain from rolling my eyes, not that she has the brain power right now to notice. "Can you stay somewhere else tonight? I think whoever killed Paige was actually trying to kill you. They thought you were in the pink costume, but you and Paige switched."

She stops and turns around to face me, no longer giggling. "What are you talking about? Nobody wants to kill me," she dismisses. Her happy drunk takes a nosedive into sad drunk. "Who would want to kill me? I've got no money, nothing good going right now, a kid to take care of." She uses her fingers to count as she lists.

"I'm sure that's not true. But seriously, can you stay somewhere else? Can you go back home tonight? Just until the police figure out what happened."

"I don't have anywhere to go right now…" Her head falls, wallowing. She's still not getting it.

"Alright, hang on. Maybe Nancy has an opening," I mutter, glancing up to see the last few remnants of Danni's happy drunk state melt as the severity of the situation settles in. I put the phone to my ear, listening to the ringing.

"Nest B&B, this is Nancy speaking," the sweet, motherly voice answers.

"Hey, Nancy, it's Maudy."

"Oh, hi there. Is everything okay, dear?" she asks.

"Yep, everything's fine. Do you have a room open tonight? A, uh," I look up at Danni as she takes another gulp from her cup. She's staring off into space in front of me. "A friend needs a place to stay."

"Sorry, hon, we're booked up all week. Nothing at the campground?"

"She's not much of a camper," I reply, thinking about Danni alone in the woods right now.

"Well, sorry, dear. Wish I could help you. Come for breakfast sometime soon."

I hang up the phone, rubbing my temples. Danni is in danger. She needs help.

"Danni, you can have my couch for the night."

She runs over to Eli, no longer sad, distracted by the bumping music. "I'm staying with her tonight." She points to me, throwing her arms around his shoulders. Eli and I lock eyes, just for a moment. She kisses him on the cheek, leaving a red stain. He rushes to rub it off with his jacket sleeve and tilts his head, clearly confused. I reciprocate the confusion, shrugging.

* * *

The sun and wind act as opposing forces, toasting and chilling my face as I sip my third cup of coffee on the back porch. Zipping my jacket a little tighter, I warm my gloved hands on my mug. It's probably in the low forties.

The latch on the fence makes a quiet, tinkling noise as a certain blonde police officer walks into the yard, receiving a hearty welcome from Mr. Martin Short. She carries a white paper bag with grease stains lacing the bottom, and the Java Jones's logo stamped on the side.

Kelly joins me on the patio and drops the bag, beginning to unload the goods. "I brought two for Danni if she wants 'em." She sits next to me and cranes her neck to peer through the glass door.

"She's still sleeping, at least she was when I last went in for a refill." I stand up. "Let me grab you a thermos for that; those cardboard cups won't cut it out here for long."

I poke my head inside to get her a thermos and check on Danni again. She's still asleep.

"Okay, run this through for me one more time." Kelly rubs her hands down her face, takes the hand-painted *World's Greatest Aunt* to-go mug, and pours her coffee into it. It's shaping up to be a long day, and it isn't even noon.

We both have our handy-dandy notebooks, hers a fancy red leather and mine teal with polka dots.

"Sure. But if I show you some stuff that *maybe* wasn't obtained through proper channels, do I get arrested or anything? Friends and family immunity deal?" I smile and bat my eyelashes.

"Ugh, Maudy. What did you do? You said you didn't take anything from Eli's place…" She ties her hair up in a messy bun. "On second thought, don't tell me. Just tell me what you found. The less I know, the better. I'm reminding myself again that Eli lets you into his house willingly," she jokes.

I pull out Paige's iPad, still tucked in my backpack, and unlock the password. She looks at me with disbelief.

"Where'd you get that?" she asks, sternly.

"Kevin gave it to me…" I admit. "I didn't take it from Eli's, I swear." I cross my heart. "Paige left it at the bar. He was afraid to turn it in. He thought it'd make Eli look guilty."

"It does," she confirms. "I'm going to need to take this from you. What's the password? We have her phone, but she didn't have a fingerprint or face unlock set up. I've had a zillion calls with Apple support to access her accounts, but we haven't gotten in yet."

"Well, I'll save you some time. It's her and Wesley's anniversary. Halloween, 2002." She jots that down, along with a few things I can't read from this angle.

I open Paige's photo app and show her the picture of them together before they went trick-or-treating. Paige is in the yellow costume, and Danni is in pink. The three boys are in their respective costumes; nobody else swapped throughout the night.

"When I saw Danni and the rest of the group downtown," I explain, "she was wearing the yellow costume. Paige was passing out candy on the front porch in pink."

Kelly nods, following so far.

"Paige was in pink when we got to the scene," she confirms.

"When I saw this picture, which they took earlier that afternoon—see?" I point to the timestamp in the photo. "They swapped costumes before the group left to take Charlie out. Here, Paige is in yellow, and Danni is in pink. They recreated a group costume from high school."

"Why, though? Why'd they switch?" Kelly scribbles like a mad-woman.

"We need to ask her again; she wasn't very coherent last night when I asked her. She told me that it was Paige's idea, that the yellow one didn't fit well or something."

"Got it… But not the boot covers?"

"I don't know. We need to ask her." I shrug.

"Interesting. So, we found yellow diamond boot covers in the dumpster, which Paige was wearing that night."

"Yes," I confirm. "Danni said she kept the pink boot covers on the entire night. Plus, you said there was no Danni DNA on the covers from the dumpster, right?"

"Correct, just Paige's. So, you're thinking," she continues, "the killer *meant* to go after Danni, who was the original Pink Power Ranger. They realized it was Paige after they already poisoned her, so they took Paige's yellow boot covers and threw them in the dumpster so we wouldn't find them and realize they swapped."

"That's what I'm thinking. The killer messed up. I mean, the group took pictures that night. You might've still realized the costume swap without Paige's wrong boot covers, but that would've made it super obvious with the colors not matching." I sip my coffee. "Whoever it was, they turned to defense mode and scrambled to cover up their mistake. They didn't account for a dog with a hyper-sensitive nose and an affinity for disgusting garbage."

We both eye Martin Short, butt up in the air with dirt flinging behind him. He's busy working on one of his many holes pocking the yard.

"That brings our list down to Wesley or Eli," she considers. "If Paige is the one who died, and Danni was the one who was supposed to die, that only leaves the men. The timeline and statements still have us narrowed to someone in that house that afternoon.

"Then it's Wesley. It has to be Wesley."

"Urgh." A throaty croak passes through my back door, interrupting us from beneath a heap of blankets on the couch.

"Oh, you're awake! Good morning." Kelly calls, knocking on the glass. The pile of blankets stirs.

We go inside, and I throw Danni a life preserver (breakfast sandwich).

"Rise and shine, cupcake. We have to talk." Kelly jostles the blankets.

"Wow, you guys are chipper this morning." She smooths out her hair, looking like death warmed over. Well, not even warmed over that much, just nuked in the microwave for a few seconds.

"It's almost noon, so not really morning." I pull a chair over from my kitchen table and sit down.

"It's noon? Crap. I have so much to do today." She sits up, scrambling for her things.

"We need to talk before you leave, Danni." Kelly straightens up, with a slight formality. "Some things have...developed in Paige's case."

"Do you remember our talk last night?" I ask softly.

"I don't remember much after the parade... I don't remember sleeping here, to be honest..." She pats the blankets, searching for her phone.

"We thought so." Kelly takes over. "The long and short of it is that we think you could've been the killer's intended victim, not Paige. You two swapping costumes caused them to go after the wrong person. They poisoned the Pink Ranger, thinking it was you."

I lean back in my chair, hiding behind my coffee mug.

"What?" Her stirring halts, and her head whips to Kelly. "They wanted to kill *me*?"

"We're not positive, but it's certainly possible," Kelly confirms.

"Marty here," I add, scruffing the dog's ears, "found Paige's yellow boot covers in a dumpster downtown. The killer took the boot covers off her body and threw them away later."

"We think," Kelly chimes in, "they wanted to hide the fact that they messed up. If we saw Paige's yellow covers when we responded, we might have realized it sooner."

I don't know if it's her hangover or shock that's causing her brain to misfire. She's slack-jawed, circling from Kelly to mine, and back again.

"Who would want to hurt *me*?" she asks. "Oh, my god. Charlie! Is he okay? Where is he?"

"He's fine," I reassure her. "He's staying with one of his friends from school."

"Thank god. Where's my phone? I can't believe this." She resumes her search.

"Danni, do you think you and Charlie could go back to your place in Hemlock Pond?" Kelly asks. "I don't want you or your nephew in Eli's house. It's not too far away, right? Fifteen, twenty minutes? You could still do all the public things. We'll have officers stationed at the events."

"I arranged to move this week." She sighs, pressing into her temples. After a deep breath, she digs around the folds of the blanket, trying to put her life back together. "I've been in a one-bedroom apartment, and Charlie has been sleeping on a cot in the living room. He needs his own bedroom for me to get custody. My cousins are moving our stuff over and giving the place a fresh coat of paint while we're here. I don't have a place until this Sunday…"

"You and Charlie can stay here, Danni. Until your new place is ready," I offer, a little begrudgingly.

"Thanks. That's really kind of you. You won't even know we're here."

I look around my small home and laugh. "That's for sure not true, but you're welcome, regardless." We all chuckle, trying to release the awkwardness before opening up the inevitable can of worms.

"Danni, did Eli or Wesley know you two swapped costumes? When exactly did that happen?" Kelly asks.

"Uh," she finally finds her phone and begins checking messages. "Okay, Charlie's okay." She leans back. "What? Oh, right. Eli and Wes." She pauses. "We swapped in the afternoon. We were hanging out in Eli's yard, and Paige kept picking at her costume. It wasn't fitting her well. We all went back inside after a while to refill drinks, make some dinner, that sort of thing. Paige and I went upstairs and helped Charlie with his homework for a while. We swapped our costumes up there before going trick-or-treating."

"So, Eli and Wesley knew you swapped?"

"I don't think they knew ahead of time; it's not like we planned it, but they could tell for sure after. I mean, our voices, heights, and stuff give it away. We all kept our masks on most of the night. Charlie kept asking us to."

"Hmm." Kelly scrawls furiously in her notebook. "Well, here's where we stand," she continues. "I'm still coming back to when and where Paige died. This doesn't change the fact that nobody came in or out of that house during the time window when she was poisoned. Now knowing you were the likely intended victim and the fact that Paige is dead, that leaves Wesley and Eli as possibilities. And technically, Charlie, but I'm not considering him right now."

"Oh, my god, I just remembered something," Danni exclaims. "We swapped cups, too! Paige bought us all color-matching tumblers to go with our costumes. When we came back downstairs, Paige and I swapped cups to stay color coordinated. The boys made drinks while we were upstairs with Charlie…"

"Well, there you go," Kelly replies. "What were you all drinking that night?"

"Some fruit punch thing," Danni replies. "It was sort of an homage to crappy jungle juice we used to make in high school. There were fruit slices, vodka, juice, and all kinds of stuff in there. It was really sweet."

"Sweet enough to cover up crushed-up pills?" Kelly asks cynically.

"I guess. It was strong." Danni's eyes dull, her thoughts elsewhere.

"So, why might Eli or Wesley want to kill you? I have thoughts myself, but am curious to know what you think," Kelly continues.

"Well," she stutters, stealing nervous glances at me.

I shrink further into my chair, my heart rate quickening. The very edge of a panic attack creeps into my mind. *It can't be Eli... He'd never do something like this.*

"This is awkward," Danni mumbles, taking a moment to collect herself. "Eli and I have dated on and off since tenth grade," she explains. "We haven't connected much in the last few years, though." She looks directly at me while saying this. "But we've always stayed in touch. When we were making our plans for this week earlier this year, sometime around April or May, he asked that I not stay with him."

"Did he say why?" Kelly prods. *Jeez, Kelly. Read the room. We all know why. Don't make her say it out loud.*

"No, not exactly... But I think he didn't want things to be weird between us. He had feelings for someone else." Her eyes slide to me.

Kelly looks at me and falters. "Oh, right. That whole thing."

"I said 'no' to him, by the way," I add, mostly for Danni's benefit.

Danni continues, "I think he thought it'd be weird if he were dating someone else and his ex-girlfriend stayed at his house for the week. For everyone involved."

Blood rushes to my cheeks, totally mortified, unsure what to say.

"This created a rift between you two? Recently?" Kelly asks, unbothered by the uneasiness seeping into the moment.

"Yeah, you could say that. I think we both sort of expected that eventually we'd end up together. At least I always had that in the back of my mind. Neither of us really dated other people seriously; we always came back." She shrugs, hanging her head low and closing her eyes.

"And when he asked you not to stay with him," Kelly nudges.

"It felt different," Danni admits. "It felt like he was saying we're over. We drifted apart for a while, and then he started reaching out again this summer. He apologized and invited me to come. It was perfect timing, actually. With the move and all, I didn't have to pay for a hotel."

"Where's the conflict here? Why would he want to hurt you?" Kelly urges her on, getting a little impatient.

"Guys, seriously? Eli didn't do this. He couldn't," I insist. My voice hitches.

Danni and Kelly look at me with doubt.

"When I got here a few days ago," Danni continues as if I didn't say anything. "We were starting to pick up where we left off, if you know what I mean." *Ugh, I wish I didn't.* "I saw him writing in his journal. He was writing something that upset me." She looks at me again. "I told him right then and there that I didn't want to be a second choice, rebound, or whatever he was doing. We got into a fight. He said I was a leech and wouldn't leave him alone. He said I was holding him back and he needed space. He said he needed to get rid of me."

"You don't think…" I gasp. "He meant that like metaphorically, right?" I ask.

"I—I thought so at the time. But maybe…" She doesn't finish the thought, unblinking.

A deep sadness overcomes Kelly's usually stoic face. "Goddammit, Eli."

"Let's not jump to conclusions, Kelly." My palms sweat as panic shocks through my body. There's no way he could've done this.

"Maudy, I hate this as much as you do. The two have been *fighting*. Like a lot. They've been dating on and off for years. Who else would want to hurt her? She's got no political motivations, no known enemies, just a pissed-off ex-boyfriend. He threatened her for Pete's sake!" She throws up her hands, equal parts disappointed and exasperated.

She gets up abruptly and shuffles out the back door, slamming it shut behind her.

"Kelly, wait!" I shout, chasing after her, rustling loudly through the fallen leaves. "He didn't do it! He couldn't have!" She heaves open my back gate, yanking it through the tall grass, and storms into Eli's yard.

"Go home, Maudy." She sticks an arm out, holding me behind her as she pounds on his back door.

"Are you crazy? You can't do this! You can't arrest him!" I cry, confused and angry. *He'd never do this. I just know it in my gut. He'd never hurt anyone...*

"I've got no other options. I have to." Frustrated tears well in the corner of her eyes before she turns and wipes them away.

Eli and Wesley approach the glass, tentatively sliding it open. He catches my crazed face as I shift my attention between him and Kelly.

"Elliot Nett, you have the right to remain sil—"

"Kelly, stop!" I plead, sobbing in desperation. "This is ridiculous!"

The very core of my being lurches. It feels like my soul is nauseous. Like my heart is ripping through my chest.

"To remain silent. Anything you say can and will be used against you in a court of law. You have the right to an attorney," she drones on.

Eli's face falls so slowly, shocked, that what's left of my heart sinks into my feet. He doesn't resist her before responding, holding my eye contact.

The look he gives me is one of knowing, of understanding. I wonder what *my* expression is saying that he's responding this way.

"No need for cuffs, Kelly. I'll come with you freely. Wes, make my bail, please. I'll be back soon, Maudy."

Kelly puts her cuffs back on her belt, a groan escaping her pursed lips. "Thanks. I really don't want to have to do this, Eli."

He walks out the door with Kelly following closely behind, as they march through my backyard and into her police car parked in my driveway.

Chapter Fifteen

The Stone's Throw Community Center, an open room on the library's second floor, is set up like a makeshift council chamber this afternoon. A long table at one end faces rows of public seating. This space hosts fitness classes, serves as our polling station, and is everything in between.

Danni slouches in the front row, a baseball cap pulled low over her face, arms tight to her body like a shield. She writes on papers spilling out of her bag, hard at work. The greasy breakfast sandwiches didn't help her much, and she's still battling the hangover with an occasional shudder between trips to the bathroom.

I sit at the head table beside my fellow Park Stewardship Committee members, each clutching an agenda. Today's topic: a new river clean-up initiative I want to start. Danni doesn't bother taking an interest and remains buried in paperwork. Her head stays down, pen fervently scrawling, attention elsewhere.

Kelly was clear—borderline militant, actually—that Danni is not to be left alone until the case is solved. So here she sits, in my work meeting. After that, she'll park her butt downstairs in the library for a couple of hours under the watchful eye of Matthew, our librarian.

Two other members of the public join this meeting. Colin, who holds a tape recorder, twitching with judgment, and Leonard, who nonchalantly opens his mail, slicing envelopes with an antique silver letter opener. A copy of the Birch River Current sits next to him, waiting to be read. The heinous photo of me stares back from the front page, jeering me on.

I try not to go down the rabbit hole speculating why Colin is recording this meeting; it's probably ammunition for Monday's debate, the last one before the election next week.

"Charlotte, I don't care if you think it looks messy. Mowing the grass on the riverbank is a bad idea. It creates runoff problems and puts more car pollution into the river. Remember how flooded it was last spring with those big thunderstorms? It'll be ten times worse with cut grass. By river 'clean-up' I meant picking up trash, not mowing down the entire riparian zone."

I try my best not to raise my voice, but my nerves are grated like Parmesan cheese after Eli's arrest this morning. Just showing up to this meeting was a Herculean effort, let alone playing nice.

Danni continues to frown, organizing dozens of papers. Craning a little to get a closer look, I notice the bold legal heading on one of them. Charlie's adoption papers. She's flushed, the reddish pink minimizing her hangover's green undertone.

"*Maude,*" Charlotte purrs, "the scruffy shrubs and unkempt grass along the river look awful! Those rental cabins could charge another fifty dollars per night by simply landscaping."

"May I make a suggestion?" Leonard raises his hand and stands up, facing the committee.

"Yes, the public may comment," I add, signaling Matthew, our designated secretary, to enter this into the meeting minutes.

"The matter of the riverbank shrubs is small potatoes compared to what this group needs to be discussing," Leonard states, setting aside his correspondence. "The entire park is a wasteland, and we should be discussing the *potential* for that property."

Over my dead body, stronzo.

"Thank you, Councilman Henley, for that comment, but I'll remind everyone that the state of Michigan owns the park. The land can't be developed." I shuffle papers in front of me and glance at Matthew, who nods back in subtle solidarity.

"Things can change, Ms. Lorso. Never say never," he responds before burying his nose in the newspaper.

We go back and forth about the grass for another ten minutes without reaching a resolution, and agree to pick up the topic again at a future meeting.

Fifteen minutes later, I'm crossing the bridge, heading into the park after dropping Danni off in the library.

"Hey, Zach," I grumble, sitting at my desk in the ranger station.

"Yikes, look what the cat dragged in."

This has been the absolute worst day. Please don't make it worse.

"How busy are you right now?" I ignore his comment, but the misery shows on my face.

"Not too bad." He backs off, sensing my mood. "We don't have any more classroom visits or field trips this week, and now that float-gate is over, I'm in good shape. Why? Do you need something? You look like you need something. The committee meeting was that bad, eh?" He takes a sip from his water bottle, eyes peeping out from under his beanie. "There's never a dull moment working with you, Maudy. What's up? Spill it."

"The meeting was annoying, but that's not the problem," I clarify. "Eli was arrested. For Paige's murder. Kelly's keeping it quiet, but it's bound to get out soon."

"No *way*," he thunders. "Eli? Seriously?"

"Believe it." I deflate, resting my head on the desk. "What are you two up to? I need to know everything."

"I *swear*, it has nothing to do with this. And I *really* don't want to ruin the surprise. Cross my heart." He mimes the gesture.

I pause, eyes narrow.

"Seriously, Maudy. I promise. Swear on my Grandma's grave."

"*Fine*," I concede. "But if you won't tell me, tell Kelly. I don't want us hiding anything from her."

He agrees, and we continue with our workday.

"Will I see you at the football game tonight?" I ask as we shut down our computers hours later, getting ready to leave. "Want to come with me during the halftime show to talk about the hayride? They're making an announcement about it. Maybe we can ask for a donation or something." *Anything to give us a little buffer before we go out on our own in January.*

"Great idea, I'll be there. I'll print up a QR code poster with our donation page."

Now, just a couple of hours before gametime, Main Street is again lined with popped trunks and open tailgates. The wind whips through the street like a bowling ball down an alley, perfect for whiskey and warm apple cider. Cornhole boards set on the sidewalk and camp chairs litter the street.

Spots of purple and white intermix with orange and black, a patchwork quilt of hometown pride. People are in high spirits despite red noses and watery eyes from the dropping temperature. Gloves and hats emerge from coat pockets, along with homemade fleece-tied blankets adorned with footballs and school colors.

A pleasant chime quietly alerts as I walk into the library. Matthew is behind the circulation desk, typing away.

"Ms. Lorso. I take it you're here to pick up your ward?" He grins, gesturing to a back room where a bank of computers sits alongside town archives and historical records. The same room where I found the information that unlocked Michael Price's murder this spring.

"Right as always, Matthew. Was she a pain?"

"Nope, not at all. She just sat there. Took a few phone calls but was quiet and respectful of other patrons."

"Good. Anything new you'd think I'd like?"

"Hmm…not you, but I did get Will Shortz's book that Eli will enjoy. Let him know, will you? I put it on hold and haven't seen him here lately."

"Um, I'm not sure he'll be grabbing that anytime soon," I confess. "He's got a lot going on right now. Probably best to take it off hold."

Subtle surprise spreads across his face, like he sipped a bitter drink. "Noted," he replies.

I leave Matthew without elaborating and walk back to Danni. She's talking on the phone in a hushed whisper. Hanging up, she starts packing her worn satchel the second she spots me.

"Hey, ready to roll?" I ask.

She's revived since I last saw her. The hangover looks largely gone, with some color back in her face. A cup of coffee from Java Jones is in front of her.

"Did you get that coffee?" I ask, accusation in my tone. "Kelly was clear. You can't be out alone. Someone's trying to hurt you, Danni."

"I know, but I was *dying*. You saw me this morning. I almost puked in your meeting. I just popped out for a second; it was no big deal. Eli is in jail," she dismisses. "He can't get to me from jail."

I sigh, not dignifying the behavior with a response, and we walk home together. She's texting and frowning at her phone the entire way.

How'd I get to be this woman's babysitter? She's Eli's ex-girlfriend. She wanted me to stay away from him. Now, here she is sleeping on my couch.

"Remind me where I need to be tonight?" I ask.

"Just be at the football game. I'll call you down during the halftime stuff. If you can, wear your ranger outfit." I scoff at the term outfit. "Uniform? Whatever."

Since divulging her and Eli's history this morning, the tension between us has intensified.

"Okay. Should I be anywhere in particular?"

"No, sit wherever you want. The stands aren't big; come down when I call you." She's short with me.

"Got it," I reply. "Danni, I need you to know nothing is happening between Eli and me. Seriously. I turned him down months ago, and he's been weird ever since. That's it, I promise." *Am I saying this to convince her, or me?*

"You're not the problem, Maudy." She tilts her head and looks at me sympathetically before changing the subject. "Speaking of, I talked to Wes. Eli isn't going to make the game tonight, given well…you know."

"I thought he was going to bail him out?"

"Not yet, at least. Wes said they'll *probably* let him post bail soon, but I doubt Eli will want to be in public even if he can. I'm relieved, honestly," she confesses. "He hasn't tried to get in touch with me yet, which I think means he's still in jail."

"You're actually worried about him? You really think he did it? I just can't picture it."

"Of course, he did it. I'm terrified that getting arrested will just make him even madder. I feel like I should pretend nothing happened and keep talking to him, so he thinks I'm on his side." Her voice shrinks. "He can't try again. He just can't. Charlie wouldn't have anyone left."

"This is all so surreal." I shift awkwardly, unsure of what to say. "This is so unlike the Eli I know." Disbelief rings in my voice, unable to picture him so conniving and hostile. *Let's not think about how upset I was when he was arrested...*

"Well, the police have him now. At least for a little bit."

"Just keep your eyes out, will you?" I plead. "Even with him put away. It could still be Wesley, or some other option we haven't thought of yet."

"It was Eli. He's the only option that makes sense."

Chapter Sixteen

The energy is thick; the buzzing cheers of these two tiny towns rival any professional football game. I bet almost every single Stone's Thrower is here.

Our school district draws students from all corners of the rural county, some riding the bus for over forty-five minutes each way. The entire student body barely tops three hundred. Hemlock Pond is about the same.

From the sidelines of the patchy field, I watch as vibrant pride erupts from the stands, everyone bundled in warm jackets, noses red under the stadium lights. Cheerleaders toss and tumble as mittens clap, hyping them up even more. It's hectic, but in the best way. It's unpolished. It's alive.

I think back to my own time in high school. It felt like the opposite. I was in a Detroit suburb with halls packed with over two thousand kids. Bells rang like cattle calls, herding us from one room to the next. My graduating class could swallow the entire Stone's Throw School District whole.

Maybe I would've been more at home here. Who knows. Maybe things with Eli could be different.

Maybe I should talk to Jeremy.

I sit smack dab in the middle of the stands with Peyton, Anna, Nellie, and her two girls. As we crunch on buttery popcorn, I clock Wesley walking over to Danni and Charlie on the sidelines. Danni flits around with Charlie in tow, making sure everything runs smoothly. She, on behalf of the Alumni Association, is coordinating a halftime tribute to Paige, handling event announcements, and presenting the final school rivalry scores from over the course of the week. The football match is the final game left to tally, besides some other silly contest at halftime.

Kelly and I text the entire game. She and plainclothes state troopers are stationed around the field, keeping eyes on Danni and everyone in the stands. They're checking bags at the gate to make sure nobody gets hurt.

After a few minutes of conversation, pain evident on Danni's face, I watch Wesley climb into the metal bleachers and sit across the aisle from me.

"So, how was your day? Better than mine, I hope?" Wesley asks me sarcastically, in between sips of hot chocolate. He's not engaging in the game, eyes on his phone.

Wesley could have done it. It just couldn't have been Eli.

"It's been a day," he continues unprompted. "I helped Eli make bail right before coming here. He had to put his house up for collateral." He shakes his head. "I dropped him off at home. He said he just wanted to be alone for the rest of the night."

"Yeah, well, I don't blame him," I reply. "You think your day was bad, his was worse."

"I can't believe Kelly arrested him," Peyton interjects from beside me, gloved hands under her chin. "It's just so bizarre."

"I know, poor guy. He'd definitely be the, uh, spectacle for the night if he came," Anna replies. "Probably smart to stay home."

"I bet Kevin is having a conniption," Nellie groans. "We should go check on him later. Lydia," she turns to her daughter, "want to draw Mr. Nett a picture?"

"Sure!" Lydia squeals, flipping to a new page in her coloring book.

"This one has a big flower. He'll like that."

Wesley leans over to me, across the aisle. "Eli wasn't in good shape when I picked him up today. He said he had a bad headache."

I lean back across the narrow aisle, under the guise of trying to hear him better, and glance down at his phone. He's looking through his text thread with Paige. The most recent message from her reads: *I can't, Wes. The money is gone, but that's not it. My work isn't done. I just can't drop out of the race. Not now. I'm sorry.*

His response? *You always knew how to gut me like a fish, Paige. I should've known by now.*

Whoa, whoa, whoa. This isn't that lovey-dovey, decades-in-the-making reunion he made it out to be.

"Ah, man," I reply, zooming out to reality and leaning back to hide the shock on my face.

My words get lost in an uproar of boos as Hemlock Pond scores another touchdown. Chants of *"Pond Scum!"* loop through the stands. The extra point brings the score up to zero to fourteen. I know nothing about football, but even I can tell their team is way better than ours.

So Paige and Wesley were also fighting? He wanted her to do something, and she refused. To drop out of her Senate race? Be together now that she's divorced? And what about money? Maybe she had the money she gave Danni set aside for something with Wesley?

"So, how's Danni been? Driving you nuts yet?" He puts his phone down and takes a sip of his hot chocolate. "She can be a handful."

"Your house has been busier than The Nest this week," Nellie adds.

"I know, right? I should be charging by the night. And to answer your question, Wesley, she's been fine. Charlie stayed with some friends last night, and I think he will again tonight. It's not a big deal. Happy to have her."

The less he knows, the better.

A buzzer goes off, marking the end of the first half, and the fans settle down. Danni, Charlotte, and a small group of other Stone's Throw and Hemlock Pond leadership walk out to the center of the field, where a wooden podium sits. Both towns' marching bands flank either side, still as statues, waiting for their drum major's signal.

"Vote Colin! Maudy stinks!" A gaggle of lanky teenagers, holding posters with Colin's smarmy face, rush the field, chanting in unison. "Vote Colin! Maudy stinks! Vote Colin! Maudy stinks!"

Seriously? I feel my face go beet red, skin crawling with embarrassment.

"Boys!" The school principal booms into the podium's microphone. "That is enough. This is not the time or place."

I shrink in my seat, wishing I could just disappear.

Holding Charlie's hand, Danni stands between the principal and Leonard, our Town Council President. The principal hands her the microphone. The waxy, sickened skin tone creeps back up her neck. She looks like she might puke. *I guess that hangover must not have entirely left her.*

"Thank you all for being here today to celebrate the lovely Homecoming traditions of these great schools. While our rivalry is strong, our friendship is stronger."

Hundreds of people fall silent, listening to Danni. Kelly paces in front of the stands, studying everyone and scanning the crowd. We nod to one another. *So far, so good.*

"We're going to kick off half-time with the last competition of the week!"

The brawny players haul a massive, fifty-yard rope onto the field. Cheerleaders from both schools take each side and begin a tug-of-war to end all tug-of-wars. With mesh pennies thrown over their uniforms, spray-painted with funny names for each person, the field looks more like a pro wrestling match than anything else.

Stone's Throw has a coordinated plan, chanting calls, and heaving the rope in an organized pattern. After maybe thirty seconds, the Hemlock Pond team inches right over the center line, marking the end of the match. The orange-and-black-clad mob roars as the football players hoist the squad up on their shoulders, celebrating the win.

"Hey, remember that one movie Eli—" I turn, forgetting he isn't here.

Peyton sees me frown. "What?" She's clapping to the music while the marching bands take the field. Danni is about to resume her announcements.

"Oh, nothing. I just forgot Eli wasn't here. The cheerleaders reminded me of a dumb horror movie we watched together," I reply. Turning to the larger group, "Did you guys still want to play Euchre tonight? I know it's Friday, but the bar will be slammed."

Nellie, Anna, and Peyton all scrunch their faces in unison. "This might be enough for me tonight," Anna says, tilting her head. "I don't know, what do you think?"

"Let's play it by ear," Nellie reasons. "We should check on Kevin. Who knows, maybe we'll be jazzed and want to keep the party going. Or we could go to someone's house and play after we see how he's doing." She sips her cherry slushy and turns back around, giving Danni her full attention.

"And on that note," Danni's voice rings through the stands. "I'd like to welcome Maudy Lorso, Head Park Ranger, and Zach Duffy, Naturalist and Education Instructor of Stone's Throw State Park, to the field! They will talk about one of our key events tomorrow, the hayride!"

I pop up, lock eyes with Zach, sitting a couple of rows over, and walk down the steps and across the muddy grass.

She shakes our hands, steps aside, and hands me the microphone. Looking out into the stands, hundreds of expectant faces regard me. I see Leonard and Charlotte, scowling, Charlotte with a bun so tight her hair is bound to fall out. I see my friends with big smiles and thumbs up. I see Wesley, absent-mindedly staring off into the distance, and

Kelly, talking into a walkie-talkie while scanning the bleachers.

"Thank you, everyone," I begin, pulling the microphone away from my mouth, wincing at the feedback screech. "Ope, sorry about that. Anyway, we're thrilled to partner with the Alumni Association this year and are excited to host a revival of the State Park hayride! Those of you from here and of a certain age," I grin, "will remember the old tradition. We're happy to bring it back this year, hopefully for many years to come.

"Tomorrow's event will be a ton of fun. The scare level will be appropriate for ages ten and over. No actors will be involved, so nobody can grab you, just mechanical props and special effects.

"Stop by or call our ranger station to register if you haven't already. We anticipate a full night. There's no fee to enter; however, we'd appreciate a donation to the park to help support future events like this. Zach here," I clap him on the back, "has this code set up to accept donations." Zach holds up a posterboard with a large QR code. "Even five dollars will go a long way towards education opportunities for little Stone's Throwers and Hemlock Pondlings, making sure everyone in our area grows up loving and appreciating our natural world. Thank you."

I hand the mic back to Danni as Zach and I clap and pump our fists to the sea of sunny faces as we jog off the field.

"Look at you go, *Maude*. It's nice to know you're not above begging." Charlotte sneers as I walk by.

With responsibilities for the night over and Danni safely tucked under the watchful eye of Kelly and her officers, I buy Zach a thank-you hot chocolate from the concession stand, appreciating all his great work this week, and return to my seat.

"Nice job." Peyton squeezes my shoulders as I sit back down next to her. "Put us all down for an open timeslot together." The rest echo their support and excitement. "There may or may not be a few-hundred-dollar donation in your Venmo." She smiles, and I tackle her in a hug with the fervor of a Hemlock Pond linebacker.

"Are you guys invested in this game?" Nellie asks. "What do you say we beat the rush and head to Pop's now? Maybe we check in on Kevin and get a hand or two in before it gets crazy." She looks down at antsy little Lydia, squirming in her seat. With none of us football fans, the group unanimously agrees and meanders over to Pop's, leaving Wesley to himself.

"Kelly, I'm taking off," I call, grabbing her attention from the outer edges of the stands where she's posted. "We're headed to Pop's if you need anything."

"Hang on, one sec," she yells back, jogging over. I signal to the rest of the group to go on ahead.

"Eli made bail," she says. "He just got out, right before the game. I'm keeping my eyes on Danni. I'll drop her off at your house tonight. Is she still okay to sleep on your couch again?"

Danni huddles on the other side of the field, under a small event tent that looks like the logistics headquarters. People with clipboards zip in and out, big boxes of equipment stack high.

Charlotte and Leonard sit under it, too. Leonard is right behind Danni, who's keeping her head down, focused on a clipboard in her lap.

"Of course she can. And yeah, Wesley told us. Can you come by again in the morning? I feel like we need to talk more about all this and figure out what to do next. She can't stay on my couch forever. And I really don't think Eli did this."

"I'll stop by early."

We agree, and I catch up with my friends, piling into Peyton's old pickup truck to drive back into town.

I huff under my breath as we dip between jam-packed tables. It's standing room only already. We make our way up to the bar as Kevin rushes around, trying to fill orders.

For the first Friday in literally years, other people occupy our booth. The usual *Reserved for the Lake Michigan (card) sharks* sign is nowhere in sight.

"Hi, ladies, hang on a minute." Kevin runs credit cards and pours beers, doing his best to thin the line. Peyton ducks behind the bar to help him out.

"Hi, Kev," Peyton says. "We wanted to come by and see how you're doing. Looks like you could use a hand." With her help, he clears the line in a few minutes, and they come back to us.

"Eli is, well...you know." Kevin can't bring himself to say it. "The kids we have as food runners are all at the game, so it's just me tonight. I closed the kitchen; I can't handle all that right now."

He swallows hard, the corners of his lips turning into a trembling smile. He's barely keeping it together, but he's trying. "Can I get you gals something to drink? Oh, shoot! I forgot to reserve your table!" Dismay colors his face as he looks at the booth behind us.

We look around at one another, deciding what to do.

"That's okay, Kevin. Don't worry about it." Nellie waves. "Lydia made something for you." The girl climbs onto a barstool, kneeling to reach. She hands him the coloring page.

"Well, Lydia, this is just beautiful. Thank you very much." A tear runs down his weathered cheek. He wipes it fast, rubbing his eyes. "Sorry, girls. It's been a day." He takes the drawing and sticks it behind the bar, on display.

"I'll stay and bartend, Kev." Peyton offers, serving someone a pint. "I'm happy to. It's been a few years since I've been back here. I should shake off the rust, anyway."

"If you don't mind, Peyton, that'd be great. Take whatever tips we get tonight. This old man is starting to slow down. Will one of you check on my boy for me? He's not answering my calls. I'm worried."

He wrings a rag in his hands.

We agree, say goodbye, and all go our separate ways. Unlocking my front door, hinges creaking, three orangish brown eyes, and one scarred, foggy one, greet me. Gumbo and Marty.

"Hey, boys." I bend down to pick up the cat, instantly purring in my arms, and let Marty outside. "How was your evening?" Gumbo nuzzles into my chin, giving me loving headbutts and chattering away, filling me in on their adventures. Looking out into the backyard, I see Eli's lights are off already. Maybe he's asleep. Wesley did say that he had a headache.

"What do you think, Gumbo? Is Eli already asleep? Want to say hi? Kevin asked that we check on him. Some of your cuddles might do him good."

I tuck the little cat into my jacket and walk through our back gate, lightly knocking on his patio door. No response. We walk around to the front and ring the bell. Still no response.

After jangling the key for an eternity, we stumble into the dark house.

"Eli, it's Maudy," I call. "You up? Your dad asked us to see if you need anything." Pausing in the living room, Gumbo squirms out of my coat and onto the floor. He dashes upstairs without hesitation. "I brought Gumbo with me. He misses you," I shout again.

I creep over to the staircase and listen for anyone stirring upstairs. "Eli? You okay?" I slowly walk up the wooden stairs, debating just how intrusive is too intrusive. The door to his room cracks open just enough for the cat to skirt through. I hear him meow from inside.

"Knock, knock. It's Maudy. Just checking on you," I say again, trying not to startle him. The cat howls.

Opening the door, I see Gumbo's silhouette perched on Eli's back. He's under the quilted crossword covers, lying on his stomach. *How can he sleep with Gumbo yelling like that?*

"Eli?" I ask, louder. "You okay?" I gently rock his shoulder. His head looks away as Gumbo paws at his hand. He doesn't respond.

"Eli," I cry, shaking him more violently. "Eli! Wake up!"

He's not waking up. *Oh, my god. No. Eli, wake up!*

My heart drops into my feet as I dial 911. "This is a medical emergency," I wail, in between sobs. My...my friend is unconscious," I stammer. *"Friend" feels wrong.* I give the operator his address and say the front door is unlocked.

I take his pulse, which is there, but weak. "Stay with me! Please!" He's breathing, but barely. I keep my hand on his neck, monitoring his heart rate. *This is not a freakin' headache.*

A pill bottle is on his nightstand. I saw it a few days ago while snooping through his medicine cabinet.

"Eli, what the hell did you take?" I ask him. I feel faint, scrambling to grab the bottle. "Don't do this, Eli," I whisper. "C'mon, Coach. Stay with me."

I turn on his lamp and look at the label. The bottle is mostly full. I don't recognize the drug name, but the prescription instructions say to 'take two as needed for migraine.'

I place my fingers back on his neck. His pulse slows. "Hang on, Eli. Help is on the way. Stay with me. Please, stay with me. I can't lose you."

Why couldn't this be me? I can't stand watching him like this... What would I do without him? I—I just can't...

I press down and pop open the bottle's safety cap, pouring the pills onto his side table. They scatter on the nightstand as I play keep-away with the cat, trying to get a closer look.

I swipe them into my hand, and my own heart stops.

There are two kinds of pills in the bottle, although they're *almost* identical. Both are white tabs. One is slightly more yellow and oblong than the other. They're just like my sleeping pills—the same kind of sleeping pills that killed Paige.

He poisoned Eli...

"It was Wesley." I descend into shock, right as emergency responders inundate the room. "It has to be Wesley."

Chapter Seventeen

"We have to stick with the plan," Kelly exclaims, curling up on my couch with a cup of hot cider and Gumbo on her lap.

It's late. Or I guess early, now.

"I'm out of options," she stammers. "I'm in hot water with Sheriff Landry. I don't like this any more than you do, Maudy, but we have no other choice."

"Eli almost *died*." I insist.

"I'm not giving the state troopers the satisfaction of catching the guy. Sheriff Landry will take my badge if we get scooped. He's furious that I arrested the wrong guy."

I bite my tongue as the acidity of an *I told you so* hits the back of my throat.

"The plan will work," Kelly says, for the fifth time. "If I bring Wesley in, the Sheriff might lighten up a little bit."

"When was the last time we heard from the hospital?" I frantically pat the couch cushions for my phone. I won't be able to sleep until I know he's okay.

Eli almost died. I found him literally on his deathbed. I can't imagine...if he were to...I wouldn't know what to do with myself. Especially if we left things on these terms. I really need to talk to Jeremy. This isn't fair to him.

"Now we know for sure!" I huff. "We have to do something right now." I slam my hand on the coffee table. "Wesley is who-knows-where, traipsing around town, while we're sitting here, knowing he killed Paige! And he tried to kill Eli, and might come after Danni, too! There's no other option. Danni was with us all day. It has to be Wesley."

The three of us have been sitting (or pacing) in my living room for the last few hours. I check my phone to make sure it's working.

"Maudy, I know this is hard. I know you're upset. But we need to think about evidence here. If we present the perfect opportunity for Wesley to confess, and get it on camera... Danni, what do you think?" Kelly turns to her. "This concerns your safety. What do you want to do? Do you want me to grovel to the state troopers to arrest Wesley right now, or stick with the sting operation at the class reunion? Where we can get some *real* evidence." She glares, clear on her stance.

Danni hesitantly sips her cup of cider, pausing to think it through or for dramatic effect. I'm not sure which.

"I think we should move forward with the plan," Danni says, definitively. "Kelly's right. We can't mess up."

"You guys are killing me! I can't believe I'm the voice of reason here. Am I the only one who realizes that he almost died?" I toss up my hands, frustrated.

It's because he means more to me than he does to them.

"Look," Danni states. "Charlie is safe at a friend's house. Kelly, you guys are checking in on him, right?"

"Yep, we have a car going by every few hours," Kelly confirms. "Maudy, what hard evidence do we have that Wes did it? Something that'll make a murder charge stick. Something I can take to the state force and tell them *for sure* he did it. He'll be out again in no time with the circumstantial crap we have right now. If we wait until tomorrow, rile him up, allow him to *fix his mistake* and catch it on camera..." Kelly shrugs. "That'll be much more convincing in a court of law. Just saying."

"Process of elimination is circumstantial?" I snort, knowing full well it is, but digging my heels in more. "If we wait until the event, and corner him into confessing publicly, I get that that'll be harder to argue against. But if we wait…" *Eli could get hurt again.*

"Innocent until proven guilty, Maudy." Kelly winces, giving me a sympathetic look.

"Let's review what we know," I retort, not ready to give up. "Wesley was in the house when Paige and Eli were poisoned." I nod to Danni, who pales. "He was the only one who saw Eli after he got out on bail. That's opportunity."

"Yeah, we know," Kelly replies with a sigh, indulging me.

"Wesley was in love with Paige. It sounded like they had plans to run off together now that her divorce was final and her Senate term was up. She was going to drop out of the race, maybe because of the slander accusations that Leonard was throwing her way. I don't know. She saved some money or got it in the divorce, or whatever," I continue. "But then she lent it all to Danni and broke things off with Wesley."

Danni hangs her head, arms hugging her middle.

"What did you need that loan for?" Kelly asks.

"Stuff for my brother," she admits, head still low.

"Like funeral arrangements and Charlie's adoption?" Kelly prods.

"Something like that. I didn't realize it would cause a thing between those two, though. I don't know what she was planning on using it for."

"Well, through the convoluted grapevine," I go on, "Wesley could see Danni as the reason he and Paige can't be together, since losing that money might be what prevented Paige from dropping out of the race and running away with him. Couple that with him accidentally murdering the love of his life… That's motive."

"Like I said," Kelly interjects. "Circumstantial."

"Why did he go after Eli, though?" I ask, more to myself, ignoring Kelly's rebuttal.

"Maybe he was onto him?" Kelly offers. "Or maybe it was an accident. He could've stashed Paige's sleeping pills in Eli's prescription bottle. The troopers checked pill bottles for anything fishy when they searched the place, but they looked so similar to his migraine medicine that it's possible they missed it. We never found Paige's sleeping pills."

"Or maybe he wanted to hurt me," Danni squeaks quietly, eyes still down. "It'd be suspicious if he went after me again directly. But going after Eli...I end up suffering the same way he is."

"Jesus," Kelly shudders. "Alright, let's focus on what we're going to do about it."

"You're sure he'll show?" I ask Danni. I hate waiting, knowing he's out there. Knowing he hurt Eli. I want to kill the man myself.

"I'm sure he will be there. Between the optics of *not* showing up and the opportunity we're giving him, he will. We're putting my head on a silver platter; it'll be perfect. It's what he wanted in the first place, right?"

"Fine, you guys win." I throw up my hands. "But I'm not happy about it."

"I know you're freaking out about Eli," Kelly says. "He'll be okay. They're just monitoring him for a little longer. He didn't have nearly as much of the drug in his system as Paige did, and his bloodwork wasn't all out of whack like hers. He'll be okay, I promise."

* * *

Smoothing out my favorite forest-green slip dress, I strap on a pair of heels I've had since prom and toss an old crewneck sweatshirt into my backpack.

My fuzzy audience sits patiently as I get ready. Marty gives me side-eye as if to say, *You sure about those heels?* Kelly and Danni wait downstairs. It's time to get to the marina for the class reunion.

Gumbo leaps up, releasing a surprised screech like a steam whistle, and flies down the stairs. My phone buzzes from his spot on the bed.

"Hello?" Wedging the phone in the crook of my neck, I pack up my backpack and pin my hair out of my face. A chocolatey curl boings into my eyes.

"Hey, how are you?" Jeremy asks.

Well, Gumbo threw up on my rug this morning, I'm about to help Kelly set up a sting operation to catch a killer, and I might have feelings for someone else... You know, the usual.

"Oh, fine. A little nervous…" I can't tell him what's happening. Not now. Kelly made me swear to keep this between the three of us. If word gets out, the whole plan is busted. He'd kill me, knowing I'm sticking my neck out on the line for Eli (of all people) like this. We're already on thin ice; no need to go stomping on it.

"You're going to the park tonight, right? Working the hayride thing?"

"Yep. I'll be at the park all night." My fancy outfit says otherwise. "Are you coming into town? I'll be super busy." I fidget, hating to lie like this. "Maybe we can hang out another night."

"I got an invite for the class reunion party as a plus one. A client of mine is going and wants to talk business. I'll stop by the park and see you. I hate that things are still weird between us. I want to fix it."

"Oh, great." I hope the insincerity isn't detectable. "Well, now that I think of it, I'm making a quick announcement at the clubhouse about the hayride first, and then I'll be in the park for the rest of the night. I'll find you at the marina before I leave." We say goodbye, as the knot in my stomach tightens.

Looking over the loft railing, another curl breaks out from its pin. Kelly and Danni eye me suspiciously. "Jeremy's going to the reunion." I wince.

"We have bigger fish to fry tonight," Kelly reminds me. "He's a big boy. He can handle himself."

"He'll get in the way," I lament. *Maybe I'm just avoiding him.*

"It'll be fine. Blame me for blowing him off if you have to." Kelly smiles weakly, waving me downstairs. "Time to roll."

The three of us head out the door. I put a Halloween bandana on Marty for the special occasion and tell him to wait here for Zach. "I'll see you in a bit, Martin! Zach will come get you, and I'll meet you in the park. I swear. You won't be here long." I give him a bone as a bribe, which he takes without complaint.

Before leaving, I stroke his head, his big brown eyes filled with love. I can't help but think about how he saved my life when Lucas, the last deranged killer I got entangled with, threw me off a sand dune. I wish I could bring him, but there are no dogs at the fancy cocktail party; it'd be suspicious. Zach will have him at the hayride, and I'll meet up with him before anything gets out of hand.

Walking to the party, I'm intoxicated by the town's energy. Now that the children's celebrations and Homecoming events are over, it's the adults' turn to party. Charlotte and her Chamber of Commerce members added even more festive decorations, blocking off Main Street to put up a hay bale maze, outdoor shopping, and a massive blow-up projector screen for Halloween movies.

The main event of the night will be the park hayride, coupled with the class reunion for the 2000-2010 graduating classes at the marina. The different event options create a funny sight. People in black-tie attire strut down the street towards the beautifully renovated space, right next to a family of bloody werewolves devouring spools of cotton candy.

Danni sighs. *With anticipation, maybe? Relief that things are finally in motion?* I'm not sure. She's been buzzing all day, making frantic phone calls and scribbling on scraps of paper, trying to ensure all details are in place.

The clubhouse looks stunning. I don't know if it was Danni, Charlotte, or someone else, but cobwebs and enormous spiders drip down the brick house, giving it a spooky, but elegant makeover. Strange gourds and bright orange jack-o'-lanterns cover the front steps.

The inside is just as gorgeous, drenched in black crystal garland and silver skulls. If Gatsby were to host a Halloween party, this is it. The house isn't as grand as Gatsby's mansion, but anything grander would be out of place here.

Photos of old gangsters and the house in previous lifetimes hang on the walls, showcasing more of Al Capone's gang for Halloween. *Is macabre chic a design aesthetic?*

"Alright, let's get to work." Kelly doles out instructions, which I follow to a tee. With about an hour before the party begins, we plant microphones and cameras all over the building, setting up a makeshift headquarters upstairs in one of the empty rooms.

Charlotte "approved" all of this added security. And by "approved," I mean Kelly ordered her to stay out of the way. I think the bit where she's not in charge of this case hasn't quite reached Charlotte yet.

Kelly winds through the house with skilled precision, hooking up small microphones in the floral centerpieces and hiding cameras in Halloween decorations. Out back, Danni hangs off the side of the hayride tractor, wiring it up as well.

Peyton arrives early and posts up in the kitchen, chef's coat already on and sleeves rolled. She's juggling both dinner and dessert menus now. Eli prepared a lot of the food and left her clear instructions, but the empty space beside her doesn't go unnoticed.

I try not to dwell on it, but I do. How could I not? *I hope he's okay. I'd give anything to make sure he's okay... Guess we'll find out soon enough. Hopefully, he shows.*

The house fills fast; it's the who's who of Stone's Throw millennials. My friends drift in not long after Colin, as well as dozens of others I don't know, all returning home for the reunion. I only recognize maybe a quarter of the guests in attendance.

Town leadership circulates the space, all polished and smiling, greeting guests as they arrive. Charlotte, Leonard, and others make their rounds with self-absorbed pride in their step, *and a stick shoved up somewhere else*, talking about the renovation like they laid the floorboards themselves.

I do my best to fly under the radar. Since most of the room doesn't live here, they don't know me or care about our local politics. Occasionally, however, someone throws a worried glance my way, or I pick up on a whisper swirling the room.

"Wow, she actually came tonight? That ad was rough…"

"Don't get in her way; her best friend was just poisoned."

A volunteer checks names off the list as Charlotte flutters, welcoming everyone. Beautifully eerie music streams from a string quartet in the corner, equal parts classy and festive.

Silent auction items line the ballroom. There are some impressive options, including a sunset sailing cruise on Lake Michigan, guided hikes and foraging excursions from us, a cookie-decorating class from Peyton, and all kinds of other things. I bid on a basket of dog goodies donated by our veterinary clinic. Marty deserves all the treats.

One by one, everyone arrives, dressed to the nines. Nellie adds an exquisitely crafted masquerade mask to her ensemble, getting into the Halloween spirit.

"Hey," Nellie and Emma walk towards me, swooning over one another. *They're so in love…so happy.*

"Hey, you two. You both look great." I give them each a hug. Emma squeezes a little too tight, a sinking smile on her face. "What's wrong?" I ask, pulling her out at arm's length.

"Emma," Nellie warns, her mouth a thin line.

"C'mon, what is it?" I press.

"It's nothing," Nellie insists, but I don't buy it. "Okay, fine. New polling numbers are posted." She reluctantly holds out her phone.

I'm tanking. Comments on the post are all about how Eli, my best friend, was just arrested for murder. *Ugh. Great. Just what this night needs.*

Eli, as sick as he is, walks through the door. He's wearing a costume tuxedo, like something the Phantom of the Opera or Dracula would wear. His red, shiny vest and matching fake blood drips on the corners of his mouth. Despite all he went through the last few days, he still manages to dress up.

The proverbial record scratches as he walks into the room. All eyes are on him. He raises a hand, acknowledging the attention, which is welcomed by meager cheers and intense apprehension.

I can't believe he came after what happened. He looks so cheesy. So adorable. So sweet...

Those thoughts end there as Danni walks over and wraps her arms around his neck, pulling him in for a *long* hug. "You came!" she squeals.

"Of course I did." He staggers back at the force of her hug, and my stomach flops.

I thought they were fighting? She said he broke things off with her and then blew up... This doesn't look very broken up to me. I'm glad he's okay, though. He's standing upright at least.

Wesley, our guest of honor, arrives as planned. He's come alone, wearing an impeccably tailored dark gray suit and a simple black tie. Kelly watches as he integrates into the party, taking a drink from the bar.

He joins Danni and Eli, clapping them both on the shoulder as he goes to hug Eli. I see the muscles in Eli's back tighten, slightly recoiling from the contact. Danni also obliges him with a hug, but quickly takes a step back, plastering a smile on her face to keep up appearances. She and I make brief eye contact, a look of concern on her face.

Wesley doesn't seem to be the wiser and carries on the conversation, grabbing appetizers off a nearby tray.

"Hello, Maudy." He approaches me after a few minutes of pleasantries (at least from his perspective). "Great party."

"Yes, it is," I appease, unsure what else to say. My fight-or-flight response teeters, debating which way to go. Right now, I just try to smile and keep him happy.

"Might want to steer clear of the dessert table, though." He takes a sip of his wine. "I got a bit of frosting on my shirt, and a bee stung me not long after." He shakes his head, pointing out a stain on his cream Oxford. "Just my luck, too."

"Oh, no," I reply, with a frown. "Are you alright?" *Just keep it light. Don't let him on to the fact you all are backing him into a corner tonight...*

"I'm fine. I'm not allergic or anything. A little hot, maybe."

"It is warm in here." I nod, taking a sip out of my own glass to cover up my shaking hands. "Would you excuse me? I need to chat with Peyton about the menu." At first pause, I rocket to the kitchen, putting distance between us.

Laughter echoes from the downtown party, adding to the feverish energy of the night. A John Deere tractor pulls around to the front of the house, in clear view of the main dining room, towing a hay-covered trailer adorned with thick, flannel blankets. Our chariot awaits.

"How much did you mess with Eli's menu?" I ask Peyton, taking shelter in the kitchen. Munching on roasted asparagus, I lean against the marble island as she preps trays of hors d'oeuvres.

"Eh, what he doesn't know won't hurt him," she muses. "I didn't change much. The guy's been through enough; he deserves to relax."

Relax, yeah. That's what's going to happen tonight. Just a normal class reunion. That's all.

"You're a good friend," I reply.

Eli walks into the space as if his ears are burning, moving slower than usual but moving, nonetheless. He sprouts a crooked, embarrassed half-smile and joins us around the island.

"Don't think I didn't notice that cumin, Peyton."

"Don't bite the hand that feeds you, or, for that matter, the hand that feeds an *entire party for you*, Eli," she pesters, chuckling.

"You're a lifesaver, douse everything in cumin if you want to. Thanks for your help tonight." He takes a seat on a barstool.

We lock eyes, feeling a magnetic pull. Peyton grabs two platters and walks out of the room, sticking her tongue out at him along the way.

"I thought you would've been in the park, running the hayride?" he asks, quietly. "Not to say I'm not glad to see you."

Jeremy joins the party, talking to a client in the distance. He raises a glass in our direction, an accusing look shooting at us like arrows through the open kitchen door.

"I'm heading there in a bit," I reply. Eli's green eyes look at me, really look at me, and the heat rises in my neck. "I have something to take care of here first."

His eyebrows raise, wanting more details.

"Later," I reply. "How are you feeling? I was worried about you. Seeing you unconscious like that..." I admit, trailing off.

"I don't know what would've happened if you didn't show up." His smile warms, and his eyes gloss over.

"Thank your dad. He asked me to check in on you." My vision blurs as I tear up, too. "What happened?"

"I had a migraine all day sitting in that holding cell. When Wesley got me home, I went upstairs and took what I thought was *my* medicine. My head was killing me, and the lights were off, so I didn't really pay much attention, just shook the pills into my hand and took them." He shrugs. "It's not like I mix pills; I pulled the right bottle from the medicine cabinet."

"Someone dumped other pills into your prescription bottle."

"I sure as hell didn't, so yeah." He runs his fingers through his strawberry-blond hair, glancing towards Wesley. "I took a couple, didn't feel better in an hour, and took a few more."

"Well." I blanch at the thought, reaching out to give his arm a gentle squeeze. "I'm glad you're okay. I was so scared. I actually wanted to talk to you about somethi—"

"Hey, babe." Jeremy strolls in, immediately scrutinizing my hand on Eli's arm.

Merda.

Chapter Eighteen

I snap my arm back and fiddle with the pins in my hair.

"Jeremy, you made it." My face warms, embarrassed.

"What am I walking into here?" he asks, sliding beside me.

"Nothing, I just haven't seen him since he left the hospital. Glad everyone's okay." Before leaving Eli's eyeline, I turn back to him and mouth, '*Sorry.*' Standing up, I grab Jeremy's hand and drag him back to the party.

Who am I kidding? We all know.

After a few more minutes of mingling, the tension between Jeremy and me growing, Charlotte turns down the music, and steps onto the small platform in the corner of the room. Danni joins her, standing slightly behind, unable to fit side-by-side.

It'll just have to wait.

"Thank you all for joining us today, as we celebrate the reunion of the Stone's Throw graduating classes of the 2000s." She smiles, waiting for the group's polite applause to die. "I'd be remiss if I didn't mention our fantastic venue, the newly renovated marina! What a fascinating piece of history. If you're interested in learning more, please find one of our village leaders. I will now turn it over to Danielle Mauer, the President of the Stone's Throw School Alumni Association. She is the driving force behind this operation."

A compliment from Charlotte? Has that ever happened?

Charlotte golf claps, urging the audience to join in, as she steps down and takes a seat. Danni grips the microphone and steps to the center of the platform.

"Thank you, thank you. And let's give a round of applause for Charlotte, eh?" The room claps again as Charlotte takes a non-humble bow, waving everyone off like her involvement is no big thing. Danni continues.

"This year, on behalf of the Stone's Throw Alumni Association, I'm thrilled to showcase one of our community's greatest assets. Show of hands, who has been in the State Park before?"

A few rowdy chants of *"hay-ride! hay-ride!"* boom from the back. As I take in the room, almost every hand shoots up. Almost.

Colin's mouth couldn't pucker more, reminding me of another body part closely matching his personality. Charlotte sips a glass of wine, skimming documents piled in front of her.

Chants grow, with supportive claps from the entire room. Gratitude swirls as I blot away a small tear.

"It's my pleasure to welcome Maudy Lorso, the Head Park Ranger for Stone's Throw State Park. She's going to go over how tonight's hayride will work." She claps as well, stepping down and handing me the microphone. She walks out of the ballroom, grabbing her clipboard, probably coordinating the next piece of the evening. She's been running around all evening.

I beam in their applause, taking center stage.

Wesley sits at a table off to the side of the room, with Kelly standing behind him. He has a weird look on his face, almost a wince, and keeps his gaze down at his lap. I make eye contact with Kelly, and she nods subtly before leaving to man her next post. Cameras are working, we're good to go.

"Thank you, thank you, everyone. I'm just as excited as you are!" The cheering subsides. "Before we go over hayride stuff, I'd like to acknowledge the black cloud hanging over our heads today. State Senator Paige Ramos, who tragically lost her life earlier this week, is a big reason why the park is still in operation." The tone shift kills any side conversations, and the room falls silent.

"You see," I continue, "Paige has been a longtime supporter of our park. I would receive letters from her office thanking us for our hard work and service to the community. It meant a lot to me; I've saved these letters and revisit them often.

"Paige went to bat for our park. And after years of keeping us funded, we unfortunately lost in state budget negotiations this year." I raise my hands in an *I'm innocent!* gesture. "I wish I could've thanked her. She kept us afloat much longer than we would have without her support. I know the hayride is free, but if anyone's inclined to donate, I think doing so in Paige's name would be a lovely gesture."

A soft, polite applause rumbles from the audience. I bow my head for a moment, unsure how to transition.

"Okay, now for the fun stuff!" I clap. "Let's talk about the haunted hayride." The chants of the hundred or so alums swell once more. "There are two tractors running tonight. One will be solely for you all." *Because it's crawling with microphones, surveillance cameras, and a couple of other surprises.* "The other is for the public. Given how big that forest is and how dark it is outside, we've got set groups already worked out. A list is posted by the front door. If you don't want to go, you can cross your name off and initial it. But for the sake of Danni's logistics, we ask that you don't switch groups with other people."

A few grumbles and groans meet that statement. "Don't worry, don't worry," I reassure. "Danni knows who you're all friends with. This town isn't that big," I laugh. "We did our best to keep you with your pals.

"Hayrides will leave at the top of the hour from here." I point out the window to the John Deere purring outside. "If there aren't any questions, we'll be off! First up is…" I make a show of pausing and reviewing my notes, as if I haven't been freaking out about it all afternoon.

"The class of 2005! Danni, Wesley, Eli, Nellie, and Colin! Peyton, you're staying here, right?" She gives a thumbs-up, holding up a shiny metal serving tray. "Right, then let's go!" The volume of my voice masks my nerves, hiding the shake.

Yes, let's go. Into the woods. To trap a killer.

* * *

"I know you said no switch-ups, Maudy, but I have to stay here. There's too much to coordinate. The silent auction isn't getting enough attention. Plus, Charlotte's watching me like a hawk." Danni whispers to me near the front entrance of the gorgeous home.

"Danni, this was the whole plan. We need you," I hiss between my teeth. "He's not going to crack without you there to put on the pressure."

"He'll crack. Have you seen him tonight? He's freaking out already. I don't think it'll take much. You'll be fine! Thank you, thank you."

Not waiting for a response, she bounds back into the party, playing hostess.

"Any chance there's an opening in this group?" Jeremy croons, nuzzling my neck and pulling me close in front of everyone. In front of Eli.

"Cut it out. I have a lot going on right now." I pull away.

"Jeez, fine." He takes a step back and puts his hands in his suit pockets. "Sue me for just wanting to spend some time with my girlfriend. I thought it'd be fun to cuddle up under the blanket together."

"You can come." I give in. "But I'm on ranger duty, and some things are in the works that you're not looped in on," I say quietly, trying to avoid others overhearing. "I need you to play along."

"I'll stay out of your way, I promise."

In the foyer, we pilfer the coat check, zipping up and pulling hats over our ears, ready to embrace the late-October night. Still in my green, silk dress, I throw on the sweatshirt from my backpack and layer it underneath my work jacket. The orange and black puffball on Eli's beanie sits on top of his head like the star on a Christmas tree, while Nellie's fuzzy earmuffs give the illusion of Princess Leia buns. The elegance of the night deteriorates into puffy jackets and brightly colored scarves.

The four alumni, one realtor, and I wave goodbye as the inaugural voyage departs. Nostalgia runs deep, as the party reminisces about childhood and the old hayrides that were staples of their youthful fall seasons. Danni sends us off, *rather chipper for someone who knows what's about to happen, if you ask me,* raising a champagne flute.

Snug under the blankets and settled in the hay, our bundled-up tractor driver honks the horn and turns over the engine. I'm between Jeremy and Eli. Eli braces himself with the trailer's low, wooden railing, looking like he might be sick. Across from us sits Nellie, sandwiched between Colin and Wesley. Both of them aimlessly scan downtown as we rumble down the street.

Jeremy tucks my hair behind my ear, smiling with a deep sadness. "Things got away from us, didn't they?" he asks as we hit the heart of downtown.

"Can we not do this right now?" I whisper, eyes darting between Eli, Wesley, and Colin.

"I'm trying to apologize to you," he replies curtly. "I want to get back on track."

"Jeremy. There is a lot happening tonight, and I don't think now's a good time," I say quietly, gently gripping his arm. "Later. I promise."

"It's never a good time, Maudy. You're always busy. You always brush me off."

"Fine. You want to do this now? Let's do this now. I think we should break up," I reply, a rush of relief overcoming me as the words fall out of my mouth. I've been holding onto that longer than I realized.

I feel his arm tense through his sleeve. A stoic, stone look slams on his face like the closing of a drawbridge.

"It's him, isn't it?" He tilts his head in Eli's direction.

The chef turns to us, surprised.

"You flinch every time I touch you. Especially in front of him," Jeremy states.

"We're just not a good fit," I reply, words much softer than his. *And, notably, not denying his accusation.*

Jeremy turns his body away from me.

"I'm not about to get into a big, public argument, Jeremy," I whisper. "You insisted we talk now. So, there you go. That's how I feel."

"This conversation isn't over," he scoffs, frustrated, and pulls out his phone.

Whatever. Am I glad these other four had to witness it? No. But at least Nellie's encouraging, sympathetic looks help curtail the sting.

Colin and Wesley thankfully aren't engaging in any of my embarrassing drama. Wes faces away, body out towards the road, keeping to himself. We hear a slight groan or sharp breath as we bounce, but otherwise he's silent. Nellie and I share a couple of confused glances when we can; she doesn't know what's happening with him. *Maybe he's onto us? Does he know what he's in for?*

"This place is something, eh?" Nellie asks as we roll slowly past rows of people in beach chairs watching *Young Frankenstein*. Kids run through a small hay bale maze, parents watching from the sidewalk, sipping warm drinks. Everyone waves as we amble on, the roar of the tractor engine revving everyone up.

"It really is," I mutter back, more to myself than anyone else.

Jeremy keeps his head buried in his phone, probably too embarrassed to engage. Fine by me. I turn away, giving him as much space as possible without launching myself off the trailer.

The town is ablaze with black and orange. Jack-o-lanterns' crooked smiles beckon us forward. It gets darker and darker as we leave downtown's festive mayhem and cross the Birch River Bridge into the park's shrouded cover.

Zach waits at the entrance, clipboard and Marty's leash in hand.

"First class reunion trip, I presume?" He asks the driver, whose face is barely visible from underneath a thick winter parka. They nod. "Great." He walks back to peer into our open trailer. "That means you're here." He smiles, pointing at me. "Marty, she's here!" he laughs, gently tugging on the leash until a black and white scruffy mutt appears from nearby bushes.

"Marty! Come here, bud." I beckon the dog onto the trailer and into the hay. He sneezes immediately and wedges himself between Jeremy and me. "Thanks for grabbing him, Zach. I'm going to go through with this tour, and then I'll be with you the rest of the night." The tractor idles, waiting for the official go-ahead.

"No problem, I'll be here. The first non-reunion group doesn't start for another thirty minutes, so nothing crazy will happen before you get here."

If only he knew.

"Sounds good, see you soon."

Zach gives the tractor a thumbs up, and after an initial lurch forward, we steadily rumble across the gravel parking lot.

The trails that watch over me, welcoming me every day, are completely transformed into an ominous, dark wood. The tractor roars as we're swallowed by trees, heading toward cackling laughter and ghost wails that swell as we crawl deeper.

As we pass motion sensors, a werewolf howls from just off the trail, and animatronic monsters pop out in front of us. We jump, laughing, clinging onto each other for safety. Jeremy ducks down into the hay, moving next to Colin across from me.

"C'mon," I whisper, tapping my foot. "The turn off has to be close…"

Coming to a fork in the road, the driver veers left, and the props get fewer and farther between as we go. The production value drops significantly, but everyone is busy cuddling, chitchatting, or doesn't care. No one seems to notice.

This must've been the best Danni could do on short notice. It's working, just enough to keep everyone distracted…

The generic monsters and scary soundscapes slowly morph into familiar faces. Posters of Paige, Danni, and Eli wrap around trees, their eyes spray-painted out. *She better not have gotten any paint on those beautiful sugar maples.*

"What the hell is this?" Nellie asks with owl eyes, staring right at me. Wesley looks around, confused as well. I hold up a subtle hand and gesture to Nellie that everything is okay. She climbs over and sits next to Marty and me, filling Jeremy's vacancy.

The group's confusion turns to worry. The tractor keeps pulling deeper and deeper into the woods. Worry morphs again into fear. I stare at Wesley as his eyes frantically dart, waiting for him to crack. I might need to push him over the edge.

The hayride music ping-pongs through the trees, a low, rumbling undertone growing as we venture further. He turns away from us, standing up and staring into the woods.

"What's happening?" he shouts, out of breath.

We pull into a small clearing, where I instructed the crew to put their supplies.

Our engine cuts.

"We know what you did, Wesley. Time to come clean." I stand up, bracing myself against the trailer's rail. Heads swivel between him and me, waiting for someone to make a move.

He keeps his eyes and body away from us; I can't see his face. Everyone's frozen, unsure how to proceed.

"Wesley?" Sitting next to him, Colin leans over the side of the trailer, trying to get a better view of his face. Wesley starts to shake (nerves, maybe? It's working!) and Colin gently touches his shoulder.

Wesley sways from Colin's touch, tumbling over the side of the trailer.

"What the," I whisper. Jumping over the rail and onto the squishy, leaf-covered ground, I rush to him, pepper spray in hand, in case he tries to run. He's face down, writhing on the ground.

He's seizing.

"Back up!" Kelly jumps out from behind the tractor wheel and quickly sheds her jacket, pushing me out of the way to assess his vitals.

"Somebody help him!" Eli shouts over the music, watching Wesley shake before hobbling over the edge of the trailer, trying to stay upright himself. "Kelly?" he asks. "What are you doing here?"

Kelly rips through Wesley's layers, getting directly to his chest. She checks for vitals, not bothering to answer Eli's question. "Everyone back," she barks, hovering over the man, putting her jacket underneath his head. I hear her radio asking for an ambulance. "Paige did the same, according to the medical examiner's reports. Not this bad, though," she admits to me, much quieter.

"Someone call 911, now!" I order.

I kneel next to Wesley, staying out of Kelly's way, watching his muscles contract, rippling over his body in jerky spasms. A small bruise on his abdomen, maybe the size of a quarter, catches my eye as he thrashes.

Using my phone flashlight, I shed light on the mark and find an almost imperceptible prick in the center. That's no bee sting. I know bee stings.

"Kelly," with her so close to me already, I lower my voice, so others don't hear. "Kelly, he thought he was stung by a bee earlier. That's not a bee sting." I point to the spot, glancing to meet her eyes. "It wasn't Wesley," I stammer, in utter shock, watching the man seize.

"He was injected with something," Kelly confirms, eyeing Eli. "It wasn't Wesley."

Chapter Nineteen

"We don't have service out here," Nellie shouts, pacing in small circles, her phone up to her ear. "Is he going to die?"

"He's not going to die. But he needs help," Kelly grunts, stuffing her jacket underneath his head. "Nobody answered my radio call."

Wesley's body skitters over the wet forest floor. Kelly hovers closely over him so he doesn't hurt himself more. I join her, desperate to be helpful.

"You're okay, Wesley. You'll be okay." I use a soft, even tone, hoping he can hear me.

"Does anyone know if he has a seizure disorder?" Kelly looks around. "Eli?"

"I don't think so." Eli's eyes are wide and fixated on Wesley. He's so pale he could be mistaken for one of the animatronic ghosts haunting the woods tonight.

Colin whimpers from the mounds of hay back on the trailer. He's wrapped himself in a blanket and is rocking back and forth.

"Is he going to die?" Colin cries in between sniffles. "This is horrible!" *At least I don't crumble in an emergency.*

"Shut up, Colin," Kelly orders. "You're not helping. No, he's going to live, but this is serious. Maudy, find a doctor. I think there's one at the party. Take the tractor back. I have to stay here with…" She looks down at Wesley, his body between us, and hands me the key. "We shouldn't move him in this state. He fell hard."

"On it." I scramble, Marty's leash tight in hand, as Eli picks himself up to accompany me. *If Wesley didn't do this...* I glance at him, truly suspicious for the first time.

"I'm coming with you," he says, not inviting questions. "A guy I graduated with is an emergency doc now. He's at the party."

Before I can object, another, deeper voice does it for me.

"Hah," Jeremy sneers. "It hasn't even been thirty minutes yet." He shakes his head. "I knew this would happen."

"Stop it, Jeremy. It's not like we were madly in love." The venom in my voice is clear. I have zero patience right now. A man is seriously injured; I don't have time to placate fragile male egos. "Stay here and help Kelly."

"I just saw this coming, that's all." He jabs back, dismounting the trailer and joining Kelly near Wesley's head.

"C'mon, man." Eli takes a step towards him. "Now's not the time." He tugs his knit hat on tighter, and we clamber into the tractor's cab, wobbling as he climbs. His body went through a lot in the last day.

With Nellie and Colin still in the trailer behind us, Marty wedges himself in the middle of the tractor's cab between Eli and me, mining for body heat.

"Sorry about him," I offer once we're out of earshot. The rumble of the tractor's engine is the only sound. "He's a little...sensitive right now." I drum my fingers on the steering wheel, meandering back up the trail.

"Yeah," Eli says. "I may have heard something."

"Hey, weird question," I say, changing the subject. "You don't have any marks or bruises on your stomach, do you?"

"Not that I've noticed, why?"

"Wesley was injected with something. There was a small bruise around an injection mark, and he commented earlier about a bee sting."

"What? He was injected?" he probes.

"I know. Something's causing the seizure. I saw the mark; it wasn't a bee sting." I reply. "How long would that take to kick in? Could it have happened hours ago, or are we talking a few minutes?"

In the warm tractor cab, he takes off his jacket and unbuttons his shirt, checking for similar poke marks.

"Anything?" I ask, trying hard to look without him noticing.

"No marks. And I have no idea how long it'd take; it probably depends on what it was." He buttons his shirt again and rezips his parka. "It's safe," he jokes, putting his clothes back on. "Who do you think poked him?"

You, maybe. There aren't a whole lot of other options out there.

"I don't know. He was sitting next to Colin on the hayride?" I ask, not wanting to admit my true suspicion. I pause, chewing on something he said a minute ago. "Did the doctors say that you seized at all? When you took the sleeping pills?"

"No," he confirms. "And no needle pricks." He taps his stomach.

"There must be two different poisons. You're okay because you only took the pills; you didn't get pricked. But nobody saw Paige seize…don't you think somebody would've caught that? Everyone was outside that night. The medical examiner said she did, but it was small. Not like this."

We sit in silence, rumbling towards the parking lot, before I pull out my phone and try 911 again, now that we're closer to town. It rings; we're within range. I put it on speakerphone.

"This is Park Ranger Maudy Lorso," I start.

"And Eli Nett," he adds.

"We have an emergency in Stone's Throw State Park. Send medical attention ASAP. A man is having a severe seizure, brought on by some sort of drug. I'm not sure, but he has a needle prick on his abdomen with no known medications." Trying to keep a steady voice, I funnel my frenetic energy into petting the dog. Eli does the same. Our hands brush against one another; we both recoil.

"Sorry," he mutters, jamming it into his jacket pocket, as if punishing it for bad behavior.

"All officers are out already," the dispatcher replies. "The phones are ringing off the hook tonight. We've got calls from all over the county. I'll try my best, but it will be a while. Do you know the exact coordinates?" I hear phones ringing and urgent voices scrambling on the other end of the line.

I get her as close as possible from memory, giving turn-by-turn trail directions and land markers before hanging up.

Trying to keep my eyes on the dark trail ahead, sufferably slow minutes pass as we roll steadily towards the entrance. Only a handful of bushes pay the price for my deficit in tractor-driving skills.

Approaching the parking lot, the lights of the hayride entrance provide much-needed respite.

"Whoa!" Something crosses the tractor's path, scampering in front of us. *A deer?* I slam on the brakes and throw it in park. Turning off the machine, we tumble out of the high-up cab. Marty leaps with grace, crashing right into my legs. Nellie and Colin unload from the trailer behind us as well.

"Danni?" Eli asks, calling to the person in our path. "Shouldn't you be at the party?"

Danni turns around, clipboard in hand, carrying a large backpack. Not a deer.

"Just checking on things over here and offering snacks to our crew." She pats the bag. "Things are fine on that end. How are you guys? What's wrong?"

"Do you have a car here?" Eli asks. "Wesley's hurt, and we need a doctor." He spills his words, out of breath.

Our panic registers, and her jovial attitude morphs into something else. *Confusion, maybe?*

"He's having a seizure, out in the woods. We came to get help," I interject while she processes. "Eli said there's a guy at the party who's an ER doctor. The police can't come for a while."

Danni looks at me with disbelief, then over to Eli. "You," she whispers, taking a step back from him. "It *was* you," she whispers again.

"Danni, no, of course not. Don't be ridiculous. Can we talk for a second?" he pleads.

"Eli, we have to go! We need to get a doctor!" I shout, desperate. Marty barks at him, too, joining the pile-on. *What the hell is he thinking? We have to move, now! Wesley needs help!*

"Muddy, it'll just take a second." He steers Danni a few steps away, trying to provide some semblance of privacy in this open parking lot.

"I'm leaving." I decide, throwing him the tractor keys and turning towards the Birch River Bridge. "C'mon, Marty."

"I'm busy, Eli." Danni's pitch is higher than usual. As I leave, I see her pacing, kicking small rocks, arms crossed.

I hear him talk to her. "I need to get something off my chest," he pauses. Probably nervously running his fingers through his hair, like he always does. I can picture it. "I can't do this anymore, Danni."

"Did you hear that?" I whisper to the dog, surprise on my face.

"We're using each other." Eli continues. "We both know this isn't real. I need to work through some stuff, and this week has made it worse."

I feel his eyes on the back of my head. It's me. I'm "some stuff."

"And same for you!" he continues. "You just lost your brother. You inherited his kid to raise. That's a lot."

"It's not all I inherited," she's angry, her voice wavering.

He's breaking up with her. I pick up my pace, giving him space, feeling guilty for eavesdropping in the first place.

As Marty and I jog into town, the growing thunder of the tractor engine gains on us a block later.

"Hi." Eli pulls up, grunting in pain and a meek, smiley wince on his freckled face. We climb back in the cab. "Sorry about that," he says.

Don't be. I'm not.

We continue rolling through town, passing the Sheriff's Office on the way. I hop out and peer through the window. It's dark inside. "Where is everyone?" I ask.

We keep driving, heading into the heart of downtown toward the marina. We go in silence, but inside, I'm in a cage match with head-to-head conflicting feelings. I want to jump for joy that he and Danni are over. And, if I'm being honest, I'm scared that he could be the one behind all this. That he could stab me with whatever is in that needle. That he killed Paige.

The end of *Young Frankenstein* plays on the big, inflatable movie screen in the street, pulling me out of my head without a resolution. Nobody's watching. It's a ghost town. Beach chairs sit empty. Shops are closed.

"Eli, what's going on?" I ask shakily from the tractor's passenger seat, hugging Marty tight. The guard-dog ridge of fur along his spine pricks on end.

"I don't know…" He looks around. "Let's go to the marina. Get that doctor. One problem at a time, right? We need to help Wesley."

He steps on the gas, both of us creeped out by the mass disappearance. As we approach the marina, decibels rise in mixes of shrieks and cries, drowning out the roar of the tractor's engine.

"Well, that answers that question," he says, turning off the machine and sliding out of the cab. The marina is surrounded. Twisting our way through the throng, I bump into Anna.

"What's going on?" I ask, tapping my friend on the shoulder.

She turns around, ponytail whipping like a jump rope. "They're trapped inside," she divulges. Pushing our way through, Eli and I get to a window. Worthless attempts to bust through the glass leave it scratched.

"It's bulletproof," an officer nearby shouts, watching us inspect the glass. "A lady inside called the security company to unlock the doors. She doesn't want us breaking these new windows and would rather they wait it out."

"They're trapped." I look at Eli, bewildered.

His mouth sets into a thin, straight line.

Eli circles the house, hellbent on getting the doctor, while Marty and I try to gather more information. "What happened?" I ask Anna.

"I don't know. We just saw a bunch of police officers rush through downtown, so everyone left the movie and came over to check it out. Emma called me, freaking out about Nellie out in the park with you guys, so I closed up the surf shop and came over like everyone else." Anna points to a few state and local police officers, standing by just as confused as the rest of us. They don't seem to know what to do, either. "All the doors are locked."

"How long ago?" I ask.

"Maybe fifteen, twenty minutes?"

"Wesley was attacked." I lower my voice. "He's in the woods having a seizure. We came to get a doctor."

"What?" she shrieks. "You're kidding." She pulls a tie-dye orange headband lower, over her ears.

"Shhh, keep your voice down," I hush. "I wish I were kidding. He was injected with something. This has got to all be connected, right?"

I look over at Eli, watching him try to pry a door open with a crowbar he found somewhere. Even if he wasn't weak from the pills, there's still no way he's getting through. He gives up and walks over to the police officers. After a quick conversation and a lot of arm waving, he returns.

"Security system malfunction, yeah right," he grumbles. "I got those officers to call dispatch again. I told them about Wes," he says. "All ambulances are out already. No one else is available to pick him up. Come with me." He grabs my hand and pulls Marty and me away from the scene, back into town. This time, I don't recoil. *Don't read into this; he's on a mission. That's it.*

"Eli, where are we going? We need help!" Two minutes later, he drags me through Pop's front door, uncharacteristically chill about Marty coming inside.

The remnants of a Halloween party are evident, with most patrons siphoned off to gawk at the marina. It's not a rowdy dance party, but a few groups linger, including a gaggle of Ghostbusters playing arcade games in the corner, a coven of vampires shooting pool, and a handful of space aliens saddled up to the bar.

Dressed as the Big Lebowski, Kevin pours drinks, mostly White Russians. A huge, knit sweater loosely hangs over the trim man. A scraggly wig and drawn-on goatee round out the outfit.

"Dad," Eli rushes behind the bar. Marty and I hover nearby, not wanting to overstep.

"I'm not Dad. I'm the Dude." He belly laughs. "Glad to see you aren't stuck over there at the party. What bad luck, eh?" He *tsks.* "They'll get 'em out soon. At least there's enough food and booze in that house to last a few lifetimes." He smiles. "You and Peyton made sure of that."

"It's not an accident, Dad. Wesley's out having a seizure in the woods. Someone pricked him with a needle. Something's going on. It's too weird to all be a coincidence."

This gets Kevin's attention, and he puts down a cocktail shaker.

"We have to get inside," Eli adds. "Well, actually, we have to get them out. An old classmate of mine is a doctor now, and Wes needs his help,"

Eli continues, desperate. "I was thinking…"

"The hole." Kevin cuts in. "Worth a shot, kid."

The two men rush into the kitchen, Eli waving for Marty and me to follow. "Don't lick anything in here, Martin. Try not to shed too much either," I whisper.

Eli pulls up an old, gray mat, unveiling a rectangular cutout in the wooden floorboards. Using a paring knife, he pops it open, revealing a rickety staircase descending into darkness.

"This has been here forever," Eli quickly explains. "We always thought it might be an old Capone tunnel, but never tested it out all the way. The stairs are rotted, so we boarded it up for safety. I almost broke my leg down there exploring when I was a kid."

"Whoa," I ogle, taking it in. "Wait, the map! The one in Charlotte's office."

"Yes, I noticed that too on the tour we got. It only has a few buildings on it. This is one of them," Eli confirms. "When Charlotte said they found secret passages in the basement but thought the other ends were long gone, I was confused, considering there's a massive hole in my kitchen."

I remember him looking skeptical down there.

"Well, no time like the present. Kevin, will you keep Marty for me?" I ask, handing Lebowski the leash and squeezing the pup tight. "See you soon, buddy."

Eli and I descend underneath Pop's, using the grimy, cobblestone walls to steady our balance. The staircase goes deep underground, maybe two stories, and flattens into a narrow dirt tunnel. Decades-old trash lines the path. Everything from cigars, bottles, pieces of barrel, everything.

Eli crouches, the ceiling a little low, as we follow our phone flashlights. There are no forks, no branches. Just forward.

"This is wild," I whisper. We keep a quick pace and are careful not to trip on the uneven surface.

We walk for maybe five or six minutes before the tunnel narrows even further. Coming in on us from all sides, we curl over, bending at the waist, and creep forward on a slight incline.

"I bet we're getting close to the house," I speculate. It constricts even more, forcing us on all fours.

After only a minute, my knees already coated in dirt and skinned from crawling (goodbye, favorite dress), we come to another wooden door in the floor. Eli lifts it open, no knife required, and peers inside.

The surprising yellow glow of lit lanterns scatter around the room below. It blinds me for a second, eyes adjusted to the claustrophobic darkness.

Eli lowers himself through the hole and drops into a room. He lifts his arms, waiting for me to follow.

"You're weak enough already. Get out of the way." I wave for him to step aside.

He insists and catches my fall. My arms slip around his neck as I hop down; our faces within inches of one another.

"Sorry about that." He compulsively runs his fingers through his hair after gently setting me down.

"Don't sweat it." I smile, dust myself off, and turn to take in the rest of the space.

The room is built of the original lake stones, like we saw in the basement, with the occasional glass bottle thrown in. A large wooden table rests in the center, with old liquor barrels serving as high tops around the perimeter. A modest desk tucks into the back corner, and a ladder leans against the wall next to me, not far from the door we fell through.

The room is disheveled, with papers and books tossed on the floor. It reminds me of an office where old-timey explorers might hang out. Maps are taped to the walls, all lumpy from the underlying stone.

The ceiling hangs low; I can brush it with my fingertips. Peering up, two wooden doors are inlaid into the stone ceiling, not including the one we came from. One is right next to the door leading to Pop's, and another is off in the corner of the room.

This could have been an old headquarters for illegal activities back in the day. Someone else has been using it lately, too.

I walk over to the worn desk, soaking it all in. The lantern light is just enough to make out a shadow of a carving on the top. Etched into the wood, I feel the shape, unable to see it clearly. The edges are soft from decades of damp, heavy air. This is old, not freshly done.

"TB," I whisper, tracing the letters.

Chapter Twenty

The lanterns are odd. They're small, modern-day camping ones that run on batteries. Not old kerosene lamps. Someone turned these on tonight; they have horrible battery life. I grab one and hand another to Eli as we sift through the room.

Pilfering the desk, I rummage through drawers, finding a mix of old and new, like the rest of this place. There's nothing really of value, dozens of old Birch River Current clippings, and yellowed scraps of paper with numbers scrawled on them. A pack of black, elastic hair ties and a tube of lipstick are tossed in.

"Maudy, look." Eli points to an old whisky barrel in the corner. On top sits a rotary phone.

"Would you look at that," I say with a dry laugh. Pulling out my own phone, I redial the number the TV station gave me. Eli surveys with curiosity, and I hold a finger up to him, *one second.*

Sure enough, the phone rings, and he picks it up. "Hello?" he asks, confirming the connection.

"This number placed the slander ad on my campaign."

"That's bizarre." He resumes snooping.

I leave the desk and shuffle through the dozens of loose papers, map scraps, and other random things on the floor, making my way to the barrels scattered across the room. On one near the desk, a planner sits open. This past Monday has a meeting blocked off titled, "Debrief

Paige Ramos." Paige had "TB" written in her calendar at the same time.

The maps on the walls are also a blend of old and new. There's a copy of the one Charlotte has in her office, the original settlement of what's now Stone's Throw. This one has hand-drawn dotted lines snaking through it. One goes to Pop's, another out to the ranger station. There's also a modern-day topographical map marked with red and blue ink. The edits flatten the dunes and reroute the Birch River channel.

"Eli, look." I point to the map, noting the line to Pop's. "Someone's marked the tunnels."

"Ever notice anything in the ranger station? A line goes right to it."

"No. Maybe they covered the tunnel door when they redid the floors." I study the other door in the ceiling. *Do you go to the park?*

The large center table is cleared except for a lantern in the middle and a single crumpled piece of paper. It's almost funny. The uncluttered, dust- and debris-free wooden surface stands out against the room's chaos. I pick up the lone paper to inspect it closely. It's a list.

- *Hinke Farm, 1192 West M-22 - animals loose*
- *Copper Lake Apartment Complex - fire*
- *Great Lakes Credit Union – robbery*

It goes on.

"Eli, did the police mention where they were all sent tonight? What's keeping them busy?" I ask, continuing down the list.

"A bunch of stuff, I guess," he says. "A fire, bank robbery, all kinds of things. They said Halloween is usually bad, but tonight has been insane."

"Uh-huh," I continue reading. "They're all fake. Or planned at least." I hand him the list and start rummaging through the desk. "Someone wanted to keep the cops away tonight."

"Whoa," he skims it. "Who the hell are you, Tiller Brazas?"

"A woman, it seems." I pick up a tube of lipstick from the desk drawer.

"What women do we know have access down here?" he asks.

An answer immediately comes to mind. An *I told you so* look sprouts on my face.

"C'mon, Charlotte? Really?" he asks skeptically. "She's super annoying, I'll give you that. But all this?"

"She's conspiring with Colin; she led the renovations of this building," I list. "Do you have any other guesses?"

"Charlotte is a neat freak," he argues. "She wouldn't leave it looking like this."

Some of the papers on the floor look like contract drafts, many of which are written over with ink, making revisions. I try to understand a couple of them, but out of context, it might as well be in another language. Others appear to be bank statements or account spreadsheets, or something. Parts of a business ledger?

"We've lost sight of what we came here for," I declare. All this new, weird information rattles around my head, and I can't make sense of it. "We need to get help for Wesley. We need to get upstairs."

"You're right." He nods. "Let's go through the basement." He walks over to the only standard door in the room and leaves.

It only takes a moment to find my shoe scuff marks, standing out against the layers of dust and lake grime. I hadn't been far off, just a few missed turns from reaching the office when I poked around last time, almost like the house had been teasing me.

We snake our way up to the original staircase, steps smooth and well-worn, to the main floor of the home. We're in the back landing with a door on either side. To the left is the house's back entrance. I can see the crowd outside through the thick window. To the right is a door connecting this small foyer to the rest of the interior. A door that is also automatically locked.

"Hey!" Eli shouts, pounding on the inside-facing door, hoping someone can hear us through the glass. "Peyton! Charlotte! Anybody!" After thirty seconds, he becomes impatient. Descending the staircase back into the basement, he clangs around for a minute before returning.

"Stand back." He motions for me to drop down a few stairs and bashes a hammer into the window, trying to break the glass. A few web-like cracks spider over the pane, but it stays intact. This one is also bulletproof.

We shout and pound until Leonard's confused, hunched-over body appears on the other side of the door. "Are you okay?" I ask the man as he approaches, his figure coming into focus, holding a glass of wine.

"Ms. Lorso? Is that you? We're just fine," he replies. "We're waiting for the security company to come. There's been a glitch in the new alarm system. It triggered, and we can't undo it without them."

"Leonard, is John in there?" Eli asks, shouting. "We need a doctor!"

"No, no. I said everyone's okay!" Leonard shouts back, confused. "We don't need a doctor. Everyone's fine." He waves us off and walks away.

"No, Leonard, come back!" I yell. Too late, he's already gone.

"Find another way?" I turn to Eli and descend back into the basement. We loop our way back through the labyrinth and into the office.

"Oh no," I groan, as the room closes in on me. Someone's been here since we left. All of the papers on the floor are gone. The maps on the wall are gone. The planner is gone. The room is wiped clean.

"Eli, they're still in the house. We've got to get the doctor and get out of here."

Looking up at the tunnel doors, we make the incredibly uninformed guess that the one next to Pop's door goes to the ranger station. Without knowing anything about the smaller one in the corner, Eli props up the ladder as I climb through the square hole, finding this tunnel much nicer than the last.

"C'mon." I lean over and extend my hand, waiting for him to join me.

"I'm going to stay here in case they come back again," he states. "You go."

"Eli, that's redicu—"

"No arguing. Go," he orders. I climb into the ceiling, and he hands me a lantern.

A layer of cardboard lines this tunnel's floor. With the lantern light, I make out the brand names of furniture, dishware, and other items bought for the renovation on the flattened boxes. I don't think Pottery Barn was a thing a hundred years ago.

I crawl for maybe ten feet before the tunnel turns vertical, with footholds carved into the wall grout, creating a makeshift ladder. I scale higher, but not for too long, before the stone turns into fluffy, pink insulation, covering studs and drywall. I'm inside a wall on the main floor. The passage keeps going. Shining my lantern above my head, it continues all the way up to the second story.

I bang on the wall, peeling back the thick pink batting, letting it fall down the chute below. My hand tingles with a thousand glass insulation splinters. The passage is too narrow for me to get my leg up and kick it, but I finagle a stiletto off my foot and hammer it into the wall, taking a page out of Eli's book, really throwing my upper body into it.

After a few good hits, a hole rips through the drywall. Now with something to grip, I pry chunks away, the gray drywall staining red and brown from blood and dirt.

"Arh," I huff, pulling hard. Chunk after chunk falls down the tunnel as I break them off, fueled by feminine rage. I have a big enough hole to crawl through now. Peering in, my face is inches away from piles of cooking pots. It's the inside of a kitchen cabinet.

As quietly as someone teetering on a grout ladder in one stiletto can manage, I scoot the pots out of my way and leverage my torso into the cabinet, legs dangling down the chute, when voices enter the room.

I hear her unmistakable piercing tone through the cabinet door. Charlotte is humming to herself. Her heels *click-clack* through the kitchen as she paces. "So far, so good," she mutters. A metal tray clinks on the kitchen island before her quick footsteps leave the room.

I press on the cabinet door until it opens just a crack. Peyton's shoes are right in front of me. "Psst," I hiss and hoist myself up.

"Who's there?" She pivots, knife in hand, as I open the door and flop onto the floor.

"Jeez, Maudy. What the hell are you doing down there? You scared me half to death. How'd you get in here?" she hisses, looking around to ensure nobody is around.

"It's a tunnel. I climbed up through the basement."

She bends over and helps me up to my feet, surprise dancing on her face.

"Thanks." I attempt to brush off the muck from my dress and detangle my snarled hair, to no avail.

"What the heck is going on?" she asks, eyes still darting. She pulls a hair tie off her wrist and hands it to me. "I'm freaking out over here."

"Wesley had a seizure in the woods, and Eli and I came to get help. I guess there's a doctor here? Someone you went to school with? Then we saw you all trapped, so we broke in."

She pulls me in closer, lowering her voice to a whisper. "It's been really weird. Charlotte says it's a glitch in the security system, but I don't buy it. She's been running around holding everything together and told the police not to bust through the windows. I guess they're expensive or something." Peyton scoffs, rolls her eyes, and pops a mini eggroll in her mouth. "I've been keeping my eyes out, but something is definitely up."

"I'm glad you're all okay." I try to brush myself off, a halo of dust falling around me.

"Here," she hands me a dishtowel.

"Thanks."

"Oh, hey, who has diabetes?" she asks while I clean myself up, walking over and opening the refrigerator to grab me a water bottle. She points out a bright blue plastic pouch with a medical vial of insulin on the top shelf.

"What?" I ask, scrubbing myself off.

"Who's diabetic? Nobody marked any sugar stuff on their meal requests, but there's insulin in the fridge."

"I don't know," I utter as I open the fridge to see for myself. The metaphorical lightbulb clicks on as I look at the small, glass vial. "But I think I know what else that's been used for today. Wesley had a needle mark on him when he started seizing. He told me earlier he thought he was stung by a bee."

Peyton's eyes saucer.

"Stash that somewhere safe," I tell her. "It's evidence, I don't want whoever's responsible to hide it."

She squirrels the pouch away in her baking supplies, burying it deep under layers of trays and chafing dishes, as I fill her in on what I found in the basement.

"Tiller Brazas is in this house," I explain. "Or at least whoever is using their office now. They swiped a bunch of stuff from down there just a second ago, so they're still around. I don't think it's a security glitch. They called in other emergencies tonight, all over, to jam up the police. I think everyone is locked in on purpose. Maybe it's a distraction so nobody could help Wesley? Or maybe they have something else planned for tonight."

That thought hits me like a ton of bricks.

"Somebody else might get hurt," I whisper, panic leaching out of every pore. "We have to get the doctor for Wesley."

"Wait, Maudy. If someone poisoned Wesley...does that mean...Eli?"

"I...I have no idea. I hope not. I've been with him most of the night. He wants to help."

We march out of the kitchen to get the doctor and find Charlotte standing at the top of the stairs, arms on her hips.

"How in the world did you get in here?" she accuses.

"You would think you'd be a little more gracious to the person coming to your rescue." I retort.

"Ugh," she scoffs, following Peyton and me as we join the others in the ballroom. "The security company will be here soon. We do not need a *rescue*," she replies. "This isn't an emergency. I've been trying to keep everyone calm. Don't go in there, riling everyone up."

If it's not an emergency, then who is jamming 911?

Stepping into the main party space, I'm surprised to see most guests still together. Charlotte's right: the tone is nervous, but not outright panic. All in all, maybe eighty or so people scuttle about, in quiet voices, huddling close to one another. Peyton's not the only one who suspects something's off.

"Hey, everyone." I raise my arms and walk over to the podium. "Is there a John here? A doctor?" Blank, disgusted stares look back at me. After dashing through half of town in underground tunnels, I look like a swamp thing with my ruined outfit and bird's nest hair.

"I'm John." A tall man, dressed in a gray linen suit, chimes in from the back of the room. "Everything okay? Can you get us out of here?"

Peyton nods at me, confirming that's who Eli was referring to.

"I'm fine, but Wesley isn't. He needs your help." I clap, trying to get moving towards the kitchen. "There's been an emergency. Come with me."

The room ripples with gasps, everyone already on edge as it is.

I jog into the kitchen; the doctor and others follow closely behind. Crouching down, I open the cabinet and swoosh all the remaining pots out of the way.

"This hole leads to a room in the basement. Eli—you know Eli, right?" John confirms he does. The rest of the group chatters away, ogling at us. Their whispers slowly escalate, almost drowning out my instructions.

"He's down there already. You'll go from there into another tunnel that leads out to the park. Eli will show you which one it is. I need you to take the four-wheeler that's in the shed. The trail is wide enough; ignore the *No Vehicle* signs. Wesley had a bad seizure out there and fell hard."

"I'll do my best, but I don't have any supplies with me. How long has it been since he started seizing?"

"Maybe an hour," I guess. "Kelly, the police officer, is with him. She said it didn't seem like this was life or death, but he might've hit his head. He fell off the hayride."

"Okay, I'll do my best."

After scrambling to give some directions to Wesley's location, the doctor is on his way.

Okay, one emergency down.

"What's happening?" a woman shrieks.

"When can we get out of here?" a snippy voice shortly follows.

The urgency crescendos. Charlotte stands nearby, leaning against a doorframe, watching the order devolve. She smirks.

"Everyone!" Charlotte screeches, clapping her hands. The chatter continues. "Everyone! That's enough!" she insists, even louder. This time, they notice, silence crushing the space. "Please take a seat in the ballroom. I won't have us acting like animals."

Grumbles break out as folks shuffle into the ballroom, sitting at the banquet tables. Charlotte and I lock eyes, and I follow as well, taking a seat next to her.

The doctor is on his way. That's good, but Tiller is still in this house...or at least someone working with them. One of the people sitting at this table might be who I'm after. Do I want to show my cards? Tell everyone I found their office?

On the other hand, somebody already cleared the creepy office. They already know we've been down there. Maybe we just try to get everyone out safely? What's the right move here? Keep everyone here together, or get everyone out?

I pause to look at the curious faces sitting around this table, taking stock. Four sit with me: Charlotte, Leonard, Peyton, and Emma. Tonight has been like herding cats. I can't keep track of everyone. I hope Kelly is having better luck than I am.

Leonard looks relatively unbothered, scrolling through his phone. His shoulders tense, but he seems content in his own little world. Next to him, Emma looks like a deer in headlights. Peyton and Charlotte are both stone-faced.

"Is Nellie okay?" Emma asks, pleading. "If you're here...did something happen on the hayride?"

"Nellie's fine," I reassure, a wave of relief washing over her. "Wesley had a seizure. We were out of cell range, and then 911 was jammed. Eli and I went to get help, and Colin and Nellie rode back here with us. She's probably outside right now, worrying about you." I smile.

"She's okay." Emma takes a deep, slow breath, shoulders relaxing. "She wasn't answering her phone."

"She probably just left it here. I bet it's in her purse." I smile. "She's fine. I promise."

"You didn't answer me earlier," Charlotte reminds me. "How did you get in here?"

"We walked through this tunnel underneath Pop's," I explain tonight's escapades. "It led to this room in the basement. It's old, like it was from all the gangster stuff. Someone is using it as an office. It was the same person who paid for all the crappy ads against my campaign."

I study Charlotte, gauging her reaction. She's mildly surprised but not shocked.

"Anyway," I continue. "A few passageways stem from that room. One got me back into this part of the house, through the kitchen."

"It's like we're in the frickin' *Clue* mansion," Peyton adds.

"You don't know the half of it," I mutter to her under my breath, so the others don't hear. She raises her eyebrows and slyly looks at me as if to say, *We're going to talk more about that later.*

On the table, amongst us, are half-full glasses, long abandoned. On one of the wine glasses, I notice a lipstick smudge. A *familiar* shade of red lipstick.

"Whose glass is that?" I point, leaning forward to grab it and hold it up to the light.

Jeremy rushes into the room, coming to a screeching halt when he sees me at the table.

"Maudy, what are you doing here?"

I know whose glass that is.

Chapter Twenty-One

"Jeremy, what are you doing here? Did you follow me?" Confused, I push him away, holding on tight to this new theory. *It's possible...*

"What is it?" Emma asks, leaning towards me.

"We need to get out of here." Abruptly, I walk into the kitchen and open the cabinet I came through. "Everyone, come with me, now!" I shout to the entire room, uneasiness erupting. "Peyton," I bark, turning to address my friend who stands with nerves of steel as she gets up to follow me, no questions asked. "You lead the way. This chute takes you right back into that office I was talking about. Where the tunnels meet. Go down there. The other two in the ceiling go to Pop's and the ranger station. Go to Pop's. Eli will point out the correct one."

"Pop's? Holy cow, Maudy. That's blocks away," Emma replies.

"Yeah, well, there's a killer in this house, and they're clearly up to something. This is the only alternative I've got. If I'm right, nobody at the alarm company is coming tonight."

Gasps ripple through the party guests.

"The tunnel ceilings are low," I rush to explain. "But not low enough that you need to crawl very long. You guys can get there in a few minutes. Peyton, stay in Pop's kitchen and guard the tunnel door. Make sure nobody comes *or goes* through it." Peyton descends first, and the rest follow her down into the dark hole behind the pots, one by one.

"Stay safe, guys. I'll see you later. Promise," I mutter as they go. Watching them climb into the wall of a gangster house was not on this year's bingo card, but here we are. At least they'll be safer. Jeremy stands behind me, leaning against the kitchen island.

"'Scuse me," I hear voices rattle through the wall just a few minutes later, pushing someone out of the way." It's Peyton again.

"Hey, Eli's not down there. Didn't you say he would be? All the tunnel doors are open. Which one goes to Pop's?" she asks.

"What?" Baffled, I run scenarios of where he could be. I take a deep breath and climb back down after Peyton.

Flopping into the office, no mind for poise, I look around the room once more.

"Dammit, Eli." The room is empty, except for the handful of people who crawled down after Peyton. Both hatch doors hang open. Nobody's sure where to go.

Pausing for a moment, I groan. *"He's mine"* is written in red lipstick in the middle of a sloppy heart, on the door to the hatch leading into the park.

"You didn't," I growl, pulling out my phone and swiping through apps.

Opening Marty's GPS collar tracker app, I see a blinking red light in the park. Eli isn't in the basement. He's out in the woods with a murderer.

* * *

I push through the pain shooting through my hands, insulation splinters cutting my palms. I'm running as fast as possible through the claustrophobic, dark tunnel, but it's still too slow. The rest of the trapped partygoers are on their way to Pop's.

"What the," I whisper, tracing my finger over letters written in sandy mud coating a wall. We're below the water table this close to the lake; everything is damp. "Don't," it reads.

A few feet further, I find another. "Come," it reads.

More and more words reveal themselves as I travel down the tunnel in the dim lantern light. Finally, after stringing them all together, the message reads, "Don't come, mud. It's a trap."

Hot tears stream down my face. *Why would he do this? Why would he walk in here with her? Did she have a gun or something? He's not in good health right now, but he towers over her. He could pin her down or knock her out easily. God, Eli, I almost lost you once. I can't again.*

A deafening roar overhead disrupts my wallowing. "I'm under the Birch River..." I realize. The powerful water rushes to meet Lake Michigan, like two old friends who haven't seen one another in years.

"Not much farther," I reassure myself as I keep moving. Pushing through the pain, my palms press firmly into the walls of the tight, rocky tunnel, keeping my balance on the uneven terrain.

After maybe fifteen minutes underground, the incline of the tunnel turns into a chute, like the one in the marina's kitchen. I climb a similar makeshift ladder and push on the wooden door above, but it doesn't budge much. Something's on top of it.

"Hello? Anybody there?" I shout, pounding on it with my fist.

"Ruff!"

I know that bark.

"Marty! Hey buddy, I'm here!"

I hear the tapping of his black-and-white nails against the wooden floor above me, picturing his wiggly, happy dance.

Not much in the way of brawn (or thumbs), the dog can't open the door. But his moral support gives me the gall to keep trying.

"Something's blocking the door. We can work with this." Using the knobby, loose stones in the tunnel, I leverage myself at a weird angle, slip an arm through a small gap, and fish for whatever's on top of me, wrenching it forward. After a few tries, I'm free and flop onto the floor of the ranger station. It was a leg of our couch.

"Hey, Marty." I throw my arms around the dog and hug him tight. He licks my hand and nuzzles in, slobbering all over my already-ruined dress and ripped-up sweatshirt. "You were right, I should've never worn heels." The exasperated puppy gives his version of *I told you so* in the form of a paw lick and sassy grumble, tail thumping loudly.

"How'd you get in here? I left you at Pop's. You're supposed to be with Kevin," I ask, looking around the station.

"Oh, no." My petting halts as I take in the room. It looks like someone robbed the place. I don't know why anybody would; we have nothing valuable, unless moth-ridden squirrel pelts count.

Ripped-up, broken floorboards litter the room, exposing the original tunnel door underneath. The renovated floor covered it before. That's why I never noticed it. Someone threw the couch back over the door to block it again.

"What happened?" Getting up, I turn on the lights and analyze every inch of the space, trying to figure out what exactly went down. "It's no robbery," I tell the dog. Nothing is missing. Not even the squirrel pelts.

A spare pair of work boots is on the floor with the rest of our supply closet. I lace them up, put on a pair of gloves, and continue searching through the debris.

Crouching, I find a knit hat with a bright orange puffball underneath my busted computer. "This is Eli's," I whisper, noting a large smear of blood, almost hidden in the black yarn. "A fight, maybe? Eli, what the hell did you get yourself into?" Marty's ears perk up when he hears "Eli." His tail wags.

There's no way this anarchy would be for a fight between only him and her. He is so much bigger… I look at my fallen, ancient computer like an old comrade who's been in the trenches with me. A fist-sized impact at the center of the screen shatters the glass.

Opening the creaky station door, Marty and I walk into the night, a growing wind ramping up around us. The sky is dark, but the parking lot glows with hayride décor.

"Zach!" I scream at the man standing with a clipboard, facing the river.

He spins around, surprised. "Uh, hey, Maudy. How'd you get back there?" He jogs towards us but stops at the ranger station door. "Whoa, what happened to you? What happened in here?" He scrunches his face like he smells something rotten, stepping back.

"Has anybody come in or out? Did you hear anything? There was a fight. Eli's been captured."

"What?" His eyes bug. After giving him a second to take everything in, I show him the door in the floor.

"Did the doctor make it out here?" I ask.

"Yes, they just got Wesley out a second ago. Kelly drove him to the hospital. I haven't seen anyone else come in. Marty came running on his own." He bends over to pet the dog. "He ran across the bridge and came right to me." He inspects the room, awestruck. "I thought he just escaped again, so I put him here for safekeeping. That was a while ago, and it didn't look like this…"

Probing the chaos all over the floor, I find my walkie-talkie and make sure Zach has his. I search the station for a flashlight brighter than this small lantern.

"Help me cover this up." We pile the heaviest things we can find on top of the tunnel door. Desks, the couch, and boxes of Zach's teaching stuff, everything. Nobody else is using it tonight.

With the door as secure as can be, the three of us step outside, double-checking to make sure the ranger station door locks behind us.

At one side of the parking lot is the hayride entrance, toward the campground. The other is our main trailhead.

"Which way did they go?" I spit, urgency seeping out in fidgets and nervous tapping. The dog looks up at me and barks. "Right." I pull up his collar tracker app and find the red, blinking light. "Hayride it is," I sigh. Marty pulls me towards the campground with his nose to the ground. I see the trail he's following. Small drips of blood pull us down the hayride path.

* * *

Cursed music chimes through the blustery, wet air. Fog machines and strobe lights make it hard to see. Motion-triggered scares activate as Marty and I run down the path, nervous and flinching at every little noise. Marty's nose is right on Eli's blood trail, his protector mode taking over. A low, rumbly growl broods in his throat.

"Eli? Where are you?" I cry, searching through bushes and behind trees. I can't let him die. "Where are you?" I shout over the intensifying music blaring from speakers hidden in the canopy. Marty pulls me forward, keeping me focused.

The dog's nose is to the ground, and his throat rumbles like thunder rolling in off the lake. As we go deeper and deeper into the woods, my calls for Eli combat the haunting music echoing through the trees, punctuated by the warning caws of Bill and Ted. They followed us out here. As we go, we trigger pressure plates and motion sensors, setting off scarecrows, scream machines, and ghosts that swing overhead, swooping down at us.

This damned hayride. Why did it have to be a freaking haunted hayride full of freaking monsters?

Marty lurches forward, out of nowhere, pulling me off balance. My heart leaps with him, leaving the rest of me to stumble behind.

"Jeez," I gasp, clutching his leash tight, running after him. He zips forward to a dark patch on the trail, about the size of a dinner plate, and immediately sticks his nose in it, sniffing wildly. His growl subsides, replaced with a high-pitched whine.

"What is it, bud?" I ask, bending over to inspect it myself. I dip my finger tentatively in the thick substance and squish it with my thumb. I answer my own question. It's blood.

Pausing, I peer ahead into the darkness, the trees closing in, swallowing the forest whole. We're at the same fork in the road, leading to the clearing where we tried to trap Wesley. Marty looks back at me, determined. He's ready.

The pathway twists and turns, but I follow it closely, knowing these trails like the back of my hand. Marty confirms the route with his nose. The posters of Eli and his friends still cling to the maple trees. Minutes later, a faint light and low, mechanical grumble bubble up from the darkness.

We follow the noise. The lights become blinding. On top of the hayride's blaring music, my senses overload.

The trees are so dense they might as well be brick walls. Marty squints, hunkered low to the ground, inching slowly, unsure of what's to come.

Bright, white light drowns the round clearing, pointing towards the center. On this path less trodden, we follow two sets of footprints on either side of long, drag marks in the mud. One of them has already left—one of the shoe prints has an exit track, too.

Tied to a massive oak tree, basking in the light, is a person, their arms and legs spread out and tied around a tree. Their head lolls, slumped on one shoulder, and is covered in a paper grocery bag. Marty growls, crouching even lower to the ground.

We inch closer, hoping both of our guts are wrong. It can't be him. Desperately pleading with any god that will listen, I beg that it isn't Eli. Getting closer, and closer, I see…*a wooden stump? What is that?* I approach a hunk of wood on the ground. It's a knife block. *My* knife block, specifically. From my kitchen.

I turn in a slow circle, boots squelching in the wet earth. The hairs on the back of my neck prickle. Trees press in tight around the clearing, branches clawing at me. Nothing moves, just the sound of my breathing and the haunted music.

Strobe lights pulse from off in the distance, along the designated hayride path, catching a glint of unpacked tubs and metal props stacked off to the side. Mannequins, fake chains, deflated creatures, and all kinds of other props spill out of massive containers like a demonic garage sale. This is where we told the crew to set up, to use as their headquarters.

I keep moving, slowly approaching the tied-up person. I recognize the outfit and freckly, calloused hands. It is Eli. A twisting trickle of blood seeps from him down the rough bark of the tree.

"Eli!" I gasp, immediately closing the distance between us.

"Stop!" A screeching voice from off in the distance panics.

I listen, slowly turning around. The voice resonates from all directions. All I see is the harsh, white glow.

"Cut it out," I bellow, faking confidence. "Come out! This is ridiculous."

"I wish I could," the voice cries.

I stay silent, trying to tune out the hayride music, the lights, the voice, to focus on Eli. I feel like I'm on a rollercoaster, mind churning, unable to stop and think. *I need to get him out of here. He can't die. I can't let him die.*

The voice continues, but a little slower, sad even. "I have to do this. I'll be done for if I don't. It's you or me."

"Danni, let us go!" I shout as loud as I can. "Eli, wake up! We have to get out of here!"

A sharp ringing blasts my forehead, knocking me to my knees. With another arresting blow, I hit the wet forest floor, skin tightening against

the cold leaves. And then nothing.
Just nothing.

Chapter Twenty-Two

Blinking bleary eyes, I come to, squinting at the harsh floodlights. *Woosh, woosh, woosh,* blood pounds in my right ear, echoing my heartbeat. I'm okay.

I move to touch my temple, trying to assess damage, but my wrists are bound with duct tape in front of me. Raising both fists to my head, I gingerly feel around.

"Ah!" I suck through my teeth, wincing. There is no blood, but a lump the size of a golf ball is giving unicorn horn.

Sitting on a flimsy camping chair, I wrench my legs to run, but they're duct-taped to the chair itself. I'm in the same place as I was when I got knocked out, right in front of Eli, who still slumps over, tied to the tree.

My walkie-talkie is gone, my phone is gone, my flashlight is gone, Marty is gone. It's just me and unconscious Eli.

The knife block is on the ground next to me. I see the navy-blue handles and silvery, steel blades. Eli bought them for me for my birthday a couple of years ago. He insisted that every kitchen needs a good set of knives. *He might be regretting that right about now.*

Erratic sobs join the tinkly, eerie music that roars on. It's all too much.

The paper bag covering Eli's face falls off as he slowly wakes up, shaking his head. He's got a unicorn horn, too.

"Eli, Eli!" I shout over the crazed music and the blood pounding in my ears.

"Maudy?" he asks, disoriented. "Maudy, what's happening?" Confusion subsides as panic sets in. I see it take over his face.

"You're strapped to a tree out in the woods. We're not far off the hayride track. You're going to be okay; hang on. Don't freak out." I grab one of the knives in both of my bound hands and scoot the chair closer to him.

Gripping the knife in clenched, taped fists, I crudely stab at my restraints. It sticks to the tape.

"I don't feel so good," he admits, eyelids fluttering. I'm losing him again; his head starts drooping, and his mouth hangs open.

"Just hang on a minute, I've got you," I beg, trying to hold his attention.

"Stop this, Danni!" I shout, crying into the black void surrounding us. She's watching. I feel her eyes on me. "You're going to kill him!"

Stepping from the shadows, a woman appears. A woman whom I stupidly let sleep on my couch. "I know," she screams. She's been crying; her blotchy, swollen face illuminates as she walks into the flickering white light. "That's the point!"

"Let us go, Danni," Eli sputters, half-conscious.

"Please," I beg, twisting my wrists. "We know you killed Paige."

"Let me go." Eli tries to stay with me, to stay present, but the blood loss gets the better of him. He vomits, some of it flinging onto my once emerald green, now brownish-black dress.

She approaches sheepishly, looking haggard, tears streaming down her face, and pulls her hair back into a bun. She puts on a pair of ski gloves like a doctor preparing for surgery. Grabbing two knives from the wooden block, she advances. I try to fight back, but she plucks the knife I stole out of my taped fists. She rubs the hilts of the other knives over my skin, getting my DNA all over them.

I squirm, trying to keep her away. My elbow knocks one of the knife blades into her palm, slicing through her glove, so at least that's something. Her blood drips onto the leaf-littered ground, getting lost in the understory.

"Like I said, it's either you or me," she snivels between sobs. "I…I have Charlie to think about. It can't be me." She points at me with the tip of a blade inches from my face. "I knew you'd follow him here."

She's crying even harder, mascara running down her face like oxbow rivers. "I can't let you walk out of here. They'll take Charlie away from me. They threatened him!" She's overwhelmed and nervous, eyes darting as if someone is sneaking up behind her.

She takes one of the knives and staggers to Eli. Raising it above her head, she hovers, trembling.

"Ah!" she screams in frustration, wiping away tears with the back of her hand.

She can't do it. She doesn't want to do it.

"Danni, let me help you!" I plead. "I can help you! You don't want to do this!" I see nicks all over Eli's body; his shirt and pants are tattered. *She must've threatened him with these knives to get him into the tunnel with her.*

"Danni, stop! This is ridiculous!" I shout over the music, twisting to look her in the eye. "At least turn off the music so we can talk!" She thinks for a second and takes a small remote out of her pocket. Clicking a button, the music softens.

The rest of the forest life starts filtering into my ears, over top of a low growl I'd recognize anywhere. Marty. He's watching from the tree line.

"Why are you doing this?" Eli asks somberly. He's so pale, his eyes are barely able to open. "Why Paige? Why me?"

"I had to, Eli. Just drop it," she sputters. Her face streaks with tears, pooling along her jaw.

"You don't have to do anything," I retort. "Let us go, and we'll figure all this out. I promise."

"No, I'm sorry. That's not happening. Neither of you is walking out of here. I have to. I'm sorry. I don't have a choice." She buries a knife into the tree, catching the fabric of his sleeve.

"Argh!" he screams, life coming back into him like a lightning bolt. The blade must've caught his forearm. He gulps for air, frantic. "Maudy, help me," he chokes.

Danni stifles another sob.

"You'll be okay!" I shout back. "It's the debt, right?" I ask her, keeping one eye on Eli. "You're in a mountain of debt right now. I found the check Paige wrote you in your purse; she lent you thirty grand. Could you not pay her back or something? You were worried she'd come after you, and you couldn't pay it back."

"Hah," she exhales. "Paige was one of the nicest people I've ever met. She wouldn't have cared if I couldn't pay her back. I can't believe I killed her…"

This realization hits Danni.

"The thirty-k wasn't nearly enough. I need to do this, okay?" She pulls another knife from the block and walks with purpose back to Eli. Without flinching this time, she slices right through his hand, pinning him to the tree.

"Oh, my god! Eli!" I scream, gasping at the blood running off the blade's hilt. I wait for him to scream a scream that'll ruin me. But it doesn't come.

He twitches but doesn't stir much. He's fading.

I can't bear seeing him like this. "Eli!" I shout. No response. "Danni, you have to stop." I turn to her with urgency, completely desperate.

"I'm sorry I hurt you," he whimpers after a minute of excruciating silence, with everything he can muster. "We can try again."

He glances at me as he talks to her. I've never seen such pure sadness.

"Are you *serious* right now, Elliott Nett?" Danni scoffs. "You think I'll let you come crawling back after what you said?"

Those words aren't for you, Danni.

"What the hell could've happened between you two that was bad enough to cause this?" I interject, picking at the tape on my wrists.

Eli grimaces, eyes closed. Whether it's from the knife in his hand or from Danni, I'm not sure.

"He's not what's causing this, but it does make it a little easier, not gonna lie." She pauses, wiping her nose. "Do you want to tell her or should I?" Danni's hands are on her hips, a knife in each one.

"He can barely speak, Danni. Look at him," I snap. Eli's eyelids flutter, his pale, freckled skin even more so.

"Maudy," he whispers, just barely. "Danni used me as bait to get to you."

He might as well have stabbed me with one of those knives. *Me? This is because of me?*

"You figured it out." She turns to me. "I knew you'd follow him. Now that I have you," she points to me with the tip of a blade, "they'll let me go. They'll let my brother rest." She spits on the ground, practically foaming at the mouth. "You didn't answer, Eli. Are you going to tell her, or am I?"

While she's distracted, I keep picking at the duct tape on my wrists. I'm about halfway through it. If I could just manage the rest of the way...

Eli's head lolls onto a shoulder, kept upright only by Danni's restraints.

"Fine, you won't say it? I will." She pivots to me. I stop picking, trying to cover up my escape attempt. "Eli admitted in his journal that he's using me. That he doesn't love me; he needed a rebound to get over you."

"I didn't say 'rebound,'" he sputters slowly, voice wobbly. "I said my heart was somewhere else. And that it'll stay somewhere else." His eyes remain closed, almost passive. "And I'm not afraid to admit that anymore."

I do everything I can to not wilt on the spot. A moment passes, and I bring myself to deal with more pressing matters (knives in Eli).

"Danni, nobody with half a brain cell will think I killed Eli out here like this. What are you going for? A murder suicide pact? They'll know something's off. They'll find you. You're bleeding. They'll find your blood. It won't matter that you're using my knives. The police know you were sleeping on my couch." I try to reason with her.

She pauses, shaking her head.

"You said 'they'll leave you alone.' Who is 'they'?" I ask, pressing harder. "You said something about Charlie. Is he in danger?"

"Just shut up! I can't talk about it." She digs her nails into Eli's shoulder, holding him up. Her other hand grips another knife, slowly raising it, like pulling an arrow in a bowstring. She waffles again, unable to plunge it into him, and throws this one wide, missing the tree entirely and launching into the muddy understory.

Eli doesn't flinch, doesn't open his eyes. He just hangs there, propped up against the tree, like a scarecrow on a pole.

She wipes snot from her nose. I snap the last bit of duct tape trapping my wrists, but keep my hands close together so it looks like they're still bound.

"Where did that go?" she mumbles, going to retrieve the lost knife. I take the opportunity to start unwrapping the tape binding my legs.

The smooth metal of the camping chair makes the tape easy to remove, peeling away cleanly. *I'm almost free... Just a few more good rips...*

"He got into trouble… My brother had a gambling and drug problem," she reveals as she hunts for the knife. "When he died, he owed a ton of money to some scary people." She wipes her eyes.

"Debt you inherited…" I utter, recalling her sarcastic comment that Charlie wasn't the only thing her brother's death left her with.

"I guess you could put it that way."

"This is a job," I state flatly. "You're a hired gun." At that moment, she finds the steak knife and immediately punctures Eli's side with it.

"Groh." A guttural grunt comes from Eli, his breath forced out of him from the blow. "I—I," he gasps. "Maudy," he whispers.

"Please shut up," Danni whines.

Every muscle in my body contracts, begging to get to her, craving to protect him. The rhythmic whooshing in my right ear quickens. Twisting my legs, ever so slightly, the duct tape breaks.

I'm free.

"Hired implies payment," she notes. "But yeah, I guess. For Paige, anyway. You two weren't planned. Things went sideways, and they told me to 'clean it up.'" Her anger morphs again back into anxiety and sorrow, the river of tears flowing again. "Same with Wes."

I stand up to face her, grab the knife on the ground at my feet, and charge her. She darts out of the way but gets tangled in my legs, knocking us both to the ground.

"Rah!" she cries, falling onto her back. Marty leaps into action from the shadows, chomping hard onto her wrist as I fling my weight on top of her. "Get off me!"

Tag teaming with Marty, we pin her down as best we can. I bash the heel of my work boot into her knee and am met with a shriek so loud, *so potent*, that I'm sure she's not going anywhere. Her kneecap is in a thousand little pieces.

"Good boy! I'm so glad you're okay." I hug Marty close, stroking his fuzzy head, nuzzling my face into his fur. "Thank you, bud," I whisper into his ear.

Kissing his forehead, I dash over to Eli and cut his restraints. He falls into a heap on the ground, unconscious.

"C'mon, Eli. You'll be okay." I press my cheek to his nose, listening for his breathing. With a hand on his chest, I feel his heartbeat, and the warmth of his shallow breath on my face. I straighten his back and lay him flat.

"Thank god," I whisper, squeezing his hand. "I don't know what I'd do if you were gone." With tourniquets in place, his bleeding slows, and I get up.

"Come back here!" Danni sobs as I leave Eli's side in search of my things. Marty stands watch over her, a threatening growl ripping from his throat. Every tooth in that dog's mouth is visible, pointed right at her face like a loaded gun.

"Zach! Zach, this is Maudy. Come in, Zach," I scream into the walkie-talkie once I find it in a pile of Danni's things stashed in a nearby bush.

"Copy," he replies.

"We need help, Zach. We're right off that left bend back behind the campground, just off the hayride route. You know, near that owl we rescued last year? The natural clearing." I fill him in on our location, a couple of miles deep in the woods.

I return to Eli, checking his wounds and monitoring vitals. "You're going to be okay, bud. A little Swiss cheesy, but okay. I promise. You hear me, Eli? You're going to be okay. Stay with me. Please, stay with me."

He groans, which I take as a binding blood oath, agreeing to stick around a little longer.

A sharp, low bark booms from Marty, followed by a growl so menacing it startles me. Danni tries to maneuver onto her stomach to army crawl, limp leg dragging behind her. The dog stations himself right at her head, glancing at me, as she tries to escape.

"Stop, Danni. Don't make me break the other kneecap."

She flops back down, defeated. It's over. We all know it.

"Why the costume swap?" I ask. Why plant the boot covers in the dumpster?"

"It's not like I'm a professional or anything!" Her tears still flow. "I just needed to throw everyone off. I couldn't get caught... Charlie has nobody else! I thought the costume swap would help me look like the *victim*. I thought Eli or Wesley would mention it in their statements to the police, but nobody did. So, the boot covers got planted to nudge that along once I felt Kelly closing in on me. They were meant to be found."

"Okay..." I reply, unsure what else to say. "But pills *and* insulin injections? Seems like overkill." *Oof, literally.*

"I—I don't have weapons just lying around! I used what I had," she sobs. "Charlie...poor Charlie has diabetes. He's gone through so much! I had to learn about blood sugar over the last couple of months. I had his insulin. But that'd be so obvious. I couldn't get caught!" she screams. "I can't get caught! They're going to come after Charlie!" She's inconsolable, sobbing into the muddy forest floor.

Danni did mention Charlie taking his medicine at my house after they showered. And all those sugary candies in his backpack...they're for blood sugar regulation. That little handheld device in Pop's before he ate was a monitor, not a video game. Of course, he has diabetes.

"We're going to try to help you." I try to reach her through her cries.

"How many diabetics are in town? Not a lot," she continues crying. "But Paige's pills take a long time to work. What if she called 911 or something? That'd ruin everything!" She pounds her hands on the ground.

"The sleeping pills masked the insulin," I interject. "Which is what you hoped for."

"I'm sorry! I just needed to do it!" she wails. "I hid the pills in Eli's migraine bottle. I thought maybe they'd blame him if the police found them. I don't know."

She's out of breath and starting to calm down.

"You didn't have pills for Wesley. The police took them after Eli got sick," I posit. "The toxicology report said that Paige had no other foreign substances in her system. They thought the sleeping pills messed with her blood sugar, not that she got injected with extra insulin."

"Yeah, they didn't do a full autopsy at first, or else they'd probably see a needle prick," Danni admits in between sobs. "I got lucky," she blubbers.

"That's why your blood work wasn't all whacked out." I look over to Eli. "You didn't get injected; you only took the sleeping pills."

Danni's floodgates open, relieved to have this off her chest, but petrified more than anything. She's crying and wipes her face on her sleeve.

"Were you the one who locked everyone in the party? Why the hell would that help anything? Also, *how?*"

"When you and Kelly told me your plan for the night, I knew things wouldn't be good for me." Her breathing starts to slow as she regains control. "Wesley was onto me; he's been weird all week. I couldn't have loose ends...they told me I couldn't have loose ends. I injected him when he got to the party, then made sure he left on the hayride to die *away* from me. I stayed behind and triggered the alarm system, so everyone would think I was locked in the house. I wouldn't have the opportunity to kill him. It was an alibi."

"But we saw you in the parking lot..." I remember.

"Yeah. I snuck out to make sure things went as planned. I didn't expect to see you two; that blew my cover. And when I heard you made it into the house through the tunnels, I knew I had to fish you out. I couldn't have loose ends..."

"Danni, it's over. Who is forcing you to do this? Who did your brother owe?" I'm exhausted. With the immediate threat gone, my adrenaline spike drains, leaving a gnarly headache in its wake.

CHAPTER TWENTY-TWO

She doesn't respond, burying her head in her sleeve, crying.

"All three of us need medical attention, like now," I continue. "Let's just go. We can figure out the debt, and whoever ordered you to do all this. Kelly can help."

Panic swells her sadness like whitecaps on the lake and recedes into defeat. She looks around, not seeing an alternative. Her mind starts to clear.

Without further struggle, Zach and Kelly arrive on our four-wheeler, a state police car following closely behind. I crawl over to Eli as Kelly cuffs Danni.

He's okay. That's what matters.

Chapter Twenty-Three

With bags under my eyes the size of suitcases, a concussed brain, and hands that look like raw meat, I pry myself out of bed and stretch. Between the hit in the head and running through tunnels all over this godforsaken town, I don't think I've ever felt this sore. This is worse than getting thrown off the dune. *This is what I get for idolizing Buffy and Veronica, fictional girls who don't need a chiropractor.*

I can't help but groan as I roll my shoulders and twist my hips, trying to muster up enough energy and courage to walk down the stairs. "I need a coffee pot up here," I mutter, wincing at my stiff knees as I clamber down like Frankenstein's monster.

Too achy to tiptoe through my living room, Eli stirs from the depths of my sunken couch. He was terrified to go home to an empty house. Paige is dead, Wesley is still in the hospital, and Danni is in jail.

"Morning, well, evening," I whisper from the kitchen over the comforting bubbling of the Mr. Coffee. The pile of blankets garbles something unintelligible, and Marty's fuzzy snout pops up near his feet, Gumbo's pointy ears next to him. "Hey there, gentlemen. Coffee?"

"Happen to have a morphine drip?" Eli counters. "I should've stayed in the hospital." Thankfully, all of the knife wounds that Danni inflicted were treatable. He lost a lot of blood and cut nerves in his hand, but Danni didn't hit any major organs. It was mid-morning by the time we got home. We've both been asleep all day.

I thought I looked like Frankenstein's monster; poor guy has stitches running all over his body.

I place a full cup on the coffee table and sit near his feet, swooshing the animals to move over. "Are you ready?" I ask, somberly. Gumbo walks to the other side of the couch, settling on Eli's lap.

"As ready as I'll ever be," he groans. "It feels like a dream; I'm not even sure what happened."

"Your ex-girlfriend almost killed us."

"Oh, right. That," he grumbles, pressing his good palm to his forehead. "I'm glad you're okay." He softens.

"Back at ya." I smile. "Can I get you anything? Are you going to be able to get over to the station?" I look at the clock on my bookshelf. "We need to leave in half an hour."

Kelly said our statements could wait until we got some rest. Eli needed medical attention right away after we were found. She's been processing Danni.

"Yeah, I'll be alright." He sits up, blinking away sleep.

"Hey, I've been wondering something," I say. "Who was with Danni in the ranger station? She couldn't have done all that damage herself, and I saw two sets of footprints in the mud out in the woods."

"I don't know. A guy was waiting for us when Danni and I came through the tunnel. He jumped me."

"Any idea who that was?"

"No, he had a ski mask on. Someone tall, but that's all I noticed."

Right on time, we walk into the police station. Kelly is waiting. Her phone sits out, a voice recording app pulled up, ready to document our statements.

She looks worse for wear.

"Hey, you two." She regards us from over a form she's filling out with an empty smile. "Take a seat. Thanks for coming."

We smile back and do as we're told. Grimacing, Eli leans back into the rigid metal chair. I take off my coat and hand it to him to use as a cushion.

"How's the hand, Eli? You going to be able to cook with that thing?" she asks, concerned.

"Should be," he replies, wiggling his fingers. "They don't think the nerve damage is permanent, but I need to take it easy for a while."

"Good. You deserve to take it easy." She smiles.

"We're happy to tell you everything, Kell," I offer. "I think we'd both like a little info, too. There are still a few open questions." Eli and I look at one another.

"Sure. This is as good as done already. Danni confessed to assassinating Paige and admitted to injecting Wesley." She points to Eli, "Not to mention all the stuff in the woods last night. Yeesh.

"And I want to thank you both before we dive in. The Sheriff was happy that we made the arrest. It redeemed me. He wasn't thrilled to hear how we went about it, but it's water under the bridge."

"I'm glad it worked out," I reply with a twinge of sarcasm. *I wish it didn't involve Eli getting stabbed, running through underground tunnels, and Wesley seizing, but I guess beggars can't be choosers.*

"Okay. Let's go through everything," Kelly starts, hitting *record*.

Eli and I launch into what happened while Kelly stabilized Wesley, stranded in the woods. I tell her about the secret passageways, the basement office, everything. Eli adds his perspective, recounting how Danni used the tunnel from the ranger station to get back into the basement office. She threatened him and stabbed him a couple of times, so he followed her back through the tunnel. Another person in a mask was waiting for them, and Marty, too. They got into a fight. Eli told Kelly that he didn't know who it was, but that the man was tall. Eli got knocked out and dragged to where I found him.

Kelly scribbles feverishly as we talk, especially once we get to the part about the fiasco where she tied us up and stole my kitchen knives. It all checks out with Danni's confession.

"So, she was in debt?" Eli asks. "She asked me for money about a month ago, but I didn't have much to give her. Pop's does okay, but we're not exactly rolling in dough. At least not that kind of dough," he chuckles. *His sense of humor is coming back! Good. Well, no, it's not good, but I'm glad he's feeling better.*

"That's right," Kelly confirms. "When Danni's brother died, he owed a ton of money to some pretty nasty people. Like *a lot* of money. Whatever you're thinking, double it." Kelly shakes her head. "She borrowed from Paige, which gave her a couple of extra weeks to get the rest, but she wasn't even close."

"Jeez," I say, leaning in. "She took this as a job?"

"Yep," she replies. "Danni told us that someone was blackmailing her to kill Paige. They were starting to threaten Charlie. That's part of the reason she was moving to a new apartment, and Charlie's been staying with friends each night. Danni was worried about him."

I think back to Charlie's drawings, showing him chased by swirly, dark monsters, and the note in his backpack. *Poor kid, getting dragged into this.*

"This is terrible." Eli runs his hands through his hair. "I wish she had said something," he mutters more to himself than to us. I put a hand on his arm and give it a gentle squeeze.

"Who are these guys?" I ask. "Did she tell you who's doing this? Leonard's got the political motive. Who else has a reason?"

"She refuses to say," Kelly replies. "We're still working on her; hopefully, she'll tell us more after she calms down. In the meantime, we sent Charlie to live with extended family in Grand Rapids. An officer is driving him down right now. He'll be safe there. Danni's brother never really left the area. I'm thinking whoever it is, they can't live too far."

"That's comforting." I throw my hands in the air.

Eli hangs his head. This must be a tough *and super weird* pill to swallow.

"Did she tell you about the costume swap?" I ask.

"Yes, she said it was to throw us off. Why? Did she say anything different to you?" She starts taking notes again.

"No, she said that to us, too. She was the one who asked Paige to switch. The boot covers were meant to help you realize they swapped, to make it look like Danni was supposed to be the victim, not Paige. She thought one of these guys"—I point to Eli—"would've mentioned the swap in their statements. She wanted there to be no way she could've been the killer. I fell for her plan," I lament.

"You also solved everything before I did. So don't get too down on yourself," Kelly admits.

"If you saw the tunnels and that gangster office, you would've been ten steps ahead of me," I offer.

Her shoulders relax as she stares into the distance, deep in thought.

"Hey, there's one thing I still don't get," Eli adds. "Why'd she try to poison me? I get why she wanted me dead last night, after we were sort of onto her, to lure Maudy into the park. But why the sleeping pills on Friday night?"

"That, my friend, was simply an extremely unfortunate accident. She hid the pills in your prescription bottle. You just took the wrong ones." She cringes a little. "The state troopers searched the house for drugs when we brought the warrant. They inventoried everyone's prescriptions. Eli's was legit; we confirmed with his doctor. The pills looked almost indistinguishable, and the sloppy state troopers didn't notice two different pills in the bottle." She rolls her eyes. "I knew they ripped through everything too fast. No tact."

"When you got a headache that night, you took them by accident." I piece together. "The dose wasn't enough to hurt you too badly."

"Exactly," Kelly adds. "They knocked you out and made you sick, but nothing the doctors couldn't pump out of your system. Paige was killed by hypoglycemia, from too much insulin. That's what caused Wesley's seizure, too. The sleeping pills made it a gentler exit for Paige. Since we confiscated them after your little incident," she points to him with her pen, "Danni didn't have any more to help Wesley along. That's why his seizure was so bad."

"And before the stabbing," Eli replies, "I called it off with her. I made her even angrier." He exhales, coughing a bit.

"She said she was after me, not you." I try to reassure him. "You were just standing in her way."

Kelly closes her notebook. "That about wraps it up. Anything else you two want to know or need to tell me?"

"What's going to happen to her?" I ask. "Don't get me wrong, she should be in jail for what she did. But someone else forced her hand..." My morals waffle.

"I hope she tells us who the real bad guys are here," Kelly replies. "I think she needs support and stability more than anything. If she gives us names, and those names lead to convictions, I bet we can get her inpatient psychiatric treatment for a while and reduced prison sentencing. Plus, witness protection. If not, though, she's looking at life in prison. She assassinated a public figure," she replies. "And has three additional attempt charges."

"Wow," Eli recoils.

"Kelly, just an FYI, I think whoever is pulling the strings also sabotaged my campaign. The phone in that crazy basement office placed my attack ads. They're using the name Tiller Brazas. Could be helpful for your investigation," I add.

"Thanks, that is," she nods, jotting that down. "I'll follow up with you on that soon. After Danni's paperwork gets squared away."

"Good. I don't care if it makes me pull all of my hair out, I'm figuring out who Tiller Brazas is."

"Ha," Kelly chuckles. "Well, let's hope it doesn't come to that because I'll be right there with you."

As she wraps up her notes, Eli and I take one another in, filled with sadness, comfort, and appreciation. If I were to go through that hell with anyone, I'm glad it's him.

"Other than that," Eli says, glancing at me, a sheen starting to sparkle on his soft green eyes, "I think we're okay."

"We'll keep working on it, I promise," Kelly responds. "I'm going to need you two to testify in court, once this goes to trial. Right now, we're linking up with the IRS to try to follow the money Danni borrowed from Paige. It's the Al Capone trick. You know, after all the horrible things he did, the IRS ultimately brought him down in the end."

The three of us sit in silence before another officer calls Kelly over to their desk. "You two stay here as long as you like, but I gotta get back to it." She comes over to our side of the table and hugs us both. "Thanks again for your help. Glad you goobers are okay," she whispers to us. "And for what it's worth, Eli, I'm glad you're not a murderer."

Eli looks right at me, so profoundly, from over her shoulder as the two of them hug. "I'm glad, too."

Chapter Twenty-Four

The scabs on my hands catch on my soft, knit sweater dress as I pull it over my head, examining myself in the mirror.

"What do you think, Marty? Good enough for a Councilwoman? If they don't all have pitchforks and torches ready to run me out of town, that is." I sigh, tugging my sleeves down to hide the red, tender skin. I fluff my curly hair a little bigger, coaxing it in front of my forehead to cover the purple and blue mountain protruding from it. The dog comes over and sits at my feet, politely asking for ear scratches. I oblige.

Now that Gumbo is back with his rightful owner, Marty's been a calm, sweet little guy, catching up on much-needed sleep. I guess kitten-sitting and catching a killer is exhausting work for a middle-aged pup.

Grabbing my backpack, I leave the dog to catch some Z's and embrace the frigid November chill for the first time today.

Futilely trying to keep my hair in order in the face of a sharp wind coming off the water, I turn onto Main Street and gather the confidence to stride towards the library like I own the place. *Public speaking? No problem! Cuts and bruises all over my head? Nobody will notice.*

"Jeremy, what are you doing here?" I shout from a couple of storefronts over. *What's he still doing in town?*

Hunching over his car's passenger door, he leans in the window. Startled, he jumps, and for a split second resembles a kid caught with his hand in the cookie jar before regaining composure.

"Oh, I just came in for a meeting," he stammers. He's lying. I walk up to him and the car. None other than Charlotte Roth steps out, wrapping a scarf tightly around her neck as she does.

"Hello, Maude. Are you ready for the debate?" she sneers, eyeing me up and down. "Is that what you're wearing? How 'down-to-earth.' You know a little concealer would go a long way."

Charlotte sees me eyeing Jeremy, trying to understand what's happening here.

"Oh, you didn't know?" She smiles a slow, creeping smile like poison ivy vines. "Jeremy's been helping Colin's campaign. He's been such a nice, dedicated civil servant. Look." She points to his car's back seat.

"Is this true?" I ask him earnestly, peering into the car window. A bunch of my signs litter his back seat. He doesn't say anything. *Anna was right about him.*

Maybe a third of the signs are mine, thrown in haphazardly with dirt still on the metal spikes, ripped from the ground. The rest are Colin's, in neat stacks straight from the printer.

"I'll leave you two to talk. See you inside!" She trills, strutting her high heels into the library, heading upstairs to the community center.

Fuming, I check my phone. Fifteen minutes until it starts. Seeing a notification, I pull up Channel Seven's most recent polling numbers. Colin is still leading, but just barely: forty-seven to fifty-three percent. I'm back on the rise, even if only a little.

"What the hell, Jeremy! Care to explain? Was it you the whole time? Egging? The toilet paper? Those heinous ads?" I'm working myself up, but intermittently fake a smile as debate watchers file in the door next to us. I feel like I'm wearing both the comedy and tragedy masks simultaneously. *Or maybe Jekyll and Hyde.*

"Look, can we not talk about this now? And for the record, no, I didn't place the ads." His tone is flat, and his eyes are blank. No compassion or remorse. Maybe a hint of embarrassment for getting caught, though.

"But you did rip out my signs? You lied about printing more? You egged my house? What are you, twelve?"

"Get off your high horse, Maudy." He crosses his arms. He's a foot taller than me and stares me down like a patronizing father. "You don't know what you're stepping into."

For a moment, I feel him soften. Like I'm getting a glimpse into something deeper, more him. He's warning me.

"Why would you do this?" I ask. "I thought you hated Charlotte." I shake my head, tears coming whether or not I want them.

He turns away as Eli and Peyton walk up, about to head into the debate, like everyone else. "Believe me, you don't want to get involved," he states through a plastic smile.

"You got this, Maudy!" Another passerby cheers me on, giving me a thumbs up, blissfully unaware of what's happening.

"You okay, girl?" Peyton stops and asks, warily eyeing us both, immediately picking up on the weird energy.

"I'm fine, you guys go. I'll be there in a sec." They take a few steps to enter the building, but I see them slyly watching over me from the window.

"You know what? I'm done putting effort into this conversation. I need to go debate in front of four hundred people. Thanks for this, Jeremy. You made any guilt I felt about dumping you completely disappear."

I storm through the library doors, and up to the second floor, walking straight past Eli and Peyton. If I stop to talk to them, the waterworks will flood, and I actually put effort into my makeup for once. I need to keep it together.

After a couple of deep breaths, I walk through a sea of chairs towards the front of the room. A few people hold out their hands for a high-five, others offer supportive praise, and give much-appreciated words of encouragement. I guess this past weekend's events gave me a little boost in people's confidence in me. *Morbid silver lining, I guess?*

With another deep breath, I take my position behind a podium.

Colin waits behind another, while current Town Council members sit front and center. Jeremy lingers, leering from the back of the room.

Kevin, the outgoing Councilman whose seat one of us will fill, raises his hands, and the spectators hush to a whisper.

"It's time to begin," he declares, smiling warmly and giving the subtlest of nods from underneath his baseball cap. "But first, a brief announcement regarding our district's state Senate race. As you all know, Page Ramos passed away unexpectedly last week. May she rest in peace. We, and the other local jurisdictions, are working to fill her position with a new candidate. Leonard will just have to be patient until another candidate is named. We'll be holding a special election next month to fill that seat since she died so close to Election Day. You will not be voting on it in the regular election tomorrow.

Leonard waves his hands, grumbling something from the front row.

"Now, let's begin." Kevin smiles at me, giving an encouraging wink. He's got my back.

Deep breath. Here we go.

* * *

After the first few questions, the knot in my stomach loosens. Even with Jeremy loudly cheering for Colin (petty, much?), the crowd seems to be on my side. Almost all Stone's Throw voters are in this room. If I can win them over, I have the election.

Kevin throws me softballs; I know he can see that I'm upset. Harder, pressing questions are bound to come. I just hope I don't come off as shaky and spineless as Colin, who can't seem to take a stance on anything, not even issues he touted as his platform.

"Alright, now for audience questions. If you could please raise your hands, I'll call on you one-by-o—"

"Yes, I have a question." Charlotte pounces like a lion stalking its prey. "The state park has fallen into total disarray since Maudy took charge. It's an absolute disaster. Someone was even found dead there not too long ago, and then what happened the other night…well, it's not proper to rehash everything."

Everyone reflects on that; whispers swirl through the room. Heads bob in agreement.

"Was there a question, Charlotte?" Kevin looks down at her over his glasses.

"Of course. Quite simply, how could we trust her to manage our town if she can't even manage *one* property?" She promptly sits down, tucking one ankle behind the other.

The whispers mutate to rumbles as I watch the audience turn on me. Snippets of conversation float up to my podium. Jeremy leans back, smirking, watching my facade crumble. *Is it getting hot in here?*

The rumbles grow, and individual voices break through the noise.

"Yeah, that's true!"

"Oh, right, the dead guy!"

Each is another crushing blow to my head. My concussion pounds, begging me for a dark room and a long nap. The room spins, and my vision tunnels.

Why is it so hot?

I see Eli's bandaged hand waving in the warping mass of people. He's worried; am I worrying him? He mouths to me, '*Are you okay?*' I think I reply, but I'm not sure. *Breathe in. One, two, three, four. Breathe out.*

The voices around me muffle, and my focus scatters.

Hello, panic attack, my old friend.

One, two, three, four. Breathe out. One, two, three, four.

I give myself a minute, no doubt looking like a fool, standing with my eyes closed, breathing heavily.

"Sorry, everyone," I admit. "I'm okay. Just needed a second."

Eli is on his feet, watching me. I see him let out a long breath as he runs his fingers through his hair.

I use both hands to brace myself on the sturdy wood. Kevin looks at me from the moderator's podium. I give him a thumbs up.

"As I'm sure all of you know," I start after a minute of silence. "I was attacked a couple of days ago. I'm left with a nasty concussion, but thankfully nothing worse than that. Just a few scrapes." I hold up my pink and purple hands, covered in glass splinters from insulation and cuts from claustrophobic stone walls.

"I think this shows how dedicated I am to this place. Stone's Throw is my home. I would do anything to protect the State Park and the rest of it. I should be in bed, but I'm here."

Peyton gives a supportive "Woohoo!" through meager applause. I continue.

"It is disgraceful of Charlotte to say the park is falling apart. I have been, and will continue to be, fully transparent. The budget situation is not good. We have been experiencing cuts for years, not just since I joined as Head Park Ranger. If it wasn't for my fantastic staff..." I pick Zach from the many faces in front of me and motion for him to stand. He stands and gives a quick salute. "And without the support of Senator Ramos, the park would've been shut down long ago. We are innovative, we are scrappy, and we know how to stretch a dollar. I think all these traits would serve me well as Councilwoman."

Eli claps loudly, encouraging the rest of the room. They follow suit, thankfully. I soak in the applause, grateful to be back on track. Maybe all isn't lost.

Kevin, as moderator, takes over. "Nobody here thinks what happened is your fault, Maudy," he asserts, glaring at the town in front of him. Not a soul dares to disagree.

The dad of Stone's Throw strikes again. He fills my heart with warm fuzzies and hopefully, at least fifty-one percent of eligible voters' hearts, too. We shall see.

The rest of the debate is a blur, but I stay conscious the whole time and keep panic attacks at bay, so it's a win in my book. When it ends, people mill about. Some linger to offer polite congratulations, to see if I'm okay, to help fold chairs, and to milk the community center for one more free cookie before heading on their way.

"Ready to go?" Eli asks, with most of the room cleared out.

"I think my fifteen minutes of fame are up." I smile at him and pull myself out of a metal folding chair.

"I wouldn't be so sure, Councilwoman." He walks me out the door toward home.

"You think? I don't know. A panic attack wasn't the most strategic move I could've made today," I joke.

"It's in the bag," he says simply, glancing over before returning his gaze straight ahead. "So, what happened? Not the panic attack, the conversation outside. It looked like you and Jeremy had it out. Not that I'm trying to get in your business or anything," he backpedals.

I've bitten his head off more than once for meddling in my love life. He knows better now.

"He and stupid Charlotte pulled up my signs."

"You're kidding? While you two were still together? Wow, that's low."

"Tell me about it. I don't get it. He could've talked to me if he didn't want me to run."

"Yeah…well, he's kind of an ass." He jams his hands in his pockets as we walk up my driveway and into my backyard. I go up to my back patio and unlock the slider. He continues in the grass, wrestling with the gate between our yards.

"Are you going to be okay alone?" he asks.

"I'm heading straight to bed."

"Good. Yeah, same. Sleep tight, Muddy." He shuts the gate behind him, and I walk inside.

Disrobing on my way up to the loft, I throw on an oversized sweatshirt and crawl into bed. As I start drifting to sleep, the whirr of a machine drags me out of it, coming from my backyard. Marty's in bed next to me, also confused by the noise. Getting up and looking out the window, I watch Eli weed whack the gate between our homes.

Chapter Twenty-Five: Two Months Later

"Charlotte, I don't know how many times I need to say this, but we don't have the money to hire a town valet. Four hundred people live here; we could all park on the street at the same time if we wanted to. At most, someone would need to park two blocks away."

I reorder papers angrily, looking around the community center. Without a single member of the public and two of our council members already on holiday, our weekly council meeting is just me, Charlotte, Leonard, and Matthew, who takes notes for the public record. I don't have my usual buffer with the other members; the weasels outnumber me today. Charlotte and Leonard are against anything I suggest, per usual.

We've been going around and around in circles for over an hour. We're not getting anywhere.

"But it's such a nice convenience," she insists. "And would practically pay for itself during the busy season."

"Aren't you always talking about preserving our *charm*? A valet isn't charming. It's showy and unnecessary for a town this size," I insist.

"If I may," Matthew interjects. "Why don't we adjourn and pick up the lingering issues in the new year when we have the full council present? We don't have a quorum anyway, so we cannot legally vote on anything right now. This special meeting was called to be a send-off, more than anything."

In agreement, we pack up our notepads and laptops.

"And on that topic, Councilman Henley, it's been a pleasure working with you over the years," Matthew adds. "I wish you luck in Lansing as our new State Senator. Your term starts in January, yes?"

Leonard tosses a copy of the agenda into his briefcase, which is already packed to the gills. Faded, gold lettering glimmers on a deep green book spine, reflecting the fluorescent lighting as he stuffs everything back in.

"Thank you, Matthew. Hard to believe it's my last council meeting. What's it been, twenty years?" The older man smiles. "Yes, I'm excited to take my work to the state in the new year. Colin will do a great job as my replacement."

Leaving the meeting a little frustrated, I walk into town. Kevin and the others tried their best to mobilize a replacement candidate for Paige in the Senate race, but Leonard won by a landslide in a special election a couple of weeks ago. With him moving to Lansing, Colin is taking over his vacancy on our Town Council. The board appointed him after Leonard won the special state Senate election. I got outvoted. *Shocker.*

Welcoming the frosty December weather, I leave the meeting, trying to check my frustration at the door, and head into town. An elk from a local farm is tied to a bike rack with leather reins, snow falling on their scruffy brown fur as children pet it in the street. I wave to Zach, next to the farmer, giving an impromptu lesson about the gigantic animal's history in our area.

The usual bell that rings upon entering Pop's is swapped with a row of jingle bells, chiming merrily as I walk into the bar for our Friday night euchre game. We're starting earlier than usual; it's the Friday before Christmas, and some of us have things to do before the holiday kicks off.

The first one to arrive, I perch at the shiny, wooden bar to order a drink. Our *Reserved for the Lake Michigan (card) sharks* sign is on our usual booth, waiting for me and my friends.

"Councilwoman Lorso," Kevin greets me. His normal Detroit Tigers baseball cap is replaced with a Santa hat, the white poof flopping in his face. He's even grown out his beard a little bit. It's snow white, like the big man himself.

"Former Councilman Nett," I joke back. "How are you? Happy Holidays."

"You too, kid. I'm doing good. Hang on one second; I have something for you. Don't go anywhere." He turns to face the long row of taps and liquor bottles, mixing some sort of concoction. "Here, try this. You'll love it."

He hands me a mug, the scent of apples and warm spices carrying in the steam.

I take a sip. "This is amazing. What is it?" It tastes like a souped-up version of what we used to drink at tailgates back in college. That was just apple cider and cheap rum. This is much better, but it still evokes that magical feeling of freezing my buns off while drinking at ten o'clock in the morning.

"Hey." Eli walks out of the kitchen, holding a couple of bowls of gumbo, serving it to a group at the other end of the bar.

"Hey, yourself. Merry Christmas." I hide my smile with the rim of my mug as he approaches. "Look what your dad made." I hold it out, offering him a sip.

"Dang, Dad. That's great."

Kevin smiles and returns to bartending, clearly pleased with himself.

"Excited for your family to come for the holidays? When do they get in? Monday?" I ask.

"Yep," Eli replies. "It should be fun. We might try fishing one day if the ice thickens up a bit. What will you be up to?"

"I'm going to spend Christmas morning at Nellie and Emma's with the girls, but otherwise not much."

"That's nice. What did you get Lydia this year?"

"A microscope. She'll love seeing all the little creepy crawlies blown up big."

We pause, enjoying each other's company while he washes pint glasses.

"Hey," he says, lowering his voice. "I assume Kelly called you? To see if you'd testify?" he asks.

"Yep," I confirm. "I talked with her yesterday." I set down the drink and wince.

"Did she ever find out who was threatening Danni?" he asks, pouring himself a pint. "I forgot to ask for an update when I met with her."

"Not yet. And I haven't given up either," I add, taking another sip. "It's like they vanished into thin air. Kelly is still working on it. I don't think the trial will be for a while. Hopefully, we'll figure it out in time."

He frowns. "So wild. I can't believe it. I should've seen signs…"

"Don't beat yourself up," I reassure him.

"Well, anyway, I'm going to need a break from my oddball family," he leans forward over the bar top. "What are you doing on Christmas Eve? How about you and Marty come over? I'll cook. Just a lazy night in with bad movies and enough food to feed a horse? PJs required. I may or may not have a present for you."

I look into his clever eyes, loving exactly how that sounds.

"That sounds perfect," I reply, sipping another cup of nostalgia, thinking fondly about my past, and maybe even, for the first time in a *long* time, my future.

"Perfect," he repeats, eyes locked with mine.

* * *

"Knock, Knock." I tap on Eli's slider and peek through the glass into the kitchen, arms full.

"Merry Christmas Eve." Eli jogs over from the stove, clocking my full arms, and lets us in. Marty bounds for Gumbo, who lounges on the couch watching TV, while I knock off my snow boots. *Christmas Vacation* seems to be as amusing to cats as it is to people. *I wonder what he thinks about the cat and tree lights scene.*

I bring my big tote into the living room and place presents under his tree. Some people decorate with coordinated colors and aesthetics in mind, but not Eli. Covered in rainbow lights and thirty-year-old construction paper garland, his tree flaunts mismatched ornaments from childhood, souvenirs from vacations long past, and who-knows-what else. He's pulled out extra fluffy blankets and the crossword quilt off his bed, making the coziest Christmas Eve setup I could ask for.

"Whatcha cooking?" I ask, following my nose back to the kitchen.

"I'll give you one guess." He smiles, stirring a large pot and tending to a pile of drying linguine on the counter next to him.

"It's not Wednesday," I joke, coming in for a taste test. He holds the spoon up for me.

"I figured it was a special occasion." He smiles. "It's not quite ready, though. Let's hang for a bit before we eat."

We settle into the couch, sinking deep into the cushions and layers of blankets. "I have a gift for you," I confess as Marty and Gumbo snuggle in, all four lumps in a tight little ball.

"I do too, but mine requires a field trip." He turns and grins, full of mischief.

"A field trip? Tonight?"

"Only if you're up for it." He shrugs. "After dinner?"

"You continually surprise me, Elliott Nett. I'm up for it. My present is under the tree, the old-fashioned way." I laugh and hand him the package, allowing the couch to swallow me up again. "I hope you like it."

"I love it already." *Cheeseball. He's so sweet.*

Ripping through the paper, he pulls out a large navy leather book. Covered in silver star stickers, "Muddy and Coach" is written in puffy paint across the top.

"What's this?" He asks, grinning, gently opening the scrapbook.

"It's us." I lean, tilting my head on his shoulder.

He flips through pictures of us over the years. Mementos and bits and bobs like concert tickets, sea glass, bottle caps, that sort of thing, are taped inside. I even dug up our rec softball team photo from the first summer we met.

Looking up with the most earnest eyes, he sets the book aside and pulls me in. "This is amazing," he whispers. "Thank you."

"You're welcome. Merry Christmas."

Turning away to steady himself, he abruptly gets up and walks into the kitchen. "Uh, the sauce is probably done. Ready to eat?"

Thirty minutes later, with full pasta stomachs, we rummage through coat hooks to find snowpants. "Dress warm," he advises.

We strap on snowshoes and prepare to face the cold, bracing ourselves for the slicing chill of winter.

"Where are we going?" He's got a full backpacker's pack on and a headlamp to cut through the dark. Leading the way, he trudges towards the park entrance. "I love my job as much as the next girl, more, probably, but I wasn't planning on working on Christmas Eve." I laugh.

"Trust me." He playfully nudges me with his shoulder.

"I do." Nudging him back.

Getting back into the festive mood, we head deeper and deeper into the woods, making Yeti-sized prints in the fresh powder. The clear, inky sky stretches endlessly above us. Bill and Ted, our nosy crows, follow us as well, flying from tree to tree, filling the air with not just snow but scratchy caws. They blend into the night so well; if it weren't for their chatter or the occasional eclipse of a bright star, I wouldn't know they were here.

"Oh, I don't know, Eli." He starts veering off at the same fork in the trail where we confronted Danni this fall.

"You've been avoiding this part of the park ever since. Trust me, remember?" He holds out his hand, and I reluctantly follow him.

I squeeze it tight. "This better be good."

He walks over to the middle of the natural clearing and opens his backpack. Pulling out a double sleeping bag, we climb inside and lean back, using the pack as a pillow.

"Exposure therapy? That's my present?" I ask, entranced by the stars. The Milky Way is in full view, like a river of light meandering through the sky.

"This is your present." He hands me a piece of paper as he pulls out a thermos and pours two cups of hot chocolate.

It's a printout of something. Nothing fancy, just a piece of computer paper. "Here, take the headlamp." He pulls the light off his head and smushes it over my winter hat.

After reviewing the presented documentation, the International Dark Sky Association is pleased to approve Stone's Throw State Park as an official, registered Dark Sky Park.

"Remember Zach and me sneaking around out here all fall? We had to submit a ton of paperwork, take photos, get land survey copies, and a whole bunch of other stuff to submit this."

"This means…" I keep reading.

"Astronomers up the wazoo. Hobbyists, but also real scientists. There's only a couple of other International Dark Sky Parks in the state, and they're nowhere near here." I hear the grin in his voice. "We're by far the biggest, too. Cha-ching."

"We can do field trips, research retreats, all sorts of things." I start to brainstorm.

"Zach is already working to host the next annual meeting of the Michigan Astronomical Society this summer. I think MSU's Astronomy Department runs it. He's been dying to tell you about it, so you should call him soon," he chuckles.

"This is incredible, Eli." I turn myself towards him. "You're incredible."

"I thought this would be good for the park," he trails off as he pulls off his hat and runs his fingers through his strawberry hair. "I thought you'd like it."

"I love it." We lean back and gaze at the stars, shoulder to shoulder in the sleeping bag. He turns his head towards me. *The stars have nothing on those green eyes.*

"Hang on." I reach over him to pick up a piece of litter from the ground behind him, exposed by the headlamp. "I cannot get rid of these things. It's one of those gross ads from the campaign."

Paid for by Tiller Brazas peeks out from the folds of the soggy paper, that stupid name still taunting me.

"It's just trash," Eli replies.

"Yep," I smile, crumpling it up and stuffing it in my jacket pocket. "Just trash."

I grab his hand in the warmth of the fleece and lace his fingers in mine. We lay there listening to winter, watching the brilliant stars.

His smile is bright and gentle, but it's careful, waiting to be sure.

"It's always been you, Eli. I just…"

"You were scared," he finishes, gently. "I get it. You weren't ready."

"But not anymore," I whisper as I lean in. "I'm done running away."

HOT HEAD
MAUDY LORSO
VOTE COLIN!
PAID FOR BY
TRAIL
BLAZERS

Acknowledgments

Writing a book is not as solitary a process as one might think. Without my friends checking in on me, my family's encouragement, and my husband Alex's unyielding love, this book wouldn't have made it to your shelf. I can't thank you all enough.

Thank you to my developmental editor, Siobhán Jones, for her impeccable eye for detail and creativity, and to Shawn and Deb at Level Best Books for their tenacity and can-do attitude. And, a big shout out to the dozen beta readers who provided constructive (and hilarious) feedback that shaped the final version of this story.

Lastly, hugs to my Northern Michigan community for their overwhelming support of this series. Between booksellers, friends, family, press, and everyone else who has joined me on this journey, thank you. I've never known a home like this.

About the Author

Eloise Corvo grew up in the suburbs of metro Detroit, eagerly awaiting trips to her family's "Up North" cabin near Traverse City, Michigan. It was there, on the shores of the countless lakes and dense forests, that she discovered her deep love for the natural world and nurtured a curiosity that still drives her today. This passion led her to Michigan State University, where she earned a Bachelor of Science in Zoology with a focus on Marine Biology. While at MSU, she founded the MSU SCUBA Club (which immediately died after she graduated) and nearly adopted a baby turtle from an eccentric herpetology professor. She later completed a Master's degree in Marine Biology.

Corvo now works as an environmental policy analyst by day and writes by night. She specializes in state and federal environmental law, helping to protect the landscapes she fell in love with as a child exploring Northern Michigan. Her heart remains in Traverse City, where she now lives full-time. To learn more about Eloise and her other publications, visit EloiseCorvo.com.

AUTHOR WEBSITE:
  EloiseCorvo.com

SOCIAL MEDIA HANDLES:
  Facebook.com/EloiseCorvo
  Instagram.com/EloiseCorvo
  TikTok.com/Author_EloiseCorvo

Also by Eloise Corvo

Off the Beaten Path (A Stone's Throw Mystery #1)

www.ingramcontent.com/pod-product-compliance
Lightning Source LLC
Chambersburg PA
CBHW051147130726
47988CB00005B/2027